IMITATION OF DEATH

"Who's going to arrest you?" Nikki asked. "Jess, I can barely hear you. What's going on?"

"The police. The paramedics. They're all here. But I didn't do it." She sounded as if she was about to burst into tears. "You have to believe me."

"I believe you. What didn't you do?"

"Kill Rex."

Nikki almost dropped her cell phone. "Pardon?"

"I didn't kill Rex March."

She didn't kill Rex? What was she talking about? Were the police saying she was with Rex when his plane crashed? That was absurd. And impossible. The day he died, Jessica was with her and a thousand other California real estate agents at a convention in San Francisco. "Of course you didn't kill Rex. He died in a plane crash six months ago. Are you drunk?"

"He's here, Nikki. Rex. He's here dead," Jessica said in a tiny voice. "In my bed."

"In your bed?"

"Someone killed him, Nikki. Not in a plane crash. Here. Today. In my apartment. He was alive and now he's dead. He's been murdered and the police think I did it!"

Books by Cheryl Crane

THE BAD ALWAYS DIE TWICE

IMITATION OF DEATH

Published by Kensington Publishing Corporation

The Bad Always Die Twice

CHERYL CRANE

𝒌

KENSINGTON BOOKS
http://www.kensingtonbooks.com

KENSINGTON BOOKS are published by

Kensington Publishing Corp.
119 West 40th St.
New York, NY 10018

ISBN-13: 978-0-7582-5887-8
ISBN-10: 0-7582-5887-9

First Hardcover Printing: September 2011
First Mass Market Printing: August 2012

10 9 8 7 6 5 4 3 2 1

Printed in the United States of America

For JLR.

"Did you not know that you are my hero?"

Acknowledgments

I would like to thank the following people for their help, encouragement, and faith in me: Lennie Alickman, Evan Marshall, John Scognamiglio, Tom and Mike, Bill and Marc, and the other CC for all of the above and much, much more.

Chapter 1

Nikki Harper snagged a Norwegian salmon canapé from a silver tray as a server passed her. Checking her Girard-Perregaux wristwatch, which she rarely wore (how embarrassing was it to own a timepiece that cost as much as a three-bedroom bungalow in Boise?), she popped the delicacy into her mouth. She truly adored extravagant food; it was these extravagant parties she could do without. They were all about seeing and being seen, neither of which appealed to her. She'd spent her entire childhood in the limelight, which still left a sour taste in her mouth. Or would have, had the smoky, salty salmon not been so amazing.

This party, like most she attended in Hollywood, was business, not pleasure. She came to these events because she had to, not because they were supposed to be fun.

According to the superior Swiss timing on her wrist, if she included the time it took in line for the valet parking, she'd been here forty-seven minutes. Surely another thirteen minutes and she could bid her hostess good night and be on her way. If she was lucky, she might even be able to escape before the grand entrance of Victoria Bordeaux, the honored guest of the evening, who was already almost an hour late. The fifties screen goddess would have it no other way.

"Are you staying?" Nikki glanced at her companion. A gaudy crystal chandelier overhead caught her attention, and she wondered how she had managed to sell this white elephant of a mansion in Outpost Estates in Hollywood for the ridiculous asking price. There were five additional, identical crystal monstrosities here in the salon where cocktails were being served.

Golden-haired Jessica Martin, as beautiful as any old-Hollywood screen goddess, regarded Nikki with arched eyebrows. She was wearing a red silk sheath dress that had no doubt been purchased on Rodeo Drive that morning. She completed the ensemble with incredibly tanned, muscular bare legs and her favorite four-inch spike-heeled red Jimmy Choos.

Nikki glanced down at her own attire, suddenly feeling self-conscious. She hoped she didn't look frumpy in her vintage sleeveless sweater dress and sensible pumps.

At five-foot-ten, she rarely wore high heels; they always made her feel too conspicuous, like she was towering over others. And no matter what she wore, she would never be as curvy as Jessica. She was *willowy,* according to her mother. Translation: skinny and shapeless. The one physical characteristic she had always liked about herself, though, was her red hair—her father's red hair. Strawberry blond, she wore it just below her shoulders. And her eyes. She'd had a love–hate relationship with *the blue eyes* for years.

"I doubt I'm staying. No one's here." Jessica wrinkled her pretty nose.

"Are you kidding? Everyone is here. Mother's colorist says Angelina's looking for a new place. Heard she's adopting more children. You should go talk to her." Nikki lifted her chin in the direction of the brunette movie icon surrounded by her entourage at the far side of the room.

Jessica sighed. "I'm not up for schmoozing. I think I'm going to go, if you don't mind."

She pressed her fingertips to her board-flat abs, reminding Nikki of the avant-garde restaurant on the Sunset Strip where sushi was served on the naked bellies of well-toned waitresses. Jessica could definitely get a job there.

"I'm starving," Jessica declared.

"Starving? Here?" Nikki eyed a tray of mushroom and lobster thingies going by, just out of reach. "You could feed a small African nation with the amount of food Edith is serving here tonight."

Edith March was Nikki and Jessica's client and their hostess for the evening. Actually, *technically*, her husband Rex had been their client. He'd approached the realty company Nikki and Jessica worked for, eight months ago, about putting his tacky Old Spanish–style nine-bedroom home up for sale. The sixty-two-year-old actor had died tragically in a plane crash two months later, before the house had been sold.

His body was never recovered from the single-engine plane he'd been flying solo when he crashed in the California desert. It was a tragedy, of course. Any death in a fiery plane crash was. What was even more tragic, though, was that Rex didn't seem to be missed all that much. Edith, Rex's widow, had begun dating only weeks after the memorial service.

The tabloids had struggled to find anything nice to say about the man and his work, and the initial excitement over his untimely death had faded as fast as the luscious taste of lox on Nikki's tongue. She scanned the room for the nearest red-vested server.

Although Rex had played the occasional small role in films over the years, his one true claim to fame had been the lead in an early seventies family comedy set on a desert island; it wasn't a great hit at the time, but it had become a residual blockbuster.

Nikki hadn't personally cared for Rex. He'd been a typical soggy Hollywood has-been who'd never had any talent to begin with nor enough sense to know it. He'd had entirely too large an ego and hands like an octopus.

Edith March, on the other hand, Nikki genuinely adored. Edith was a classy lady who had remained loyal to her philandering husband to his death, and now she was making lemonade out of lemons. With the mansion sold, there was talk of buying a condo in Belize and a penthouse in New York City with her new, *young* boyfriend.

And Edith knew how to throw a party. Everyone was here: the film actors and actresses of the old Hollywood days as well as current box office draws. She was even kind enough to invite a few TV stars. Edith was saying good-bye to the mansion she had never liked, good-bye to her previous life, and maybe a final good-bye to Rex, whose larger-than-life-size portrait was painted as a mural on the wall of the salon.

"I can't eat here." Jessica looked at Nikki as if she'd just grown a horn in the middle of her head. Or maybe worn Manolo Blahniks to the gym. "Not in this dress. I haven't eaten for two days and I still had to lie down on the bed to get it zipped up." She drew her hand over the red silk and her amazingly fit torso. "Besides. You know me. I don't eat raw fish eggs. Give me a well-done burger with special sauce any day."

Nikki chuckled. She and Jessica didn't see eye to eye on fashion any better than Nikki and her mother did. Nikki was into comfort, old styles, and recycling perfectly good garments from her favorite vintage used clothing stores on Santa Monica in Beverly Hills. Jessica liked her designers big and her heels high. But Jessica was what she was, and Nikki liked her because of it. Sometimes in spite of it. One of Jessica's most endearing qualities was that she wasn't any more impressed by celebrities than Nikki was. Their only difference was that Nikki had grown up with them and Jessica slept with them. The combination of their personalities made them a great team at work.

Take this sale, for instance. Jessica had brought the client in; she had catered to him, cooed and batted her lashes at him. Nikki had hit the pavement in search of prospective buyers. In the end, they had both wound up with *phat* commissions.

"Hey, check that out. Ten o'clock." Jessica eyed the host of a new late-night talk show. She liked her men mature. Preferably *rich* and mature. Sadly, also married. "Know him?"

"Met him." Nikki glanced at the bar. She wanted a glass of champagne before she was on her way, but there was a casting executive there whom she wanted to avoid.

"*Mother's?*" Jessica questioned dryly.

"Where else?"

"Nikki! Darling! How good of you to come." Their hostess squeezed through her crowd of guests and enveloped Nikki in plump arms and yards of buttercup yellow chiffon. Hugging the breath out of her, Edith March still managed to keep the champagne glass in her hand from tipping and spilling its contents on the floor, or worse, on Jessica's red silk number. "Really, you should be the guest of honor. None of this would have been possible without you."

Nikki air-kissed Edith's cheek and extracted herself from the sea of nose-tickling fabric. "That's kind of you, but we were just doing our jobs, Edith. You remember my partner, Jessica Martin," she said, knowing full well that Edith remembered her.

There had been some unexplained friction between the two women from day one; during the process of selling the estate, Nikki had kept them apart as much as possible. Nikki knew from experience that that happened with Jessica sometimes with their older female clients; just part of the territory when working with a drop-dead gorgeous partner.

Nikki smiled at Edith. "We're just pleased we were able to work out a deal that was acceptable to both you and the buyers."

"Acceptable? It was more than *acceptable*. Wasn't it, dear?" Sipping from the glass, Edith opened and closed long red talons, beckoning to a good-looking thirty-something model/actor in a white dinner jacket.

Nikki had heard that Thompson Christopher was in the running for a role in a new romantic comedy. Word was, the part could make him a household name if Kate Hudson signed on.

"Thompson, tell Nikki how thrilled we are with the deal," Edith insisted, finishing off her champagne.

Thompson slipped his arm around Edith's thick waist. "I'm pleased if Edie's pleased." His smile seemed genuine, something Nikki didn't see all that often in these circles.

"Jessica and I are just happy we were able to make this process as painless as possible." Nikki glanced at Jessica, who had resumed eyeing the late-night TV guy, and gave her a little nudge. "Aren't we, Jess?"

"Absolutely," Jessica gushed, offering a good half of her attention.

"And I know you said you're not ready to buy yet, Edith," Nikki continued, "but—"

"Should we decide to buy in L.A., you'll be the first person I talk to." Edith handed Thompson her glass and took both of Nikki's hands in hers. "I wouldn't have it any other way. You were such a blessing when Rex passed. God rest his soul." She glanced in the direction of her husband's slightly creepy grinning face looming over the room from the far wall.

"God rest his soul," Thompson echoed good-naturedly.

Nikki couldn't help but look at Rex's portrait, wondering how he felt, gazing down from wherever he was, watching his wife play house with a man young enough to be his son. A man who didn't seem to understand the difference between a first name and a last.

"If I'd left the sale to that damned lawyer of Rex's, I'd be packing my bags for a homeless shelter."

"Edie," Thompson admonished gently.

"A wolf in Armani wool." She drew her finger beneath her beau's chin. "You haven't been in Hollywood long enough to recognize them yet, but you will. There are packs of them. He was supposed to be here, you know." She scanned the sea of celebrity cocktail dresses and suits with a trained eye. "What makes me think he'll be a no-show? It's just like Alex to insult me like this."

"Well." Nikki clasped her hands, ready to make her escape. She'd eaten her weight in seafood and spoken to her hostess. If she hurried, she could be home in her PJs with her TiVo in an hour. "Just let me know if there's anything else we can do to make the transition easier."

"You've already done so much, dear." Someone caught Edith's eye. "Oh, heavens, is that Portia Raleigh?

I thought she'd gone to Palm Springs to recover from another facelift. I do hope she was more cautious this time about her choice of plastic surgeons. I must say hello." She fluttered off, leaving Thompson holding her empty champagne flute.

He watched her go and then returned his attention to Nikki. "I really do appreciate what you've done for Edie," he said. "You've been helpful and you've been kind. And having Victoria Bordeaux here tonight as Edie's guest"—he opened his arms—"I know that was you, too. It's such an honor and a dream come true for Edie."

Nikki hesitated; comments like that always made her uncomfortable. Thankfully, Jessica always knew when to throw her a lifeline.

Jessica moved gracefully to the forefront, pumping Thompson's hand. "We're just pleased that Rex March's widow is pleased, Mr. Christopher."

"Well, thank you again. Now, if you'll excuse me, ladies." He bowed slightly, which made him appear very old Hollywood, especially in his classic white dinner jacket and black trousers. Nikki liked him better by the second. "I'd better get Edie some more champagne and rescue Ms. Raleigh." He flashed a handsome grin and pushed through the crowd.

Nikki waited until Thompson was out of earshot before she touched Jessica's arm. "What's with the cold shoulder to Edith? She was nice enough to you."

"No cold shoulder." Jessica shrugged her golden sculpted shoulders. No matter how hard Nikki worked out at the gym, she'd never have those fabulous shoulders.

"But did you see her nails?" Jessica murmured, leaning closer, cupping her hand to her mouth with her own manicured fingers.

"I know." Nikki eyed another tray of hors d'oeuvres. Was that beluga caviar? "A little long for a woman her age not working as a cashier in the dollar store."

"It's not the length I'm talking about," Jessica whispered. "Chipped."

"Chipped?" It wasn't likely Edith was serving chipped beef. Nikki was still hung up on the hors d'oeuvres.

"Her nail polish. It was chipped. Unacceptable. She needs to fire her manicurist. Well, I'm off." Jessica kissed the air beside Nikki's cheek. "What are you doing tomorrow?"

"Biking in Malibu Canyon. Wanna come?"

"Who're you going with?"

"Marshall and Rob."

Jessica frowned. "Taken."

Nikki chuckled. "So, see you Monday?"

"Tuesday. Monday I've got a seminar downtown. Downy wanted *office representation* and he's footing the bill. But I swear, if it's Zig Ziglar again, I'll commit hari-kari right in the conference hall." She gave a wave. "See you."

Nikki stood in the sea of beautiful people, watching Jessica make her way to the front foyer. She debated whether or not to track down the beluga, but decided against it, and headed in the same general direction as Jessica. The door. If she was lucky, she'd be out of here before—

Nikki had barely reached the foyer when she heard the familiar whirr and snap of dozens of cameras as the double front doors were thrown open. In this age of digital cameras, the paparazzi no longer flashed and popped. Instead, they sounded like a swarm of clicking insects.

Holy crapoli, she thought. She would never grow used to it, not as long as she lived. She glanced over her shoulder; there was no way to escape gracefully. The spaces behind her were quickly filling. Even celebrities liked to get a look at a goddess.

A smile immediately lit Nikki's face. It was the smile her mother had pressed upon her since birth, very possibly in utero. It was a well-practiced smile, intended to conceal any emotion the bearer might be experiencing. In Hollywood, feelings were better suited to psychiatrists' couches and intimate dinner conversation. One never shared with the public.

Through the crowd, she spotted a familiar face. The driver, dressed immaculately in a black suit and old-school chauffeur's cap, threw open the rear door of the white Bentley and offered his hand. Slender, gloved fingers slid into his and suddenly the dark night lit up with the sheer effervescence of the incomparable Victoria Bordeaux.

For a moment, Nikki felt trapped. Like a tiny mouse trying to escape a horde of hungry cats. Maybe not a tiny rodent, more like a tall, lanky one. But the crowd moved back, leaving her alone at the door.

Dressed in a gorgeous gold cocktail dress, matching kitten heels and an amazing faux-ermine shrug, Victoria Bordeaux alighted from the Bentley and strode toward her. The screen star may have been in the twilight of her life, but thanks to good genes and sturdy undergarments, she was as beautiful as she had been in her early twenties. Petite and a natural blond, she still had that sweater-girl curvaceous figure that had shot her from a soda fountain stool to stardom all those years ago.

And, still, after all this time, Victoria's beauty, her poise, took Nikki's breath away.

The star offered her gloved hand and Nikki took it,

leaning down to kiss her very close to her cheek, but not so close as to muss her face powder.

"Really, Nicolette," Victoria admonished under her breath. "A sweater dress to a cocktail party?"

Nikki couldn't resist a smile of amusement as she stood to her full height, towering over the older woman. Some things never changed. "Oh, for sweet heaven's sake, Mother. It's vintage Chanel!"

Chapter 2

"Staying in tonight or going out?" Victoria asked, gazing into the mirror. Dressed in a white silk robe, she sat at her rosewood vanity and carefully removed her eye makeup. She'd hosted a charity luncheon that afternoon and had been in full goddess mode, something she no longer did every day.

Nikki, who sat cross-legged on the floor flipping through an old photo album, glanced up at her mother. Even seen this way, as a reflection in the old mirror, her hair in a turban, her face wiped clean of makeup, she was a woman of extraordinary beauty, a truly golden Venus. Nikki may not have been exactly jealous of her mother's beauty, but she was certainly envious of it. "Staying in."

"You and Jeremy should go out more."

It was a familiar topic of conversation, one Nikki didn't care to delve into this evening. After a long day at work, she just wanted to relax with her dogs and not think, and certainly not argue with her mother. Her relationship with her childhood-friend-turned-lover was complicated, but weren't all relationships?

Both of Nikki's Cavalier King Charles Spaniels lounged with her on the floor among throw pillows, and she scratched one of the pups behind the ear. Victoria didn't allow dogs on the furniture, so Nikki sat on the floor with them. At the end of the day, the dogs craved her attention and she, on some level, craved theirs. It was such simple, uncomplicated love between her and Stanley and Oliver. The only effortless relationship she had.

"What do you think, Stanley?" The dog's ears perked up at the sound of Nikki's voice. "Should Jeremy and I go out or should he go to his daughter's dance recital? Or maybe Grandma should just mind her own beeswax, hmmm?" She scratched under the dog's chin and he sighed with obvious pleasure.

"I am *not* a grandmother to those canines." Victoria returned her attention to the mirror. "Stop trying to bait me. I worry about you. You say you and Jeremy are in love, but you rarely see each other more than once a week."

"His wife died, Mother. An ugly, hair-falling-out, shriveling-to-nothing cancer death. His children need him and I'm not going to foist myself upon them."

Jealous of the attention Stanley was getting, Oliver inched forward until he rested his muzzle on Nikki's leg. She stroked his soft, spotted red and white coat. Oliver was a Blenheim. Stanley, a cousin twice removed to Oliver and two years older, was a black, white and tan Tri.

"I understand that perfectly." Victoria lifted both hands in a conceding pose; for her, every movement was about perfect lighting, angle and balance, even when she wasn't in front of the camera. Victoria never,

ever got caught by the paparazzi picking spinach from between her teeth or dragging toilet paper beneath the heel of her alligator-skin pump. Nikki had had the bad fortune of both. "I understand perfectly that children are needy. I raised seven children of my own."

"You and a revolving door of nannies," Nikki muttered. She regretted the words the moment they came out of her mouth.

Victoria elegantly turned on the padded bench and looked Nikki directly in the eye. "Did you come here to pick a fight?"

Nikki sighed and stroked Stanley's head. "No."

"Good. So spare me the Joan Crawford guilt trip and tell me about your day."

Nikki smiled. This was one of the reasons she loved her mother so dearly. If there was one person Victoria Bordeaux knew, it was herself. The good and the bad, and she made no excuses for either. "I think I may have sold that place in Brentwood we listed last month."

The fact that Nikki sold real estate for a living was still a prickly subject, even after ten years, but Victoria's smile was genuine. "The one down the street from that football player who killed his wife and got off scot-free?"

O.J. Simpson had just been put in his place by Victoria Bordeaux and he didn't even know it. "O.J. Simpson. And the jury found him innocent. 7.7 million."

"I suppose you have to split the commission with Jessica."

"She *is* my partner. And the listing agent gets a cut, but I may have to buy myself that antique Victorian ring I was telling you about, the snake one with the emerald eyes."

"You must have gotten your taste from your father." Victoria slipped a cigarette from a pack on her vanity. It didn't matter who told her the dangers of smoking, or how often, it was a habit she said she'd indulged in for the last fifty-odd years and at her age she didn't intend to give it up. "Because it certainly wasn't from me." She struck a flame from the antique lighter that had not been an antique when it had been given to her by Howard Hughes. White smoke curled around her turbaned head.

Oliver wrinkled his nose and sneezed in protest of the acrid smoke. Nikki stifled a chuckle.

"Please." Victoria gazed down at the dog. "There are no Oscars for canines. Not even an Emmy," she sniffed.

Nikki absently studied a photo of herself taken on her fifth birthday. Her mother had somehow wrangled a photo-op with Nikki's favorite TV personality and thrown her a space-themed party on one of the studio lots. Somewhere, there was a picture of her and Jeremy that day, too. She flipped the page. "Speaking of Oscars, what are we watching this week?"

"*The Little Foxes* or maybe *Johnny Belinda*. I haven't decided."

Nikki set the photo album aside and gathered both dogs onto her lap to cuddle them. "*Johnny Belinda* starred Jane Wyman," she recalled. "You were friends at Paramount, right?"

"She was a little before my time, but I knew her." Victoria exhaled blue-gray smoke. "A nice enough girl."

"I can't believe you knew Ronald Reagan." Nikki's phone vibrated next to her in her bag. "He was such a hottie back then. Who could have imagined he would be president one day?"

"I said that the day he was elected."

Nikki grinned as she fumbled for her BlackBerry. "Let's have a little respect for the dead, if not for two-term presidents, shall we?" Locating her phone in her

Prada shoulder bag, she looked at the screen. Jessica. "Hey," she said, answering it. "How'd the seminar go? Learn anything—"

"Oh, Jesus, Nikki. You have to come," Jessica said into her ear in an uncharacteristically high-pitched voice.

Stanley licked Nikki's pant leg where she had spilled blue-cheese salad dressing at lunch. "Come where? Stan, stop." She pushed the dog's head away. Her linen trousers now had a wet doggy-tongue stain, but at least the oily spot seemed to have disappeared.

"Tell her to come for supper. We'll have Ina make fajitas." Victoria ground out her cigarette in a porcelain ashtray, half-smoked. Always half-smoked. Her way of cutting back.

"Nikki, please," Jessica moaned.

Nikki realized, then, that something was wrong. *Seriously* wrong. She pushed both dogs off her lap and got to her feet.

"If she doesn't want fajitas, I think there's chicken breasts," Victoria went on. "Ina can whip up a nice chicken pasta with avocado."

Nikki held up her hand to silence her mother. She couldn't follow two conversations at once. "Jess, what is it? What's wrong?" There was noise in the background. Male voices. Was that a police siren? "Are you okay?"

"Jesus, no. No, I'm not okay. I'm scared shitless."

She sounded like she was trying to whisper, but with her voice so high-pitched, Nikki could barely understand her. "Tell me where you are. I'll come right now."

"My apartment. Oh, Jesus," she moaned. "I think they're going to arrest me. They're saying I have to get off the phone. I don't want to go in there. I don't want to see that again. Not ever."

"Or we can do take-out," Victoria continued, rising from her vanity. She glanced at Stanley and Oliver, sprawled on her carpet. "I suppose doggies do take-out."

Mother, Nikki mouthed. She turned away so she could better concentrate on what Jessica was saying. "Who's going to arrest you? Jess, I can barely hear you. What's going on? Who's there with you?"

"The police. The paramedics. They're all here. But I didn't do it." She sounded as if she was about to burst into tears. "You have to believe me."

"Okay, okay, I'm coming." Nikki walked back to grab her bag off the floor. Jessica wasn't making any sense. "I believe you. What didn't you do?"

"Kill Rex."

Nikki halted abruptly; her purse hit the floor. "Pardon?"

"I didn't kill Rex March."

She didn't kill Rex? What was she talking about? Were the police saying she was with Rex when his plane crashed? That was absurd. And impossible. The day he died, Jessica was with her and a thousand other California real estate agents at a convention in San Francisco. "Of course you didn't kill Rex. He died in a plane crash six months ago. Are you drunk?"

"I've warned that girl about drinking too much." Victoria waggled her finger at Nikki as she crossed the bedroom to her open closet doors.

"He's here, Nikki."

There it was again, the shrill voice that raised the hairs on Nikki's arms. Only now her tone was laced with something akin to desperation. She was scaring Nikki now. "*Who's* there, Jess?"

"Rex."

"Rex is there? In your apartment?"

"What do you think I should wear Wednesday night?"

Victoria asked. "The ambassador to Spain is coming. You'll like him," she mused, paying no attention whatsoever to the conversation Nikki was having on the phone.

"Yes, he's here. He's here dead," Jessica said in a tiny voice. "In my bed."

Nikki almost dropped the phone. She didn't mean to sound like an idiot, but all she could do was repeat what Jessica had said. "In your bed?"

"Someone killed him, Nikki. Not in a plane crash. Here. Today. In my apartment. He was alive and now he's dead. He's been murdered and the police think I did it!"

"I'll be right there." Nikki grabbed her bag and raced for the bedroom door. "I have to go, Mother. Jessica has an emergency. I'll be back for the boys later."

"Guess it's you and me, gentlemen," Victoria said, nonchalant, as Nikki rushed out the door. "I vote for fajitas. How about you?"

Chapter 3

"I'm sorry, ma'am, but you can't enter the building at this time." The uniformed LAPD cop took a sidestep to his left, effectively blocking the entire entranceway to Jessica's Spanish-style garden apartment building with his gorilla body.

"What if I live here? I can't enter my own home?" Nikki glanced over her shoulder at the cop cars, their blue lights flashing, parked catty-corner in all the handicapped parking spots out front. There had to be a dozen of them here already and the not-too-distant sirens suggested more were on the way. How many cops did it take to subdue one real estate agent in four-inch stilettos? It was no wonder the LAPD was way over budget again.

He made no eye contact with her. "I'm sorry, but this property is a crime scene, ma'am. I can't let you pass." It sounded like a spiel. Rehearsed many times.

The knots of onlookers standing in the overgrown, tropical vegetation that surrounded the Hollywood apartment building were growing by the moment. A news van pulled up out front, followed by an ambulance. When she'd first arrived, she'd walked down the alley alongside the building, and she'd seen the apartment parking garage had its own little traffic jam going; cars couldn't enter or exit. Nikki sensed the rinky-dink circus was about to go three ring. She had to reach Jessica.

"I understand this is a crime scene." She gazed up at the cop's ape face. She wasn't crazy about the police in general. She'd had a few run-ins with them as a rebellious teen. They'd locked up her opinion of them when they botched her father's murder investigation. "That's why I'm trying to get inside." She tried to remain patient and speak slowly to assure his full comprehension of her simple words. "My friend has been accused of committing *said* crime."

"I'm sorry. I can't let you pass, ma'am." He stretched out a hairy arm. "This property is a crime scene."

So he didn't just look like a primate. He had the brains of one. No, to say that would be unfair to the world's gorilla population; this guy wasn't that bright. "Look, my friend Jessica Martin, apartment three twenty-two, called me a few minutes ago and asked me to come right away. She said that when she got home from work, there was a dead man in her bed."

"I'm sorry, ma'am—" King Kong started again.

"Hey! Aren't you Nikki Harper?" An LAPD uniformed cop approached them from the building foyer. "Weren't you in *People* magazine last week? Some big charity fundraiser at the Regal Biltmore?"

She shifted her attention to the cop trying to get around gorilla-man. Mid-thirties, average-looking guy.

"Must have been an old copy. That was weeks ago."

"Probably. Dentist's waiting room." The cop managed to squeeze past his coworker. "Victoria Bordeaux's daughter, right?" He pointed at her and grinned slyly.

"That's me." She pushed her sunglasses up on her head, put on her friendly face and glanced over her shoulder again. A local news crew was piling out of the van. Victoria wouldn't be happy if Nikki's face was plastered all over the eleven o'clock news. Mother didn't like bad publicity of any sort and being connected to a murder case would definitely be categorized as bad publicity, even if Jessica *was* completely innocent.

"My friend Jessica Martin just called me from inside. She's scared to death and she's alone."

"The suspect." The normal-size cop hooked his thumbs into the waistband of his pants. "You know, my mom loves your mom's films. I gave her one of those DVD boxed sets last year for Christmas. I think it was called *Victoria Bordeaux, The Early Years*."

Again, she offered *the smile*, the one learned in utero. "I hope she enjoyed them. What a great gift. Hey, listen." She leaned closer, shooting for quick intimacy. She hated to take advantage of her mother's celebrity status, but she *had* to get upstairs. "Do you think I could get inside? My friend is expecting me and I can't stand out here and wait." She motioned to the gathering crowd behind them. "Not with the paparazzi." She made a face as if he understood firsthand the trials of being a household name.

He looked at the news team quickly setting up a camera next to an overgrown bougainvillea behind the yellow crime-scene tape.

"I'd really appreciate it, Officer . . ."—she checked out his nameplate—"Syzusky."

He thought for a minute, glancing up at his hulky partner, who remained unfazed by Nikki's *celebrity*. "The suspect hasn't been arrested yet. I don't see why not. Shep, let her pass."

The gorilla put out his hand. "This is a crime scene. I'm sorry, but—"

Nikki slipped under his furry forearm and followed Syzusky into the front foyer of the apartment building. "Thank you so much, Officer Syzusky."

He led her across the red travertine tile lobby to the staircase. Several officers milled around. Someone was taking a dinner order for In & Out. Nikki just didn't get the L.A. obsession with the place. Jessica loved their burgers. She practically lived off them.

"So, can you tell me what's going on here, Officer Syzusky?" She spoke quietly, cultivating the sense of intimacy between them.

"It's Brian; you can call me Brian."

She offered her hand to shake his as they started up the stairs. "Nikki Harper. Of course, you already knew that." She laughed just the way Jessica did when she was trying to get something out of a man. "Nikki."

"I really can't give you any details. I'm probably putting my ass on the line even taking you up." A dimple indented his cheek when he grinned. " 'Scuse my French."

"Well, here's what *I* know. Jessica Martin called me, asking me to come right away. She said she arrived home to find a dead man in her bed. Rex March." She met his gaze. "Only the thing that's got me confused, *Brian*, is that Rex March is already dead. He died in a plane crash in the Mojave Desert in March. I know that for a fact because I attended his memorial service. I've been working for his widow. I sell real estate."

"I know. Read it in *People*."

"Right." The smile. "Soooo, how can Rex March be dead in my friend's bed?"

"We've been asking ourselves the same question since we got the 911 call." They reached the second floor and continued up the stairs. "But he looks like Rex March to me." He frowned and lowered his voice. "You know, I never got into that show of his, *Shipwrecked Vacation*. Did you?"

He went on without giving Nikki a chance to respond, which was fine with her since she thought the 70's syndicated television show that Rex had starred in had been god-awful, even for its day. The man couldn't act his way out of a wet paper bag. In a monsoon.

"Now my brother Andrew, he loved it," Officer Syzusky continued. "Or, at least he loved that girl with the blond hair. What was her name? Teeny. Only she wasn't so teeny, if you know what I mean. Always wearing that little bikini Junior made for her out of sailcloth the first day they were wrecked."

Mercifully, they reached the third floor and entered the hallway. Two EMTs, one on her cell phone, ambled past them and started down the stairs. Apparently there was no rush to get the victim to the hospital. If he was dead, why would there be?

"So getting back to Rex March." Nikki headed for Jessica's apartment at the end of the hall, ignoring the neighbors who stood in their doorways, gawking. She recognized several faces; worse, she knew they recognized hers. "If a memorial service was held for him, how is he in Jessica's bed right now?"

"Oh, he's dead now all right. Big hole where his left eye ought to be." The cop poked himself in the eye, demonstrating. "And whoever did him knew what they were doing. Killed him instantly, the EMT told me. Murder weapon went right through his eye to his brain and *bam!*" He smacked his palms together. "Dead as a doornail."

Nikki flinched at the sharp *thwack*, but kept her cool. "And they're sure it's Rex March. Not a . . ." Nikki

searched for the right word. The whole idea was so lu-
dicrous that she was having a hard time expressing it
herself. "An imposter?"

"You mean like one of those Elvis impersonators? My
wife and me, we got married in Vegas. Not at the Elvis
Chapel; they were booked, but we thought about it."

"*Could* this be a Rex March look-alike?" Nikki asked,
afraid if she let him continue, she would soon know not
only where he and his wife married, but where they
stayed on their wedding night and even more intimate
details. It was funny how people were like that, always
telling her their private business. As soon as they realized who she was—and hell, she wasn't even a celebrity
herself—they felt as though they could tell her the most
personal details of their lives. Details they should not be
sharing with strangers.

"Could be an imposter, I suppose. His body will have
to be ID'd by a family member down at the morgue.
Dental records, birthmarks checked, if there's a question." He stopped and looked at her with an earnest
face. "But who would want to impersonate *Rex March*?"

He had a good point.

The hall was filled with uniformed cops trooping
around like ants. Doors opened and closed as Jessica's
neighbors were shooed back into their apartments.
There was a lot of talking. Whispering. Someone had
their TV on too loud. A *Kung Fu* rerun. Nikki would recognize David Carradine's voice anywhere.

At the open door to Jessica's place, Syzusky stepped
in front of her, puffing up with self-importance. "I'll
have to escort you."

"Of course." Nikki followed behind him. Just inside
the arched doorway of the living room, Jessica hollered
her name.

"Oh, Jesus, thank God you're here!" She flew across

the white tile floor in her pale pink Patrick Cox heels. Nikki hated the idea that she could actually identify the designers of some of the shoes that so consumed Jessica.

She threw her arms around Nikki and dropped her head onto her shoulder. She had been crying. They were genuine tears. Nikki had never seen Jessica cry.

"It's okay," Nikki hushed, hugging her. "Everything's going to be okay."

"But it's not." Jessica stepped back and wiped under her eyes, then stared at the mascara smeared on her fingertips. "Oh, Jesus H., do you have a Kleenex?"

Nikki dug around in her ancient Prada bag, a hand-me-down from Mother, and came up with a small pack of tissues. She plucked off the lint stuck to the top one and handed over the whole package.

Jessica extracted a Kleenex and dabbed at her eyes.

"Tell me what happened," Nikki said softly, taking in the scene around her. There were cops everywhere in here, too. They looked stark in their dark blue uniforms against the pristine, contemporary living room. Everything was white here: the floor tile, the walls, the leather couch, the drapes, even the wrought-iron railing of the small balcony off the living room. No one seemed to be paying much attention to the so-called murder suspect.

The whole scene felt surreal.

When Jessica didn't answer, Nikki stepped closer, looking into her teary green eyes. "You have to tell me what happened," she repeated. "I can't help you if I don't know what's going on."

"How can I tell you what's going on? I don't know what's going on!" She sniffed and dabbed under her eyes. "I . . . I went to that seminar downtown. Came straight home. It's wash night. I . . . I went into the bedroom to get the clothes from my laundry basket and there he was." She gestured with the Kleenex, as if Rex March was right in front of her. "Rex. Dead. In my bed."

Nikki felt her forehead wrinkle. She was headed for Botox for sure. Probably sooner rather than later. "It really is Rex?"

"It sure as hell looks like Rex." She sniffed. "He's wearing nothing but a pair of gold lamé bikini briefs. Doesn't a man his age know better?"

It was a bizarre comment, even for the fashion-conscious Jessica, but Nikki let it slide. She was still hung up on the whole Rex-is-already-dead issue. "And you have no idea how he got here?"

"Of course not." Jessica hugged herself. "I was at that seminar all day. Plenty of people saw me. I don't understand how anyone could think I did this."

Nikki glanced in the direction of the bedroom. The door was open and she could see plenty of cops inside, but she couldn't see the bed from this angle. "Has anyone called Edith?"

"I don't know. I know I sure as hell didn't. How'd you like to be the one to make *that* phone call?"

Nikki would have laughed had the circumstances been different. Rex March had not been a good husband to his wife of twenty-some years and everyone knew it, including Edith. He'd been a liar and a cheat. Over the last few years, he'd made a fool of his wife in the pages of gossip magazines more times than Nikki could count. So Edith hadn't exactly been the heartbroken widow when he'd been declared dead. The first time.

And now Edith was about to be notified, if she hadn't already been, of her husband's second demise. Just thinking about it made Nikki dizzy. Or at least made her wish she had a large glass of Syrah. Maybe a whole bottle.

"That's it?" Nikki studied Jessica's pale face. "There's a dead man in your bed and that's all you know?"

"That's all I know." Jessica opened both hands. "And now you know as much as I do."

"Miss Martin?" A guy in a rumpled brown suit stuck his head out of the bedroom door. Dirty hair. Five o'clock shadow. Had to be a detective. He was a perfect example of how stereotypes were perpetuated in the media. "Miss Martin, can I speak with you for a moment?"

Jessica snatched Nikki's hand and Nikki felt the damp tissue against her palm. Jessica tugged. "You have to come with me. I can't go in there alone again," she whispered. "Not with *him.*"

Nikki didn't know if she was referring to Rex or the guy in the brown suit, but she allowed herself to be led into the bedroom.

Seeing Nikki, the guy pointed. "She can't—"

"This is my best friend, Nikki Harper. *The* Nikki Harper, daughter of Victoria Bordeaux." Jessica clutched Nikki's hand with both of hers. "I don't have to tell you what an influential woman her mother is or how big a stink she'll throw if her daughter isn't treated by the LAPD with utmost respect."

"Detective Lutz." He didn't offer to shake Nikki's hand, which was okay with her. He was wearing a latex glove that could possibly have touched Rex's body.

"This is a crime scene, Miss Martin," he said, looking back at Jessica. His cadence was weird. Almost mechanical. "She can't come in here. I don't care who she is."

"But he can?"

He looked at her with obvious impatience. "Who?"

"Him." Jessica pushed past the detective, into her bedroom, dragging Nikki along with her. "Him!" She let go of one hand to point in the direction of her bed, set diagonally in the west corner, out of direct line with the door. Good feng shui.

"At least I invited her," Jessica said in a shaky voice. "I *didn't* invite him."

Several cops in the room turned to look at Jessica, but Nikki barely noticed them. Her gaze started at the tip of Jessica's manicured nail, and followed an invisible beam across the bedroom to the bed. She tried to stop herself. She'd already seen one dead man. Enough for a lifetime. But she couldn't look away.

Nikki didn't know what she expected. Hell, she hadn't expected to see Rex March at all, no matter what everyone was telling her.

But there he was. His pale, bloated body in the middle of the bed, tangled in sky blue silk sheets. He had not been an attractive man when he'd been alive. Dead, he was worse. Stark naked, except for the embarrassingly tiny gold lamé bikini briefs he wore, he looked like something that had washed up on the beach. His protruding, hairy stomach seemed overly tight, like the skin of a drum. And his bald pate was sunburned. That was the last thing Nikki noticed before she looked away.

Her stomach did a flip-flop with the granola bar she and the boys had shared in the car ride to Mother's. "Oh, Jessica," she whispered.

"I know." Jessica stared right at him. "Hell of a sight, isn't he?"

"Miss Martin, you're going to have to come down with me to the Hollywood precinct."

Jessica grabbed Nikki's hand again. She was shaking. Jessica Martin wasn't usually afraid of anything and she didn't shake.

"Am I being arrested?" she asked in a tremulous voice that sounded nothing like her own.

"Not yet." His response was dry. Emotionless. He acted as if he found dead men dead again all the time. Or he just didn't care how many times Rex March died.

"Can you come this way, Miss Martin?" It clearly wasn't an invitation.

Jessica clutched Nikki's hand. "What am I going to do?" she begged, her eyes filling with tears again.

"You're going to answer the detective's questions," Nikki answered firmly.

"But I don't know how he got here. I didn't do this. I swear to God, I didn't."

"I'll get you a lawyer."

"I don't need a lawyer," she declared shrilly. "I didn't do anything wrong."

"I'll get you one anyway."

"Miss Martin." The detective took her arm.

"Please, Nikki. Please." Jessica let go of Nikki's hand as he pulled her away. "You have to help me."

"This way."

Nikki's eyes stung. "I'll be right behind you, Jess. You said Hollywood precinct, right?" she called after the detective.

"Yes, ma'am."

Nikki glanced back at Rex's body before walking out of the bedroom. The sight of his dead body was deeply disturbing. Even more disturbing was the situation his body had put Jessica in. *How did you get here?* she wanted to ask him. *And why the hell are you wearing those ridiculous briefs?*

Chapter 4

Outside the doors of the LAPD Hollywood Station on Wilcox Avenue, Nikki took a deep breath and closed her eyes. It was early in the season for the Santa Ana, only the first week of October, but a warm, dry breeze teased the hair that had fallen from her ponytail. On the night air, she could smell the intoxicating fragrance of the white flowers blooming in the nearby bee brush.

She took another deep breath, and rang her mother. It was nine fifty-nine; Victoria never received calls after ten p.m. She insisted on nine hours of *beauty rest* each night, unless she was making a public appearance, or there was an emergency. Jessica's arrest for murder definitely did not count as an emergency. Nikki wasn't entirely sure that if *she* had been arrested for Rex's murder, her mother would have taken her call after ten.

First, Nikki tried Victoria's personal cell phone, but there was no answer. There never was. Victoria had not yet quite gotten the knack of cell phones and constantly misplaced them. This was the third cell Nikki had bought her this year. It was Nikki's own voice on her mother's recorded message. She hung up and called the house. Amondo answered.

An Italian expat, he'd been working for Victoria for more than thirty years and served as her chauffeur, bodyguard, personal secretary, and in whatever other capacity he was needed. He adored Victoria and, secretly, Nikki thought she adored him.

Nikki leaned against the brick wall of the police station and watched the cars crawl by. Across the street, a bail bond sign flashed OPEN 24 HRS.

Cell phone use wasn't permitted in the waiting room where she'd been holed up for hours, so she'd stepped outside. She'd needed a breath of fresh air, anyway. The waiting room stank of unwashed bodies, fish tacos, and . . . despair. The stark walls stirred up memories from her past that she just didn't want roused. "It's Nikki, Amondo," she said, thankful to hear a friendly voice. "Is she still awake?"

"You're cutting it close tonight, *cara mia,*" he teased. "Let me get her." After all these years, he no longer spoke with an Italian accent, but as with most Europeans, Nikki noticed, he had a certain cadence of speech. On Amondo, it was charming and sexy, even for a sixty-year-old man.

He must have been with her in her bedroom suite because Victoria spoke at once into the phone. "I take it the dogs are sleeping over?"

"If you don't mind." Nikki exhaled. She hadn't seen Jessica in nearly three hours and no one, not the desk clerk or any cops she could waylay, could tell her anything about what was going on. The endless waiting was beginning to wear on her. She was tired and hungry and she just wanted to go home with her dogs and pretend none of this was happening. "I'm at the police station waiting for Jess. I don't know how long I'll be. I'll get them tomorrow."

"They had chicken breast for dinner. Free range."

Nikki's phone beeped. She had another call coming in. She glanced at the screen. It was Jeremy. What were the chances he'd heard about Jessica's arrest already? She didn't answer it. She'd talk with him later.

"Amondo has walked them and tucked them in for the night in your room," Victoria continued. "So I suppose they can stay."

Nikki leaned the back of her head against the wall as she watched an LAPD car zip out of its parking space in front of the station and down the street. She wondered if the cop was headed to a homicide or out for a bite. She doubted he'd be having free range chicken for dinner. "Aren't you even going to ask me why Jess is at the police department?"

"Finally arrested for prostitution?"

"That's not funny, Mother."

"Neither is being arrested for killing Rex March. Although, I suppose it is, when you think about it. Being arrested for killing a man who was already dead."

"You heard?" Nikki stood upright, gripping her BlackBerry. "How did you hear already?"

Victoria chuckled. "Darling, you know I never reveal my sources."

Victoria had an intricate web of informants in Hollywood to rival any police department's . . . probably even the FBI's . . . and the CIA's. Combined. Hairdressers, manicurists, doormen, all willing to lay down their lives to be certain Victoria Bordeaux was the first in Hollywood to know the latest news about anyone even remotely connected to her. In return, she granted them her glorious smile and the occasional ticket to a movie première or a gift bag of goodies she'd collected in a green room somewhere. She was actually quite kind to her informants and they were utterly loyal to her in return.

"How did she kill him?" Victoria continued drolly. "I sent a four hundred dollar spray to his memorial service. I hope Edith doesn't expect a second."

"Mother! How could you say such a thing? The man is *dead*."

"For a second time," Victoria injected. "Let's be honest, Nicolette, the man was always a liar. How do we know there won't be a third?"

"Jessica didn't kill him." Nikki ignored her mother's witty sarcasm. "She didn't even know he was alive." She thought for a second. "*You* didn't know he was alive, either, and I'm quite sure Edith didn't."

"Right. Otherwise, she'd have been a bit more hush-hush about that beefcake moving in with her, wouldn't she?"

Some people thought Victoria Bordeaux was too outspoken. She *was* candid, but she was usually saying what others thought but wouldn't *dare* say.

"I should go, Mother. I just wanted to let you know where I am and that I'll be by tomorrow to pick up Stan and Ollie." She heard the rumble of a male voice, then her mother's again.

"Amondo says he'll dog-sit tomorrow," Victoria said. "He enjoys walking them. I have no earthly idea why. He's going on about some kind of dog treats he's bought for them. He'll let them into your place tomorrow afternoon if that suits. He has your key."

Nikki smiled. Amondo had always been good to her . . . and to the dogs. "Tell him I'd appreciate that." She hesitated. She didn't really know what she wanted from her mother, why she'd really called, beyond checking on Stan and Ollie. She just wanted to hear her mother's voice, she supposed. Silly. "I should go. No one has told me anything about what's happening. I'm not even sure if the police actually arrested Jessica or if they're just questioning her, but I intend to find out."

"Please tell me you're not going to get involved in this, Nicolette."

Nikki began to walk toward the glass doors that led inside, keeping her eye on a guy coming up the sidewalk, headed for the same door. He was dressed like an Amish man, of all things: full beard, straw hat, highwater pants and suspenders. In Hollywood, there were impersonators walking the streets every day: Marilyn Monroes, Elvises by the dozens, James Deans. Nikki had seen some crazy things in Hollywood, so crazy that she had begun to think nothing would surprise her. Then a man impersonating an Amish farmer appears at the police department . . . and Rex comes back from the dead to die again in Jessica's bed. Nikki returned her attention to her mother, still eyeing the Amish guy.

"She's my best friend, Mother."

"I don't know if she killed Rex or not. I don't really care. I'm just saying this is a matter better left to professionals. To the police. Lawyers and such."

"The same way we left Dad's murder investigation to the police?" Nikki hugged her bag to her side. "Is that what you mean, Mother?"

Victoria sighed on the other end of the line. "Why don't you come here tonight? Ina's already gone, but I'm sure Amondo could make up your bed fresh for you." Her voice wasn't exactly gentle, but Nikki could hear the emotion behind her gruff exterior. Even though Victoria had been divorced from John Harper for many years by the time he had been murdered, she had mourned his death deeply. And gone to great lengths to hide that.

"I don't know where I'll go tonight. Probably my place. Then again, I might be sleeping in a blue plastic chair." Nikki waited for the Amish impersonator to enter the building before going through the front doors. "Talk to you tomorrow, Mother."

Victoria hung up. There were never good-byes on the phone with her.

Inside the building, Nikki watched the Amish guy walk up to the glass window, speak to the clerk, and take a seat in the row of blue chairs. Nikki stepped up to the window.

The female police officer looked up at her, making Nikki recall the saying, "if looks could kill." It was a cliché, she knew, but clichés were always based on truths, weren't they?

"I'm sorry," the officer said through the bulletproof glass between them. Her voice came out slightly muffled through the holes punched in the glass. "I don't know anything more than the last time you asked. Or the time before that. Have a seat." She returned her attention to the magazine she was reading.

Nikki returned to her campsite. At midnight, the female cop behind the bulletproof glass was replaced by an Hispanic male. Same empty look on his face, same lack of information or willingness to share. Nikki dozed on and off the rest of the night, occasionally making pilgrimages to the bathroom and to the cop at the front desk, only to be sent back to her plastic chair. At one point, a junior-size Amish impersonator was released from the bowels of the station and without speaking a word, the older Amish impersonator had escorted the younger out the front door and into the dark night. Nikki felt as if she had been awake all night, but apparently she hadn't been because eventually Jessica ap-

peared in front of her, nudging her shoulder and startling the bejeezus out of her.

"Come on, Sleeping Beauty. I can go now."

Nikki shot out of the chair; she'd been hugging her
Prada bag so close to her chest to keep it from being
lifted that it had left red marks on her forearms. "They
let you go?"

"For now." Jessica headed for the door, amazingly
still able to teeter on four-inch heels, even after an
overnight interrogation. "I want to get the hell out of
here before they change their mind, arrest me, and
send me to Alcatraz."

Nikki wiped something from the corner of her
mouth that could only have been drool. "They never arrested you?"

"I was *interrogated*. The guy had the worst breath."

"All night?" Nikki followed her out the door. The
sun was already up, bright and full of promise, unlike
Jessica's life at the present.

"Yup. His breath stunk all night. Some awful combination of raw onions, rotten potatoes, and cinnamon
Dentyne."

"I meant, did they question you all night? I'm parked
there." She pointed to her white Prius. Her mother had
given her a Jaguar XF for her fortieth birthday, but she
rarely drove it. It embarrassed her to own such an ex-
cessive car. Jessica kept telling her she should sell it and
blow the money on a trip to Monte Carlo, but Nikki
couldn't do that, either. So it sat in storage and once a
month she and Jeremy took it for a drive. Always after
dark.

Nikki fumbled for the key fob in her bag. She imagined her breath smelled as bad as the cop's who had interrogated Jessica. The corn chips and coffee she'd had

at three in the morning probably hadn't helped matters.

"They kept you all night without arresting you?" Finally managing to unlock the doors, Nikki climbed in.
"Can they even do that?"

"Do I care, as long as they didn't arrest me?" Jessica
buckled in and fell back against the leather seat, closing
her eyes.

Nikki felt the sudden urge to reach out and give her
a hug, a pat on the arm, something, but they didn't
have that kind of relationship. Nikki didn't exactly consider herself a touchy-feely kind of person, but Jessica
was off the chart when it came to physical affection. At
least between friends. So Nikki kept her hugs to herself.
"You all right?" she asked.

Jessica kept her eyes closed. "I just need a double
espresso and a shower. I'll be fine."

Nikki started the car and it purred away from the
curb. "I'll take you right home."

"Can't." Jessica sighed, kicked off her heels, and
glanced at Nikki. "It's officially a crime scene. I can't go
in, not even to get any of my stuff, until it's been released."

"Okay. So, my house." Nikki gripped the wheel. A
million things were running through her head, dis-
jointed by lack of sleep, a corn chip overdose, and genuine fear for her friend. "So we should do something
about getting you a lawyer. The sooner the better."

"I can't afford a lawyer, Nik. I owe American Express
six thousand in two days. Why would I need a lawyer if I
didn't do it?"

"Then I'll pay for the lawyer." Nikki was generally
careful about throwing money around. Her father had
left her wealthy, immensely so, but she tried to live a
lifestyle appropriate to her own income. Growing up,

she'd seen what wealth did to too many people and she had decided years ago not to allow that to happen to herself. She had enough baggage to drag around without filling it with gold. It was a subject she and her mother had agreed to disagree on. On alternating Sundays, at least. The rest of the week, Victoria made a point of telling Nikki what a fool she was to even work.

"So what happened?" Nikki asked, easing onto Sunset. "They questioned you about Rex and . . ."

"And they questioned me and questioned me." Jessica gestured wildly as she talked, her words becoming manic. She acted as if she'd already had two double espressos. "They asked me why I killed Rex. I said I didn't. They asked me how he could be alive when he'd crashed his plane in the desert. I said I didn't know. They asked me how his body got in my apartment if I didn't kill him and I said I didn't know. It kind of went around in a circle after that."

"But they believed you? They must have believed you." Nikki hit her horn as a monstrous black SUV with tinted windows cut her off. "Otherwise they wouldn't have released you, right? I mean, they would have arrested you if they really thought you did it."

"Oh, they think I did it, all right. That or they're just too lazy to get off their asses, get out there, and find out who did. Apparently, because they found no murder weapon in the apartment, no evidence I killed him, they couldn't arrest me. You know, it's all circumstantial bullshit. But they said it was only a matter of time before they had what they needed. I can't leave the state."

"So what about the fact that Rex was already dead? How did that play into the whole questioning thing?"

"Not at all. I mean, *obviously*, he wasn't dead. Even those boneheads figured that out." She looked at Nikki. "I need a cigarette. Can we stop and get a pack?"

"Sorry." Nikki made a face. "You can't smoke in my car. You know that. Or my house."

Jessica wiggled in the car seat, pulling down her fitted navy skirt. After a night of interrogation, she looked a hell of a lot better and far less wrinkly than Nikki. "There are cigarettes in my car. And some other things. Can we run by?"

Nikki hesitated. Obviously, she wanted to help Jessica any way she could, but as her friend, she felt as if she had to keep Jessica from doing anything that might rile the cops even more. "I don't know that you should be near your apartment. It might seem suspicious."

"I don't want to go inside." Jessica shuddered. "I don't know if I'll ever be able to sleep in that bed again. I just can't get that picture out of my mind, of Rex dead on my St. Geneve silk sheets." She gripped the sides of the leather seat as if she was holding on for dear life. "Please. I just want to get into my car and get my cigarettes and my bags. I went shopping at lunch yesterday. I bought the cutest Raquel Allegra tunic. I can put it on after I shower."

"The police might have already impounded your car," Nikki argued. But she was already hitting her turn signal to head back toward Jess's, on Hancock.

"If they can find it."

Nikki cut her eyes at Jessica. "It's not in your apartment garage?"

"On the street, a block down."

"Why?"

"This weirdo was following me yesterday on the way home. I parked and cut through the alley. I didn't want him to know where I lived. Why would the police want my car?"

"There could potentially be evidence."

"Evidence of what? *I didn't kill him,* Nikki!" Her last words came out in a sob.

Nikki broke the rules and gave Jessica's manicured hand a quick squeeze. "I'm telling you how the cops might be thinking, not me."

"I can't believe the police think I did this." Jessica sniffed and pressed the heel of her hand under her nose. "To . . . to Rex."

"When he was already dead," Nikki added.

"Exactly. Oh, Nikki." Jessica, breaking her own rules, wrapped her fingers around Nikki's wrist. "What am I going to do? What if they railroad me? What if they say I killed him and they put me away for the next twenty years?" She sounded as if she was going to burst into tears.

Nikki gripped the wheel, staring at the bumper ahead of her. "Here's what you're going to do. We're going to grab your bags from your car, you're going to take a shower at my place, and you're going to lie down for a couple of hours and then you're going to go to work. You're going to go about your day as if this is all a misunderstanding, you're innocent of all charges, and someone is trying to frame you, which obviously they are."

"Okay, okay." Jessica nodded, as if seeing the plan now. She looked up. "But what are you going to do?"

Nikki turned onto Jessica's street and spotted her green BMW. "I'm going to prove your innocence."

"How are you going to do that?"

"I'm going to find out who killed Rex . . . this time."

Chapter 5

Nikki hesitated at the apartment next to Jessica's, finger poised over the doorbell. Was she doing the right thing, or was this one of those instances where Victoria's words would haunt her later?

Back at her place, Nikki and Jessica had both showered and while Jessica lay down, Nikki had thrown on some clothes and run out to get bagels. She didn't want to leave Jessica alone for long, but, on impulse, she'd made a detour to Jessica's apartment building. She knew the logical thing to do was just let the police handle the investigation, but all these years of guilt about leaving her father's murder to the *authorities* told her that she just couldn't bring herself to do it. If only she had interfered in *that* case, maybe her dad's killer wouldn't have gotten away scot-free. To kill again.

So here she was. She assumed the police had questioned all of Jessica's neighbors, but she knew Mrs. McCauley from previous visits to the building. More importantly, she knew the elderly woman didn't get out much, so she made a career of watching her neighbors.

The thing was, Mrs. McCauley could be a little difficult to talk to sometimes; she rambled and she didn't always make sense. What if the police had missed something in their conversation with her, or just written her off as the neighborly nut job?

Either way, it wouldn't hurt for Nikki to speak with her. If nothing else, she would brighten the old lady's day by stopping to say hello. Nikki rang the doorbell, which chimed inside. The chimes were followed by a bizarre series of scraping, thumping sounds, as if someone were dragging a bag of bricks to the door.

"Yes?" Mrs. McCauley called from inside. She had a slight European accent. Eastern Bloc, Nikki guessed.

Nikki stepped back so the senior citizen could see her through the peephole. "Mrs. McCauley, it's Nikki Harper."

"Nikki Harper? I don't know you."

"Yes, you do." Nikki could see a filmy cataract-covered eye through the peephole. It was a little unnerving. "We've met before. I'm a friend of Jessica's . . . Jessica Martin. Next door. In 322?"

The pale eye blinked.

"I . . . I was wondering if I could speak with you, Mrs. McCauley."

"Nikki Harper," the old lady repeated.

"Yes. Yes, that's right. I'm Nikki Harper. I'm a real estate agent. And . . . and a good friend of Jessica's."

"You're Natalie Wood's daughter."

Nikki grimaced. She had nothing personally against Natalie Wood, but Victoria and Natalie had not been the best of friends, not after Natalie had gotten the part in *Splendor in the Grass* and gone on to receive an Academy Award nomination for her performance. To this day, despite its Academy Awards for Best Writing, Story and Screenplay, Victoria refused to show *Splendor in the*

Grass on movie night. "No, no, not Natalie Wood's daughter. I'm Victoria Bordeaux's daughter."

Again, the eye blinked. "Victoria Bordeaux wasn't in *Rebel Without a Cause*."

"No, she wasn't, Mrs. McCauley, but she *was* in *Fortune's Wheel* the same year."

"But not with James Dean. He's dead, you know. Such a waste. Stupid boy."

Nikki's phone rang in her bag. She ignored it but Mrs. McCauley stared. "You going to get that?"

"Um . . . no. Sorry." She reached into her Prada, glanced at the screen long enough to see that it was Jeremy calling again and hit the power button. She'd call him later. For sure. "I'm sorry," Nikki said. "You were saying?"

"I was saying Victoria Bordeaux definitely wasn't in *Rebel Without a Cause,* and don't try to tell me otherwise."

Nikki looked up and down the hallway. This was a bad idea, coming here. She'd have been better off questioning the bagels in her car. "No, ma'am."

"That was Warren Beatty. In that movie with her. He slept with a lot of women, you know." The eye squinted. "Probably with your mother. Between husbands, of course," she added quickly.

The old woman knew her 1960s movies, Nikki would give her that. "Mrs. McCauley, could you open the door? I'd like to speak to you and I . . . I don't have a lot of time."

"Because your mother's a movie star."

"No, not because my mother's a movie star. She isn't *really* anymore, anyway. She's pretty much retired." Nikki heaved her bag from one shoulder to the other. "I don't have a lot of time because I need to get home and get ready for work."

The eye disappeared. Then, on the other side of the door, Nikki heard the same scraping and banging she'd detected when Mrs. McCauley first came to the door. The door slowly opened. Mrs. McCauley stood just under five feet tall and was accompanied by a walker. It was a plastic stool she'd been dragging . . . behind her walker. A stool that, apparently, allowed her to see through her peephole.

"Mrs. McCauley, thanks. For taking time to speak with me." She tried not to stare. The old lady was wearing a very short pink and blue plaid kilt, red tights, tap shoes, and an A-Team t-shirt. Old-school TV. Not the Liam Neeson flick.

Mrs. McCauley shook Nikki's hand, studying her suspiciously. The cataract-clouded eyes were blue. Her close-cropped hair was also blue, though a different shade. "Victoria Bordeaux's daughter, eh?" She rolled the walker forward a couple of inches to get a better look at Nikki. The walker came equipped with a quilted bag holding multiple tabloid magazines, a copy of the latest issue of *The Economist*, and a toilet bowl brush.

"You're tall," she continued. "I liked her in *Fortune's Wheel*, but not in *The Widow's Daughter*. She should never have taken that part. I told my husband Sean that. I said 'Sean, Victoria Bordeaux should never have agreed to be in that film!' He's been dead twenty-two years, God rest his soul."

Nikki nibbled on her lower lip. "Um . . . I'll be sure to tell her." She looked up and down the hallway, then back at Mrs. McCauley. Apparently she wasn't going to be invited in, which was okay. The apartment smelled of brining cabbage. "I was wondering. Um . . . did you . . ." Nikki sensed the need to work on her interrogation skills. "Did the police speak to you yesterday?"

"About the murder next door?" the old lady asked

matter-of-factly. Despite the accent, her English was very good.

"Yes."

"I think the police have lost their minds. But that's obvious, isn't it? Such behavior. Racial profiling. On the take. All you have to do is watch TV. Read the newspaper. You have nice hair. Red. I always wanted red hair. No one killed Rex March in that girl's apartment," she scoffed. "He couldn't have been there. He was dead already. I'd certainly have known if a dead man was here." She squinted her eyes. "I know everything that happens in the building. You know that, don't you? Is your hair real or out of a box?"

Nikki wasn't sure how to respond. "Um . . . it's my natural color." She didn't think she needed to confess that she highlighted it every once in a while. "So . . . you didn't see Rex March go into Jessica's apartment? Or . . . anything else unusual?"

"All those policemen. *That* was unusual. We don't get many cops here. It's a quiet building, except for the loud music in 311 sometimes." She leaned forward on her walker. Despite needing assistance to get around, she seemed pretty spry for a woman who appeared to be . . . a hundred, a hundred-and-twenty years old. She looked as if she were wearing a wrinkle suit, the wrinkles on her face and arms and hands were so pronounced.

Nikki gestured. "Before that. I meant, did you see anything unusual *before* the police came? During the day. Like . . . maybe Rex March going into Jessica's apartment?"

"I already told you. I'd have noticed a dead man walking in the hallway. I usually keep my door open, you know. I have a gate I put up here to keep people out, but with the murder and all, the police say I should keep my door shut." She held up a finger. "Oh, but you know what *did* happen yesterday that was out of the ordinary?"

Nikki waited.

"Jean-Luc Picard was in the garden. In the back. I saw him from my balcony. I see a lot from my balcony. 209 sunbathes without his shorts. You know him, don't you?"

Nikki wasn't sure if she meant the nude sunbather or the TV/movie character. She shook her head in confusion.

"Of course you do. Captain of the *Enterprise.* The new starship, not the old one. Kirk blew that up." She smiled slyly, balancing with one hand so she could waggle a finger with the other. "Very handsome man, that Captain Picard. Wouldn't mind if he beamed himself into *my* boudoir, I'll tell you that."

Nikki took a step back. This was more like it. *This* was the Mrs. McCauley she knew. "He *is* handsome—Patrick Stewart—the actor . . . who plays Jean-Luc Picard." She studied the old woman's wrinkles on her face. "So, Picard was here, but you never saw Rex March?"

"Nope." She began to roll backwards. "But that doesn't mean Picard didn't beam him into her apartment, does it?"

Nikki was still standing at the door when Mrs. McCauley closed it. "I need some sleep," Nikki muttered as she walked away.

The next apartment she tried was 324, on the other side of Jessica. She was surprised when she rang the doorbell and someone was actually home. It was close to nine o'clock. She assumed most people would be at work.

"Yeah?" came a male voice from the other side of the door.

"Hi. I'm Nikki—"

"I know who you are." The door opened a second later. "I'm Pete Toro."

Pete was nice looking: dark hair, medium build with a suntan that didn't appear to be sprayed on. He thrust out his hand to shake hers vigorously. "And you're Nikki Harper, Victoria Bordeaux's daughter. Jessica's told me all about you."

"She did?" That was funny; Jessica had never mentioned *him* before.

"Sure. You're her best friend." He finally let go of her hand. "What can I do for you?"

Nikki hung onto her bag for emotional support. "I guess . . ." She gave a humorless laugh and started again. "I guess you know what happened next door yesterday. I mean, not *what happened*, but . . . what Jessica's been accused of."

"Yeah. Right. Oh, my God. Poor Jessica." He touched his forehead. He had nice hair, thick and wavy. "I can't believe the police arrested her. There's no way Jessica could have done a thing like that. Is she okay? Please tell me she's okay."

"She's okay. They didn't arrest her. At least, not yet. They just took her to the station and questioned her. She's staying with me right now." She glanced in the direction of Jessica's door, barred with yellow crime-scene tape, a piece of paper sealing the door. "She's not allowed to go back to the apartment. Not yet."

He glanced at the door, then back again. "Right. Sure. Well, tell her I was asking for her. Tell her maybe she and I can have that drink when she gets back. We've been trying to hook up, she and I. To have a drink. We're just so busy, both of us. Her with her real estate job and me at the store. I work retail."

"Listen, Pete." Nikki looked him straight in the eye. Victoria always said that was the best way to get honesty out of someone; she said it took them by surprise and they didn't have time to lie. "About this thing with Jessica yesterday. You didn't . . . happen to see anything, did you?"

"See anything?" He leaned on the doorjamb. He had nice biceps.

"Anything unusual."

"Like Rex March?" He laughed. "No. I didn't see him. Hey, you want to come in? I've got coffee." He pointed inside.

"I can't. Thanks. Gotta go home, pick up Jessica and then get to work. You were saying you didn't see anything unusual yesterday?"

"I didn't get home until six-thirty. I was heating up a bean burrito when I heard the sirens. The next thing I know, the cops are banging on my door and telling me I need to stay inside. That someone would be by to talk with me. I didn't know what the hell was going on. I was afraid something had happened to Jessica."

So he hadn't seen anything. Something told Nikki that if she banged on every door on the floor, she'd get the same answer. Either people weren't home, or they were home but didn't see anything.

She stepped back. "Well, thanks. I was just checking around. You know." She gave a quick smile. "Making sure the police didn't miss anything. But I guess they didn't. Since you didn't see Rex."

"I wouldn't tell the cops if I did see him. He deserved to die. Both times, however the heck that happened. I gotta tell you, I was just glad he was gone.

Jessica deserved better than that jackass, I don't care how famous he was."

Nikki was just starting to turn away, but she turned back, giving Pete Toro her full attention. "I'm sorry . . . Jessica *deserved better?*" When she tried the "look him straight in the eyes" thing this time, it didn't work. He suddenly became preoccupied with his shoes.

"It's none of my business."

"Pete, the police are saying Jessica killed Rex March. You don't want her to go to jail for a murder she didn't commit, do you?" She got in his personal space. "You've seen Rex March before? With Jessica?"

He still wouldn't look her in the eye. "Before he was *supposedly* killed in that plane crash. He used to come by here. He was a complete ass. He would never give an autograph or anything like that. Jessica deserved better than that old geezer."

It was Nikki's turn to stare at her own shoes. She tried to think through what Pete had said. Jessica and Rex? Was it true? What reason would this guy have to lie?

She glanced up at him. "Listen, thanks. You have a good day." She walked away.

"Tell Jessica I said hi," he called after her. "I'll keep that drink cold for her."

Nikki waited until he closed his door and then went back to Mrs. McCauley's. She rang the doorbell and Mrs. McCauley went through the same routine of dragging the stool to the door so she could look out the peephole. Nikki waited patiently until the door opened.

"It's you again. Natalie Wood's daughter. You should have been in the movies. Pretty enough."

"Victoria Bordeaux's daughter. Nikki Harper. Mrs. McCauley, did you ever see Rex March in this apartment building?"

"Of course. But that was before he was dead. The other time," she added.

Nikki stared at the little old lady. "Why didn't you say that before—when I asked you if you'd seen him?"

"You asked me if I'd seen him *yesterday*."

Nikki closed her eyes for a second. Taking a breath, she opened them again. "So you didn't see him yesterday, but you've seen him here before. Before he was killed in the plane crash?" she asked, pretty certain she was pushing her luck with that last bit.

"He used to come to Jessica's apartment." The old lady nodded. "With either Jimmy Stewart or that cute Frank Sinatra."

Nikki forced a smile. This was going nowhere. Fast. If the police had assumed Mrs. McCauley would be no help in the investigation, they would have been right.

"Well, thanks again. You have a good day."

Nikki took the steps instead of the elevator, tired and frustrated. Jessica and Rex? She couldn't believe it.

Of course she could believe it, when she really thought about it. Rex was sooo Jessica's type: rich, married, a total ass. Nikki had lost count of the number of men like him that Jessica had gone through. And now Edith's coolness with Jessica made total sense. Jessica had been having an affair with her husband before he died.

The first time.

Chapter 6

"I'm so sorry," Jessica said, sounding truly contrite. Nikki gripped the steering wheel as if she were maneuvering a tank, which was sometimes an excellent skill, driving in L.A. "I can't believe you didn't tell me. We were representing him, Jess." She shook her head. "That is *so* not cool, starting an affair with a client."

Jessica was silent long enough that Nikki glanced over. "What?"

Jessica nibbled on her berry-red lips. She looked entirely too put together for someone who had spent the night in jail being interrogated, slept less than two hours, and used the makeup in her purse to do her face. The new pencil skirt and silk tunic from K-Dash didn't hurt. Nor did the fact that she was so drop-dead gorgeous that she could have come out of a night of interrogation in a Dumpster and looked good.

Jessica spoke in a meek voice. "It kind of started before he asked us to sell the house for him."

Nikki rolled her eyes and concentrated on the black Benz convertible in front of her. The blond driver was

on her cell and paying no attention whatsoever to the
traffic ahead of her. "How could you, Jess? How could
you, and then not tell me?"

"I'm sorry. I'm so sorry. I swear to God I am." She
was teary now. "I know this is hard for you to believe,
but he was really sweet to me, Nik. At least in the beginning. And Edith didn't understand what he was going
through with his career and—"

"Oh, please," Nikki groaned. "*Do not* tell me you fell
for the 'my wife doesn't understand me' line. Not again."

"It wasn't like that. Not this time. He made me feel
good . . . at least at first," she added in a tiny voice.

Nikki pressed her lips together and signaled to pull
over in front of the shoe repair shop. Jessica had a pair
of Jimmy Choos that she insisted had to be dropped off
today. She'd fished the box out of her car when they'd
stopped for her shopping bags. "I'll wait for you here."
Nikki put the car in park.

Jessica reached around to grab the bag with her
shoes off the back seat. "Please don't be angry with me."

"I'm not angry," Nikki said. And she wasn't. But she
was disappointed in her friend. It was wrong to go out
with a married man, period, end of discussion.

"But you *are* disappointed in me." Jessica looked her
in the eye. "Oh, God, that's why I didn't tell you—I
didn't want you to be disappointed in me." She sniffed.
"Again."

Nikki dropped her hands to her lap. "I only want
what's best for you, and men like Rex—"

"I know, I know. I swear to God that I'll never do it
again." She gripped the shopping bag containing her
$1,800 shoes, given to her, no doubt, by one of her *ad-
mirers*. Maybe even Rex. "Just get me through this and I
swear I'm done with married men. I'm done with Sugar
Daddies, married, unmarried. It doesn't matter." She

rested her hand on Nikki's arm, her second display of affection in the same day. "Help me, Nikki. Help me get through this and I'm turning over a new leaf. I swear to God I am."

Nikki stared straight ahead. "Did you know he was alive?"

"Rex? Oh, sweet Jesus, no. I didn't. You have to believe me. I didn't know. We had a fight, and then . . . then the next thing I knew, his plane went down and he was gone. He . . . he was just gone."

Nikki exhaled and glanced at her friend. "Enough with the tears. Your mascara will run."

Jessica sniffed and laughed. "You believe me?"

"Of course I believe you," Nikki said gently. "Now drop off the shoes and let's go to work. We've got estates to sell and a murder to solve."

Nikki punched in the security code and waited as the white iron gates swung open, admitting her onto her mother's property in Beverly Hills, north of Sunset. It was an older, well-established neighborhood, the residence of the stars of Hollywood's Golden Age, like Jimmy Stewart and Lucille Ball.

Nikki had arrived home to find that the doggies had not been dropped off. It had taken three phone calls, one in which Victoria *accidentally* hung up on her, to learn that Stan and Ollie were still *visiting*. According to Victoria, Amondo had been busy all day with errands for her and hadn't had time to run them home to Nikki's. It was a ploy, of course, on Victoria's part, to get Nikki to come over. It worked. As tired as she was, she wanted to see her dogs, so she'd left Jessica with the TV remote control and a bag of take-out Chinese and headed over to the 1000 block of Roxbury Drive.

Nikki maneuvered her car around the piles of twigs and yard debris that her mother's gardener, Jorge, had left in the circular driveway. "Really, Frank? Really?" Nikki muttered, her favorite line from *Always Sunny in Philadelphia.*

Jorge wasn't just her mother's landscaper/gardener. He was the son of Victoria's housekeeper, Ina, who'd been with Victoria since the golden years of her cinema days. Nikki had practically grown up with Jorge, and in a lot of ways, she was closer to him than her half-siblings. Nikki had spent a great deal of her childhood hanging out in Ina's cozy kitchen playing go fish, then old maid, then gin rummy with Jorge. He had been the first boy she ever kissed—purely a rehearsal for the real deal.

As Nikki slalomed around the piles of cuttings, her phone rang on the seat. It was Jeremy. It was the fourth time he'd called since the previous night. She studied the phone for a moment. She didn't even know why she was avoiding him.

That was a lie. She *did* know.

She hadn't picked up or returned his multiple messages because she didn't want to deal with him right now. That was always a bad sign in a relationship, wasn't it?

She answered on the third ring as she parked her car in front of the two-story, white Georgian with a two-story entry. There was no sign of Jorge or any of his utility trucks. Over the years, Jorge had expanded his business from one guy and a pickup truck to four vans and utility trailers and twelve to fifteen employees, thanks to a personal loan from Victoria.

"Hey," she said into the phone.

"Nikki, I was beginning to worry. Why didn't you call me back? I left four messages."

"And how was your day, dear? Mine was terrific." She

shifted the car into park and turned off the engine. "Except for the part when my best friend found a dead man in her bed and then was accused of killing him and hauled off to the slammer."

Jeremy sighed on the other end of the line. "Sorry. It's just that I really was worried about you. And no one calls it 'the slammer' anymore, no one but eighty-year-old men, hon."

She smiled. It was nice to hear his sexy dentist voice. "Sorry about being so touchy. I'm fine. I didn't call you back because I haven't had time—" She stopped and started again. "I know you're not a big fan of Jessica's. I guess I just didn't want you to judge."

"I wouldn't judge. Innocent until proven guilty. I just wanted to know what was going on and make sure you were okay. When Victoria called, she said—"

"My mother called you?" she interrupted. She put the window down. The evening breeze felt good. The air was filled with the scent of bougainvillea and fresh-cut grass and she could hear the bubble of the massive three-tiered fountain in the middle of the front lawn. "Why, for heaven's sake, did she call you?"

"You're getting touchy again," he warned. "She cares about you, that's all. You don't always give her enough credit."

Nikki eyed the second-story windows on the end of the Paul Williams Georgian. Her mother's room. Victoria didn't like it when her daughter sat in the driveway on her cell phone. It meant Victoria couldn't hear what was being said, leaving her uninformed. A fate worse than overenthusiastic eyebrow waxing. It would only be a matter of time before Victoria was down here, staring in the car window at her.

"I'm sorry, Jeremy," she said. "You're right. I'm just beat, that's all."

"So did the police really arrest Jessica for killing Rex March?"

She rubbed her temples and eyed the window again. She thought she could hear Stanley and Oliver barking . . . in the backyard, maybe. "She wasn't arrested. Not yet at least. But she was held all night at the Hollywood precinct for questioning."

"Crazy question, but I went to his memorial service with you. How did Jess kill him if he was already dead?"

"Jess didn't kill him!" It came out louder than she intended. "It doesn't make any more sense to me than it does to you," she said, softening her tone.

"But he was definitely the dead man found in Jessica's apartment? The police didn't make a mistake in identifying the body?"

"Oh, it was him, all right." She began to dig in her bag, hoping to find something to eat. The hot Szechuan chicken hadn't smelled the least bit appetizing when she'd picked it up for Jessica, but suddenly she was starving. "I saw him with my own eyes. Dead as a doornail—more like a swollen carcass—in Jess's bed."

"Aw, Christ, I'm sorry you had to see that, Nik."

She heard the distinct crackle of a food wrapper and dug deeper in anticipation of what the Prada might give up. "Yeah. Me, too. It was pretty awful. And it was definitely Rex." She tried not to think about the hole where his eye had been or the ridiculous underwear he'd been wearing; either would make her nauseous.

"Did . . . did the police offer an explanation as to how he could have been dead in Jessica's apartment when he supposedly died in a plane crash?"

"Well, obviously, he didn't die in a plane crash," she said, unable to curtail her sarcasm. "But the cops didn't really address *that* issue." Bingo! She pulled half a pack of peanuts from her bag; they were probably stale, but she was too hungry to care. "They were more into the whole 'Why did you kill him, Miss Martin?' "

"And Jessica says she didn't do it?"

Nikki rested her BlackBerry between her shoulder and her ear so she could attack the bag of peanuts. "Of course she didn't do it. She was at a real estate seminar all day. I'm sure she's got plenty of witnesses who saw her there."

"That's good, then," he agreed. "As long as the coroner can pinpoint when he was murdered, and she's got an alibi for that window of time."

"Right." Nikki groaned. Leave it to Jeremy to always get right to the crux of the matter. "The thing is, that's going to be an issue. I didn't exactly understand what Jessica was trying to tell me this morning, but somehow Rex's liver temperature was an issue. Jess said the cops acted like her alibi wasn't that strong. Especially since she apparently spent a *long* lunch hour shopping." She munched on the peanuts. "I'm going to look into it. Once we know what time he died, I thought I could retrace her ride down Rodeo. Surely some clerk remembers her."

"Whoa, wait a minute. Go back. *You're* going to talk to the sales clerks? Nikki, that's not up to you. I agree with Victoria."

As if on cue, the upstairs window opened and Victoria popped her head out. She was never late on a cue.

"I know you're Jessica's friend," Jeremy went on, oblivious of the peanuts or Victoria's entrance. "But you can't get involved in a murder investigation."

"You coming in or do you plan to sit out there all night?" Victoria hollered down. Her voice carried well for a woman her age.

"Jeremy, hold on a sec. Mother's paging me." Nikki lowered the phone. "I'll be up in a minute. It's Jeremy," she said, hoping to placate her. Victoria *loved* Jeremy.

"Sorry," Nikki said into the phone. "I'm going to have to go. I'm at Mother's, picking up the boys."

"Ask him if he's coming Wednesday night," Victoria called down. Her turban was lavender terrycloth. She must have just gotten out of the shower.

Nikki sighed as she glanced up, then refocused on the peanut bag again. It was empty. "Jeremy, Mother wants to know if you're coming tomorrow night." She dumped the peanut dust into her mouth.

"Tell him I'm showing *The Little Foxes*, 1942."

Nikki exhaled. "She's showing—"

"With Bette Davis, directed by William Wyler," Victoria interrupted again. She was shouting now. For a woman who had been smoking for close to sixty years, she had good lungs.

Nikki dropped her head back on the headrest. "You get that, Jeremy?"

He chuckled. He thought everything Victoria said and did was amusing. He loved Victoria as much as she loved him. Their love affair got old, for Nikki, after a while. Sometimes it was so bad that Nikki felt as if she was the third wheel in the threesome. They just so *got* each other. Maybe it was the whole Hollywood star background. Jeremy had been a child star, then a teen heartthrob. He'd given it all up for the East Coast, dental school, and a sane, ordinary life. It wasn't until his wife had died and Nikki had come into his life again that his world got crazy again.

"Got it," Jeremy said. "Tell her I'm sorry, but I can't make it. Jerry's got a soccer game and there's a PTA board meeting at Lani's school. I can't get out of it."

"He can't make it," Nikki hollered up to her mother's window. "Jeeze," she muttered under her breath, realizing how ridiculous this would look to anyone watching them. Unless, of course, they knew Victoria. Nikki climbed out of the car. "He's got stuff with the kids!"

Victoria still hung in the open window. "Tell him he's going to miss the fresh oysters I'm having flown in."

"She says—"

"I got that, too." Jeremy was still chuckling. "You go see your mom. We can talk later."

"Sure," Nikki surrendered. "And maybe we could get together this weekend?" She hoped she didn't sound too pathetic or needy. She knew their relationship was complicated right now, but she really did miss him.

"I'll see what's on my schedule."

There was a silence on the phone, but it was a comfortable silence. It made her feel close to him, if only for those few seconds. "Talk to you later," she whispered.

"Later."

Nikki dropped her phone into her bag and glanced up at her mother, still hovering in the window. "You're going to fall out of that window to your death, one of these days, and your face will be plastered all over the *Enquirer*, 'Drugged-out Victoria Bordeaux Commits Suicide.' "

Victoria slammed the window shut.

Nikki smiled as she went inside and crossed the black-and-white tile floor. The front hall was big enough to be a mausoleum. Her footsteps echoed up the wrought-iron curving staircase. As children, she and Jorge—sometimes she and Jorge *and* Jeremy—had played hopscotch on these tiles, until Ina caught them and threatened to beat them with a fly swatter.

She could hear the dogs barking in the back of the

house. She went through the elegant hall, past the formal living room, dining room, and parlor (which most people called a family room) and into the enormous kitchen. Ina had her head in the refrigerator and the dogs were circling the granite island, which was big enough to build a vacation home on.

"Chiquita," Ina greeted.

"Hi, Ina. Was Jorge here today? I haven't seen him in weeks."

"Not Jorge. One of the lazy hombres who works for him." She had no Spanish accent after all these years of living in the U.S. (legally!), but she still liked to spice up her conversation with Spanish words. "I called Jorge and I said, 'Jorge, those are lazy hombres who work for you. They leave sticks in Victoria Bordeaux's driveway.' I said, 'Jorge, fire those lazy hombres before they ruin your business.' "

"And what did he say?"

She spiced up the conversation with a few choice curse words. "I had to leave a message."

"Ah," Nikki said, knowing better than to say anything further when Ina was in one of her moods. She crouched and the dogs hopped up and down, barking a greeting. "There's my boys! How are my boys?" She petted Stanley and then Oliver and then Stanley, the needier of the two, again. "Have you been good boys for Grandma? Have you?"

"This is a game with you, isn't it? A game you're making into a career." Victoria glided into the kitchen. She still wore the lavender turban, and was dressed in a floor-length, white silk robe. "Vexing me." She turned to Ina. "Tea?"

"Be ready in a second. You want it in your room or by the pool?" Ina was still moving things around in the refrigerator.

"It's a nice evening. Poolside." Victoria headed for the back door. "Nicolette."

"I'm not staying, Mother. No tea for me, Ina," she called over her shoulder as she followed Victoria outside. The dogs flew past them; they preferred their "grandmother's" yard to Nikki's. More room to run.

"I'm sorry to hear Jeremy can't come tomorrow night. Alan Ball's coming. Jeremy adores his work." Victoria took a seat in a cushioned chair on the stone terrace that looked out on an immaculately groomed garden. "Sit."

"I'm not staying. I'm beat. The office was crazy today. Apparently, people like the idea of hiring a woman who's been accused of killing a dead man."

"All the more reason why you should have a nice cup of green tea. It's energizing."

Nikki leaned on the back of a chair, letting her hair fall forward over her face. "I don't want to be energized, Mother. I want to go home, put my PJs on and crawl into my bed. I want to be comatose."

Victoria frowned. "Tell me you're not serious about sticking your nose into this business with Rex."

"It's not about Rex, Mother. It's about Jessica." Nikki watched the dogs play tag with each other as they circled the pool. First Ollie chased Stanley, then Stanley chased Ollie, their ears flopping as they sailed around the yard. They made her smile.

"I'm utterly against it, but if Jessica were my friend and I felt inclined to *not* mind my own business—" Victoria met her gaze with those famous piercing blue eyes, "then I'd start with the wife."

"You think Edith could have something to do with this?"

Victoria shrugged theatrically. "If you were Rex's wife and he rose from the dead, wouldn't you kill him?"

Chapter 7

The next day Nikki showed a house on The Strand in Hermosa Beach to an Arab sheik with a name she couldn't pronounce. Then she stopped by Edith's around noon. Security was tight at her front gate and it took two calls to the house before she was able to get in. Shondra, Edith's maid, answered the front door in her black-and-white uniform. The homes with the maids in frilly white aprons always amused Nikki. Even Victoria wasn't *that* pretentious.

But Edith had put up with so much crap with Rex that Nikki was willing to give her a bye on that issue. Besides, the woman had grown up in Echo Park. A woman who fought her way from Echo Park to the canyon neighborhood of Outpost Estates in central Hollywood, even to live in a tacky tomb, deserved a little leeway.

Still, Nikki knew for a fact that Shondra hated the uniform. A pretty girl in her early twenties with mocha skin, dark hair, and her mother's brown eyes, she dreamed of being a model. Her mother, Edith's house-keeper, had gotten her the job; Shondra only did it to

make her rent. She and her cousin shared the position
so they could both go on look-sees.

"Edith in?" Nikki asked.

"Right this way." Halfway across the front hall, Shondra looked over her shoulder and whispered, "Mrs.
March says I have to do it this way."

Nikki smiled. "You do it perfectly."

Shondra led her to Rex's library and held open the
door. Inside, Edith and Thompson were having lunch
on a hideous coffee table fashioned from animal horns
and a slab from a redwood tree. *Was that even legal?* A
footstool made from an elephant's foot, complete with
toenails, made up the furniture grouping.

"Edith, I'm so sorry," Nikki said as she walked in.
Shondra closed the door behind her.

If possible, Rex's library was decorated even worse
than the salon. There were animal heads on the walls:
bison, elk, a bighorn sheep. To Nikki's knowledge, Rex
had never hunted big game in his life. *Exactly where did
a person buy a stuffed elk's head the size of a VW bug?*

"For what?" Edith popped a morsel of sandwich into
her mouth. It smelled like chicken salad. "For the fact
that Rex is really dead, or that he lied about it the first
time?"

Edith's words sounded harsh, but her face told a different story. Her eyes were puffy from crying, her
mouth tight at the corners, making her smile lines
more pronounced. She wasn't an attractive woman, but
Nikki had always thought she did well with what she
had. She always appeared regal. Today, she just looked
sad and exhausted.

"I don't know," Nikki confessed, throwing both
hands up and letting them fall. "For all of it, I guess. I
just feel so bad for you, Edith. You don't deserve this."

"Will it affect the sale of the house?" Thompson asked.

"I don't see why it would." Nikki directed her response to Edith; she was her client, the eye-candy wasn't. "You already have a contract. If the buyers back out, you'll keep the earnest money."

"I don't want the earnest money. I want out of this house! I thought I made that clear to you and that bimbo friend of yours months ago." She pressed her lips together, pushing her plate and half a sandwich away. "I want out of this life. I want you to call the buyer and insist the sale take place as planned."

"Have another half a sandwich, Edie darling," Thompson insisted, pushing a white porcelain plate of sandwich triangles toward her. "You have to eat more than that."

"I can't possibly. I just can't." She sat back against the leather couch constructed of various animal hides sewn together like a puzzle.

Rex had referred to the room as his *big game* library. Nikki and Jessica had privately called it the *cemetery room.* Nikki had seen the work of many a bad decorator in her years as a real estate agent, but this room definitely made her top ten list of worst rooms.

"I . . . can certainly contact the buyers, just to check in with them and be sure everything is running smoothly on their end," Nikki said slowly, deciding to just ignore the bimbo remark. What could she say? Nikki knew what Jessica was, and she had a sneaking suspicion that Edith did, too. That she had known all along. "It's better that I not suggest there's any option but to complete the sale. We don't want to put any ideas in their heads."

"Good. Now, why did you come by?" Edith sipped from a glass of lemonade that Thompson had pushed into her hand. Her voice had a little edge to it; now, the blade was definitely directed toward Nikki.

"I . . . I don't know." She chewed on her lower lip, tasting the last of her Bobbi Brown lipstick. "I guess I just came by to see how you are. To see if there's anything I can do for you."

"There isn't." Thompson slid his arm around Edith's shoulders.

Nikki couldn't decide if it was a gesture of protection or isolation.

"I've got everything under control here," he said.

"Right. Sure. Of course." Nikki rocked back on her sensible-heeled black boots. "And, I guess I just wanted you to know that Jessica didn't do it, Edith. Kill Rex. She has no idea how it happened, how he got in her apartment—"

"Oh, please. He'd been there before. They'd been sleeping together for months when he disappeared."

There was more than just an edge to Edith's voice now. She was bordering on downright hostility.

Nikki stared at the cheetah-skin rug beneath her feet. Surely another illegal acquisition. "I didn't know that until yesterday," she said quietly. "So I guess I came to apologize for that, too." She looked up. "But Jessica's not a bad person. She just—"

"Did she know he was still alive?" Edith interrupted.

"No. Did you?" Nikki didn't know where she found the cojones to ask.

"Of course she didn't," Thompson put in. "I think you need to go, Miss Harper."

Nikki hesitated. This was Edith's house; Thompson was only a guest, though, granted, one with benefits. "I'm just trying to piece things together, Edith. To help Jessica understand what happened."

"I don't know what the hell happened. All I know is that Rex died in a plane crash and I started a new life."

Thompson smiled at her and leaned forward to kiss her.

"Then he comes back," Edith continued, "long enough to get himself murdered, stark naked, in some floozy's bed."

Nikki wanted to argue that her statement wasn't entirely true. Yes, Jessica was probably a floozy, but Rex hadn't been completely naked. She decided to keep quiet and let Edith continue.

"I just want it to all go away." Edith's voice cracked. "Can you do that, Nikki, can you make this all go away?"

Apparently the question was rhetorical. Thompson got to his feet. "Let me show you out."

It wasn't an invitation. Nikki headed for the door on his heels. "I'll be happy to call the buyer and feel them out, if you want me to. I can't imagine why this would affect their taking the house, though."

"We could probably charge more," Thompson commented, holding the leather paneled door open for her. "There's been more about Rex in the papers and magazines in the last year than the previous five, when he was still alive."

Nikki gave him a quick half-smile. He didn't smile back. As he walked her to the front door, she wondered why Thompson and Edith's reception had been so cool. Saturday night at the party, things had been hunky-dory. Edith obviously wasn't upset by the idea that Rex really was dead now. Was this secondhand anger directed at Nikki? Was Edith upset at Nikki because Jessica had been sleeping with Rex? That didn't make sense, because Saturday night Edith had known. She'd apparently known for months.

And what was up with Thompson's attitude?

He held the front door open for her.

Was Edith just upset with everything that had happened, or was there something else going on here? The obvious question was, if Jessica didn't kill Rex, who did? Was Edith trying to hide something?

Nikki glanced up at her escort as she stepped out the front door. "I'll get back to Edith after I talk to the buyers."

"We'd appreciate that." Thompson nodded his square, dimpled chin and closed the door behind her before she had time to say anything more.

"Interesting," Nikki whispered to herself as she made her way to her car. As she got in, she glanced back at the house. She was surprised to see both Thompson and Edith standing in the front hall, watching her through a side transom window.

Very interesting.

"Curtain," Victoria called from where she sat in the first row, raising her hand high and wiggling her fingers. A hush fell over the screening room that she'd had built in the basement of her home in the days before media rooms were the rage. She'd done it elegantly, as she did everything. The room sat twenty-five privileged viewers and was a thing of beauty, imitating the theaters of bygone years. Decorated tastefully in an art deco style, with gilt trim and comfortable velvet seating, the room, even after all these years, still gave Nikki a little thrill every time she walked in.

Some of Nikki's best childhood memories centered around this screening room. Here was where she had seen her mother's first movies and shared her first kiss with Jeremy, back when she was fourteen.

The lights dimmed, the velvet curtain opened, and the dramatic music began to play.

Nikki leaned over in her seat and whispered in her mother's ear, "I went to see Edith March today."

"Did you sell the house to the sheik? I know which one it is. Amondo drove me by. I can't believe anyone would pay fifteen million dollars for a house. A bit affected for a foreigner, don't you think?"

"I'm showing him another in Manhattan Beach tomorrow. He didn't like the pool in Hermosa Beach."

"He comes from a desert. You'd think a blowup kiddy pool would tickle him. How was Edith? Playing the anguished widow?"

"No, not really. I don't understand why you don't like her, Mother. She's always been nice to me. Except maybe today," Nikki added as an afterthought.

"They just don't make movies like this today, do they?" Victoria shook her head. She smelled faintly of her favorite jasmine perfume and the slightest hint of cigarette smoke.

"Have you been smoking again?" Nikki demanded.

"Shhhhh," Amondo hushed from one of the seats in the back. He acted as projectionist and usher on movie nights.

Nikki stared straight ahead as Bette Davis walked onto the screen.

"It's not that I don't like her," Victoria said. "I'm just not sure I trust her. When I called her today—"

"You *called* her?"

"To offer my condolences, and I must say, Nicolette, she was rather cool."

"I got the same reception."

"Was her beau there? The one in the soap commercial?"

Nikki smiled. "He was. And his name is Thompson."

"I thought it was Christopher."

"That's his last name, Mother. It's Thompson Christopher."

"Ridiculous name. And how did *he* behave?"

"It was pretty obvious he didn't want me there. The whole thing was kind of strange. They've both been so nice to me. He was genuinely pleasant at the party the other night."

"Ah hah."

Nikki glanced at her mother in the dark, light from the movie screen flickering on her face. Every hair was in place, her eyebrows perfectly sculptured, her lips a luscious hue. In the gentler light, Victoria looked twenty years younger. She could have been Nikki's sister.

"Ah hah? Ah hah, what?" Nikki asked.

"Ah hah, that's a clue."

"It is?"

"People don't change the way they treat you from one day to the next without reason."

"Meaning?"

"Shh," Victoria hushed, pointing at the screen. "I love this line."

Nikki watched as her mother mimicked Bette Davis, moving her lips as she was speaking the lines.

"Look at that shot." Victoria swept her hand. "Bette Davis never looked so good as she did in one of Willi's films. He was hard to work with, though." She snapped her fingers. "Take after take with no instruction or critique. We never knew what he wanted out of us. I think that was the key to his brilliance as a director." She glanced at Nikki. "Do you think he's hiding something?"

"Who?" Nikki had a hard time following her mother's conversations sometimes. Victoria was a conversation multitasker, if ever there was one.

"The boyfriend with the ridiculous name."

"Thompson Christopher."

"Right. Wait." She held up a finger. "Listen to this delivery."

Nikki returned her attention to the movie screen. Five minutes passed before Victoria spoke again. Nikki felt bad for their guests. She knew Victoria's talking had to be a distraction from the movie. But Victoria did as she pleased and it pleased her to talk during her weekly movie nights. Honestly, depending on who she was talking to, sometimes the conversation in the screening room was better than the one on the screen. One of the most entertaining conversations Nikki had ever eavesdropped on had been between her mother and Jack Nicholson in this very room.

"Maybe the boyfriend is who you should be looking at."

"You think?"

"Who's got the most to lose if the dead husband isn't really dead? The toy boy, of course."

"*Boy toy.*"

"Whatever." Victoria flicked her wrist.

"But you don't really think Thompson would have killed Rex, do you?"

"My dear." Victoria turned her full attention to Nikki. "If there's one thing I know, it's men. I've survived seven marriages, nine if you count the second time I married John and Syd. Let me tell you, men are ultimately about themselves. We women, we'll kill to protect the men we love. Men will kill to protect the men *they* love." She patted Nikki's arm. "*Themselves.*"

Nikki chuckled.

"Did Edith and the boyfriend know Rex was still alive?"

"Actually," Nikki said, thinking back on the conversation, "I'm not sure. I asked Edith if she knew, but Thompson answered for her, saying she didn't."

"Someone's hiding something. Oh, wait. I love this part." Victoria indicated the screen.

A few minutes later, Victoria leaned over and spoke into her daughter's ear. "I'll bet you my black pearl cocktail ring that one of them is lying. One or both knew he was alive. Probably both."

Nikki met her mother's gaze. "You really think so?"

"It's just like in *Sister, Sister*," Victoria murmured, citing an MGM film that had made her a household name in the 1950s. "Remember? Eve and Angelina told their mother they knew nothing about the money their father had hidden, but it turned out Eve had seen him at the railway station talking to the man in the black hat. Eve knew but Angelina didn't. It was Eve who knew about the money and who stole it from her mother, not Angelina, as everyone assumed."

It hadn't occurred to Nikki that the best way to investigate a murder was by using the plots of old movies, but Victoria certainly had a point. Whoever killed Rex had to have known he was alive. How the killer lured him into Jessica's apartment, Nikki didn't know. But it was a step in the right direction.

Chapter 8

The next evening, Nikki left Jessica on the couch with the remote and a cold cloth on her head and slipped into the backyard, doggies leading a merry chase ahead of her.

Jessica had a migraine, a minor side effect, as far as Nikki was concerned, of another interview with the police. This time they came to the office Nikki and Jess shared at Windsor Real Estate. Apparently, Hollywood's finest had concluded that it was unlikely that Rex had been killed in Jessica's apartment. Jessica had thought that meant she was off the hook. She was not, hence the headache and the new handbag from Fendi that Nikki had had to stop for on the way home.

The police also informed Jessica that the medical examiner's office was having difficulty placing the time of his death, but again, not letting her off the hook. Apparently, they thought the beautiful young real estate agent was far more devious than she looked. And smarter. How did a woman in four-inch Blahniks carry a two-hundred-and-fifty-pound dead man into her apartment without anyone noticing? The good news, of course, was that despite the scowls from Detective Brown Suit, Jess hadn't been arrested.

Nikki followed the stone path through the overgrown garden in her backyard, past the beds of yarrow, paper flowers and prince's plume, to the gate that led from her property to her neighbor's. Victoria was always offering to send Jorge over to cut back her jungle, but Nikki loved it, just like she loved her Craftsman-style bungalow, which her mother called *plebian*.

"Knock knock," she called as she went through the arched wood-and-iron gate. The dogs shot past her, their big ears flying behind them.

Nikki's dear friend Marshall lay in a lounge chair beside the pool, bare-chested and barefoot in a pair of shorts. For a man whose net worth was somewhere around two hundred and fifty million, he was still a pretty down-to-earth guy. Marshall Thunder was a big screen icon, at the top of his game at the age of forty-two. A strikingly handsome, full-blooded Native American, he was versatile enough to do romantic comedies, action thrillers and dramas. He was one of the top paid male actors in the business and because he was single, the number one heartthrob with females ages eighteen to fifty. He'd made *People* magazine's Top 50 Sexiest Men list the last three years in a row.

Marshall set aside the paper he was reading to look at her over his dark sunglasses. "I was wondering when you'd pop up. I've been worried about you, hon."

The dogs rounded the pool, ran to Marshall to greet him with a few licks and then took off again. He wiped his mouth. "Don't tell Rob you saw that. You know how he feels about kissing after dogs."

She smiled and plopped down in the lounge chair beside him. The sun was beginning to set, but it was still bright out. She was glad she'd grabbed her sunglasses on her way out the door.

"You okay?" Marshall asked.

She eyed him. "You shouldn't be sitting out here like that. Are you wearing sunscreen? You had that skin cancer scare last year."

"Thanks, *Mom*. But who ever heard of a pale-skinned redskin? And you didn't answer my question. Jessica is all over the news." He picked up the tabloid newspaper he'd been reading. "It says here there've been claims she had Rex's baby last year. Someone's calling her the Stiletto Stinger."

Nikki groaned and lay back in the lounge chair.

"You have to admit it's catchy," he said.

The dogs were barking wildly at something and she glanced over to see that they'd cornered a toad at the fence. "Oliver, Stanley, leave it!" she called. There was little worse than toad-tinged doggie breath. Remarkably, the dogs bounded off, headed for another adventure.

"The Stiletto Stinger? And you ask me how I am?" she said. "Worried half to death, that's how I am. And why didn't you ask how Jessica was?"

"Because Jessica's not one of my best bosom buddies in the world." He tossed the newspaper in the pile on the stone patio. Marshall was a great fan of the tabloid newspapers: *National Enquirer, Star* magazine, *Weekly World News.* Fanzines, too. He bought them all and read them cover to cover every week. The fact that it was mostly lies and he sued them regularly didn't seem to dampen his adoration. "And Jessica can take care of herself."

Nikki groaned. "I can take care of myself."

"And by taking care of yourself, you mean getting involved in a police murder investigation?"

"How did you—" She glanced at him. "Please don't tell me that Mother called you."

"Okay, I won't." He flashed his multimillion-dollar smile. "But she's right. This is none of your business." He folded his hands, resting them on his rock-hard abdomen.

Marshall was six-foot-two, monstrous for a Native American, although he'd once told her men and women of his tribe—the Oneida, part of the Iroquois League—were taller than most Native Americans. He had inky black hair, killer brown eyes, high cheekbones, and a muscle-cut bod to die for. It was really too bad he was taken, and had been for the last ten years, a fact that his fans were completely unaware of.

The house—here, next door to Nikki's—was technically Rob's house. Marshall owned a neoclassical monstrosity on Beverly Drive where he entertained when his agent forced him to. He rarely spent more than a night or two there a month. Unbeknownst to his fans, Wetherly Drive was home sweet home and had been for almost ten years.

"It's none of my business that one of my best friends has been accused of a crime she didn't commit?" Nikki asked. "It's none of my business that an innocent woman could go to jail for . . . for life, for something she didn't do?"

"Enough with the drama. You know very well she was banging him."

Nikki whipped off her sunglasses. "That's not a crime punishable by a prison sentence."

"You're probably right." Marshall tilted his head, grimacing. "Rex March was a pretty big slimy slug. Doing him was probably punishment enough."

"I can't believe my mother called you." She leaned back and closed her eyes. "She called Jeremy, too."

"That's our girl."

Nikki tilted her chin up to get the last warmth of the fall sun. "You know, you shouldn't encourage her. She's worse when you encourage her. All of you."

"It's a conspiracy for sure," he teased, but then his voice grew more serious. "So tell me what's going on, sweetie. She didn't kill him, right?"

Nikki opened her eyes to check on the dogs. Oliver had parked himself under the shade of the diving board on the far side of the kidney-shaped saltwater pool. Stanley was wandering along the water's edge, sniffing with great enthusiasm. "Of course she didn't kill him."

"So how did he get in her apartment? Dead?"

"I don't know. She doesn't know. Apparently, he was killed somewhere else and moved there."

"Did she know he wasn't really dead?"

"Oh, he was dead all right. I saw him."

"You saw him?" Marshall shuddered. "But I meant the first time. The supposed plane crash."

Nikki shook her head. "She says she didn't know he was still alive, and I believe her. Why would she lie?"

"Well, there's an obvious answer to that question."

She glared at him.

"Just sayin'," he argued.

"Well, *don't* say. I'm telling you, she didn't do it. She might be a girl with loose morals but she is *not* a murderer."

He studied her for a second. "There's all kinds of speculation as to what happened, you know. Concerning the circumstances of Rex's 'death' six months ago."

Nikki didn't respond. Stanley wandered over to look at her with big brown eyes and she tapped the chair, indicating he could jump up and lie beside her. He rewarded her with a slew of wet doggie kisses. He was such a sweetheart.

"They're saying he faked his death," Marshall went on, "because he was going to jail for tax evasion and that he's been living in Spain with his granddaughter's nanny."

"Well, I don't know about the nanny-in-Spain part. I didn't even think he spoke to his daughter. She was from his first marriage, before his Hollywood days. And who knows about the taxes? What I do know is that obviously he faked his death in that plane crash. I just can't figure out why."

"Oh, I can think of a million reasons." Marshall studied his manicure.

"You can?" She took off her sunglasses again. "Like?"

"I didn't really know him, but most likely money problems. Living beyond his means. Maybe wife problems. And his career was certainly in the toilet. Hence the money problems."

"But he had to be making millions on the residuals for that stupid TV show he starred in. Nickelodeon plays it seven nights a week."

"But who knows how he spent his money: gambling, whores, drugs?"

She scowled. "Okay, so what if he *did* run away to Spain with the nanny. Why come back?"

"It's a mystery, isn't it?"

Nikki wanted to throw her glasses at him. Instead, she perched them on Stanley's nose. They were vintage Persol and he looked pretty cute in them. "Whoever killed him obviously knew he was alive, so I've got to find out who knew."

"How about his wife?"

"That's what Mother said." She scratched Stanley behind his sunglasses. "Edith isn't a killer."

"Did she know her husband was still alive?"

"I went by to see her. She says not. She seemed genuinely upset."

"You actually *asked* her?" Marshall chuckled. "Damn, girl, you've got gonads. You going to hang a shingle, NIKKI HARPER, P.I.?"

"This isn't funny, Marshall. We're talking about a dead man. Someone put a sharp object through his eye, into his brain, and killed him."

"Ewww," he groaned, waving his hunky man-hands. "You didn't have to tell me that. I'll have nightmares now, and I'm going to call you and wake you up when I do."

Nikki took her sunglasses off the patient pooch. "See, the thing is, Edith said she didn't know Rex was still alive." She pointed the glasses at Marshall. "But something didn't seem quite right when I was there yesterday."

"What? She wasn't acting enough like the grieving widow? She thought he was already dead, Nik. And we have to keep in mind, there was no love lost between them. Rex March was a lying, cheating scumbag to the Nth degree and everyone in Hollywood knew it, most of all his wife. I was surprised she wasn't dancing a frickin' jig at his memorial service." He wrinkled his nose. "You think she'll have another? What's the etiquette here? I mean, do you throw the guy another memorial service, now that he's *really* dead?"

"Marshall, you're digressing. You're supposed to be helping me think this through. Edith was upset when I was there yesterday," Nikki said. "She'd been crying. But she wasn't upset that he was dead, per se."

"Maybe she was upset because Rex came alive long enough to make a mess of her life again?"

"Possibly, but it seemed like something more. Different."

"What about the hunky boyfriend?"

Nikki rolled her eyes. Marshall had a crush on Thompson Christopher. Marshall had wanted to go with her to the party at Edith's the other night, just so he could drool over the actor, but his agent hadn't been able to get him out of a previous commitment.

Nikki thought back to her visit. "Mr. Hunky was attentive to Edith. He was saying all the right things. Doing all the right things. But he seemed upset, too. Both of them acted like they didn't want me there. And they'd been super-friendly the night of the party—before Rex turned up again. *Genuinely* friendly."

"Hmm," Marshall pondered. "Maybe Rob will know something. He's not in the Hollywood department, but you know very well that cops talk. They're worse than teenage girls." He looked at her. "You want me to ask him what the scuttlebutt is? Maybe he knows something the police aren't telling Jessica."

Rob Bastone was Marshall's sweet, kind partner of ten years, who disguised himself as a tattooed, hard-ass L.A. police detective.

She sat up and Stanley crawled into her lap. Realizing his pal was getting all the attention, Oliver hightailed it toward her. "Can he do that?"

Marshall sat up and scooped Oliver into his lap. "For me?" He grinned and scratched Oliver behind the ears. "For me, sweetie, he'd do *anything.*"

"What about that time he refused to sneak you into the Ricky Martin concert he was doing security for?"

"That?" Marshall stroked Oliver's silky coat. "It wasn't that he didn't want me to see Ricky. He was concerned for my safety."

She grinned. "Ah."

"I'll feel him out." He wrinkled his large, well-shaped nose, somehow managing to appear both gay and heartthrobby at the same time. "He knows how much I love gossip."

"I'd appreciate any help you guys could give me." Nikki rose. "I better get back to Jessica."

"What you better do is have a hot cup of tea and get the tea bags on those bags under your eyes. You need some sleep." He deposited Ollie on the ground and walked with her toward the gate. "You need a Xanax or something?"

She glanced at him, making a face. "You know me better than that. I don't need a Xanax."

The dogs raced away, taking one more lap around the pool before they headed home, sweet home, to bed. Without a Xanax.

Nikki sat in her car on Outpost Drive, studying the gate leading up to the March house. She wanted to get inside and talk to Edith's house staff; the staff always knew the details of their employers' lives. She'd been clever enough to come when she knew Edith would be at her regularly scheduled hair appointment. It was funny how intimately she got to know a client, and then they just disappeared from her life after the sale.

So, Nikki knew Edith and Thompson wouldn't be there. He always went with her when she got her hair done. But what Nikki *didn't* know was how she was going to get in. Even though she had been showing the house regularly for months, she didn't have the code to get in the front gate. She and Jessica always scheduled the appointment and just called up to the house when they arrived. One of the servants would then let them in, as per Edith's instructions.

Nikki heard the sound of a small engine starting up
and she craned her neck to see through the iron fence
that bordered the property on the street side. It sounded
like a weed-whacker. Bingo! Jorge serviced Edith's lawn.
If it wasn't Jorge himself, it had to be one of his employees. Nikki grabbed her handbag and, on impulse,
the In & Out bag on the car seat—Jessica's lunch that
Nikki had picked up to take back to the office. Victoria
had taught Nikki it was always polite to take a gift to the
host or hostess.

She approached the iron gate and spotted one of
Jorge's employees, whom she knew. He was trimming a
bush. "Harley," she called.

He continued to whack at the bush.

She hollered his name louder, and when he turned,
startled, she flashed that smile Victoria had ingrained
in her. He smiled back.

Worked every time.

Harley cut off the weed-whacker and lifted his gog-
gles as he approached the gate. "Mithss Nikki." He had
a bit of a lisp, due to unfortunate tooth arrangement
and lack of orthodontia as a child.

She knew she blushed. She'd told Harley before just
to call her Nikki, but he hailed from the Deep South
and family traditions died hard. He'd once told her his
granny would "whip hiths heinie with a switch" if he
didn't address her with proper respect.

"Hey, Harley. Could you let me in? Mrs. March isn't
home and I need to get some info on curtains in the
house."

"You want to drive up?"

"Nah, I'll walk." She gave a little laugh. "It's a nice
day and I need the exercise."

He hit a button on the keypad on the inside and

there was a mechanical click, then a dull buzz as the gate parted in the middle and slid open.

"Thanks." She crossed the threshold, feeling only slightly guilty for being so devious. "You eat lunch?" She held up the bag, a grease stain already spreading on it.

"I don't want to take your lunch, Mithss Nikki."

"You won't be. Long story, but it's extra. If you don't eat it, it'll lie on the floor of my car until I toss it or the dogs find it." She held out the bag.

"Thankths, Mithss Nikki." He took it, nodding his head. His green hat read JORGE & SON. There was no son; Jorge was divorced with no children. He'd just liked the name when he chose it for his landscaping company. That, and he hoped someday to have a son.

"You have a good day, Harley," she said as she started up the paved driveway. "I can let myself out."

"You have a good day, too," he called after her. "Thankths."

When Nikki reached the house, instead of going up to the front door, she cut across the grass, around to the back service entrance where deliveries were made and the house staff entered and exited. The service wing, with a commercial kitchen, storage, and a maid's room, had been added to the house by the previous owner.

Nikki debated whether or not to ring the doorbell. Even though it would only ring in the kitchen, she decided against it. It would be better if she acted as if she was supposed to be there. "Hey there," she called as she came through the door.

Chessy, who cooked and cleaned for the Marches, was sitting in a chair, watching a game show on a small TV on one of the marble counters. Chessy was the blackest woman Nikki thought she'd ever met. Her skin was so black, it almost looked blue.

When Nikki walked in, Chessy was grinding out a cigarette in an ashtray inside a drawer under the counter. "Good God, you scared me!" Chessy exclaimed. She had come half out of her seat in her attempt to hide her cigarette and was now depositing her three-hundred-and-fifty-plus pounds back into the chair. "Whatchu doin' comin' in the back? The Missus's not here."

"Which is why I'm coming through the back," Nikki explained, closing the door behind her. "How are you, Chessy?"

Nikki and Chessy had gotten to be friends in the months leading up to the sale of the house. Edith liked to think she ran the household, but it was Chessy who did the actual running. She oversaw the yard work, the housecleaning, and the food preparation. On a night like last Saturday night when Edith had thrown the party, Chessy had overseen the entire catering operation, start to finish. She was a woman of many talents, with a no-nonsense attitude.

"I'm good, 'cept you scared the bejeezus outta me and prob'ly a year of my life." She opened the drawer to check that the smoking cigarette was out and closed it again. "What can I do you for?"

"I brought you those free movie tickets, for you and your boyfriend." Nikki grabbed the envelope from her bag and slid it across the wide expanse of the counter. The kitchen was massive, entirely too big for the size of the Spanish-style home built in the 1920s on three-quarters of an acre. The pricey kitchen with its miles of marble, Viking stoves, and walk-in refrigerator had been one of the reasons why the house had been hard to sell, tacky decor aside.

Nikki gave the envelope a little push. "And to ask you some questions. About . . . about what was going on, on 'onday . . . the day Mr. March was found dead."

"Ah." Chessy picked up the envelope and peeked inside. "I still get to keep the movie tickets, even if I don't answer your questions?"

"Of course." Now Nikki really *did* feel guilty. If Harley had refused to open the gate for her, would she have thrust Jessica's lunch through the fence to him, anyway?

"I really liked them cupcakes you brought last week." Chessy slid the envelope into the open neckline of her uniform and it disappeared into the mountainous region of her breasts. "Papers said your partner, Miss High-and-Mighty, killed Mr. March."

Nikki came around the end of the marble counter. "She didn't, Chessy. I swear she didn't."

Chessy reached out with a remote control and the TV went off. "Wouldn't matter to me if she did. I didn't like him, not one bit," she said matter-of-factly. She heaved her full weight out of the chair. "You know how to devein shrimp, girl?"

Nikki stared at her, having a hard time seeing the segue. "Um . . . sure."

"I always know'd Victoria Bordeaux had beauty *and* brains." Chessy tossed her an apron from the counter. "Got shrimp cocktail to make. You devein, I'll talk. I hate deveinin' shrimp, almost as much as havin' to get the missus outta bed a second time to tell her her no-good husband's dead again."

Chapter 9

"So, what you wanna know?" Chessy popped the top on a can of Coke she'd taken from the walk-in refrigerator, along with three pounds of jumbo shrimp. According to Chessy, Edith had friends coming to *pay their respects* and get tipsy over cocktails that afternoon. There was chicken liver pâté to make, too.

Nikki slid the deveiner through the back of a shrimp. She didn't have the heart to tell Chessy that her mother hadn't taught her how to devein shrimp. Nikki was pretty certain Victoria Bordeaux had *never* deveined a shrimp. Discovered around the age of seventeen (Victoria's dates were always a little fuzzy), then launched into stardom, she'd never kept her own house. Never had to. But she *had* been smart enough to hire a woman like Ina. Not only had Ina deveined shrimp for Victoria for the last thirty years, she'd taught Nikki how to devein a shrimp, how to make a true dirty martini, and how to sew up a Christmas turkey. All skills fortysomething L.A. women were sorely lacking these days.

"I'm trying to piece together what happened Monday." Letting her hands fall, she glanced up at Chessy, who was leaning on the counter across from her, sipping the Coke. "With Jessica. And . . . here."

"Keep cleanin'." Chessy waved her hand. "Can't you talk and devein at the same time, girl?"

Nikki neatly ripped out another vein. "I was wondering if you knew." She gave a little laugh. "Of course you know. You know *everything* that goes on here. I guess what I'm asking is if you could tell me what happened here Monday. Who went where, when," she said quickly, before she lost her nerve or her grip on a slippery shrimp.

"Your floozy girl got herself an alibi?"

"She does." Nikki nodded. "She was at a real estate conference downtown . . . and she did some shopping. Plenty of people saw her."

The door that led into the main part of the house opened and Chessy's daughter, Shondra, entered the kitchen carrying a plastic caddy with cleaning supplies. She threw the caddy up on the counter. "I swear, if that man doesn't stop cutting his toenails in that bathroom and *flippin'* 'em all over the floor, I'm going to kill him." She glanced up at Nikki as she headed for the refrigerator and lifted an eyebrow. "Real estate business gone sour for you?"

Nikki held up both hands, a shrimp in one, the deveiner in the other. "It's always good to have a backup plan, right?"

"She was tryin' to bribe me, get me to give up who was where that day," Chessy explained.

"I wasn't trying to *bribe* you," Nikki protested, the guilt creeping in again.

Chessy broke into a grin. " 'Course you wasn't. I know good people when I see 'em. But I got you to devein them shrimp, didn't I?" She cackled.

Nikki laughed along with her. Too few people in L.A. could laugh at themselves. "I'm trying to help out my friend Jessica," Nikki explained to Shondra. "You know, my partner Jessica."

"Oh, I know her, all right." The younger woman pulled a Coke from the fridge. "It sure doesn't look good for her, from what the papers are saying."

Nikki dropped a clean shrimp into the bowl. "The case is more complicated than the papers are saying. Rex wasn't killed in Jessica's apartment."

"I don't know why we're wastin' good taxpayer money investigating him bein' dead. I don't know no-body who liked him. You know he tried to feel me up once!" Chessy covered her monstrous breasts with her hands and readjusted the alignment. "I understand him wantin' a little taste of Shondra, her bein' pretty as she is, but me?" Chessy made a clicking sound between her teeth and took another swig of Coke. "That man was garbage. I'm glad he's dead. I'd have killed him myself, if I'd gotten the chance. What was wrong with that man, claimin' he was dead, then comin' back? But I was here all day, still cleanin' up after that party. Caterers and such come back for their stuff saw me. And Shondra had a job bein' a perfume girl downtown. And you can tell anyone you want that." She pointed at Nikki to emphasize her position on the matter.

"Actually . . ." Nikki grimaced. "I was wondering if you could tell me what Edith did Monday . . . and Thompson?"

"You think the missus killed him?" Chessy chewed on that thought for a moment. "I don't think she's got it in her, otherwise she'd'a'done it years ago."

That seemed to be the general consensus.

"So do you know where she was?" Nikki reached for

another shrimp. She was getting the hang of it now and moving faster.

"She was here. In bed most of the day. Plain worn out. That, and she rubbed the skin right off her bunions in them too tight shoes she wore to her party Saturday night. But you know rich white folk. Not a lotta sense. Except you, Nikki. You got sense."

Nikki grinned. Compliments from a woman like Chessy were few and far between and greatly appreciated. "So she was here and you saw her . . . all day."

"Yup. Now, that man of hers." Chessy did her pointing thing again. "I can't vouch for him. He left early that morning. The missus said he had casting calls."

"And when did he get home?" Nikki tossed another clean shrimp in the bowl. She was on a roll.

"Late. *Dancin' with the Stars* was already on."

"And that comes on, when? Eight?"

"Eight o'clock," Chessy agreed. "That's right. I remember 'cause I was annoyed. I like to be home to see the beginning and it was already on by the time I went out that door." She indicated the service entrance.

"Ma, I TiVo it for you every week. You can watch it whenever you like."

Chessy frowned. "I like to see it live."

"It's not live, Ma."

Chessy glanced at her gorgeous daughter. "You got more toenails to sweep up?"

Nikki smiled into her bowl of shrimp. "So Thompson was on casting calls." She nodded. "Tricky, but not impossible to track down."

"You might be wastin' your time there," Shondra said. "I'm thinking that hunky monkey's not going to matter around here much longer."

"What makes you say that?"

"Because I think Mrs. March is about to kick him out on his pretty tail."

"Thompson? Really?" Nikki stared at Shondra. "But I thought things were good with them. They seemed happy together Saturday night and when I came by Wednesday," she thought about how'd they'd been together, "everything seemed good."

"If there's one thing I've learned, it's that how rich people act in front of people like you and how they act in front of people like me, it isn't always the same." Shondra sipped her Coke. "It's like they don't acknowledge our existence, if they don't have to."

Nikki had to stop deveining for a second to take in what Shondra was saying. "So you think Edith and Thompson are having problems?"

"Sure sounded like it Saturday. I couldn't hear what was being said, but there was a lot of hollering going on in her suite, then door slamming, and next thing I know, he's taking off on his motorcycle."

"Thompson left here Saturday afternoon, before the party?"

"Sure did. Didn't come back until a few minutes before the guests started arriving." Shondra leaned on the countertop beside her mother. "I heard her tell him just before she went downstairs that he better hurry up and get dressed if he was going to *her* party."

"Interesting," Nikki commented, as much to herself as to the two women. Plopping the last clean shrimp in the bowl, she went to the sink to rinse off her hands, checking her vintage Patek Philippe watch. Technically, it was a man's watch, but one of her favorites. "I better get back to work, but I appreciate you talking to me. Not that you've done anything wrong." She grabbed a hand towel. "But you know what I mean."

"The help's not supposed to tattle on the employer?"

"You're *not* tattling," Nikki insisted, heading for the door. She was going to be late to a meeting at the office and she was going to have to either show up without Jessica's lunch or be beyond fashionably late. "Edith and Thompson didn't do anything wrong."

"Not that you know of," Chessy called after her, her tone as sassy as ever.

Nikki skipped making a second stop at In & Out and was only fashionably late to the meeting at the Windsor offices on North Canon Drive in Beverly Hills. The agents spent more time fussing over Jessica and discussing what they'd heard on talk radio about Rex March's murder than they did discussing the new properties coming on the market. Nikki tried to not let it bother her that Jessica seemed to like all the attention. It shouldn't have surprised her; Jessica was a firm believer that there was no good publicity versus bad publicity. Just publicity.

After the meeting, Nikki went into the small office she and Jessica shared; actually, it was more like a cubicle with high walls and a door. While Jessica chatted in the break room, Nikki pulled the March file. She didn't know what she was looking for, but she was hoping she'd know it when she found it. She studied the original listing sheet she and Jessica had created when the March home had gone up for sale in the pocket neighborhood of Outpost Estates in the eastern Hollywood Hills. The area had a great history dating back to the 1920s when the luxury neighborhood had been in the heart of old Hollywood.

Nikki knew the listing from memory; it had taken

hours to write. The estate was such a white elephant, it had been difficult to play up: an old commercial kitchen that desperately needed renovating, an out-of-date tiled pool, mediocre landscaping, not to mention the *coup de grace*, the mural of Rex on the wall in the salon. After glancing at the listing, she set it aside and studied the notes in the file; most of them were in her own handwriting, but there were a couple of slips of paper in Jessica's handwriting.

Jessica walked into the office. She was dressed as if ready to make a public appearance, which, in a way, she was. The press couldn't get enough of her right now. This morning, Nikki had had to drop her off on the street behind their office in order to avoid the paparazzi. She was wearing a cute little orange Badgley Mischka number and her signature sky-high heels. Nikki tried not to feel frumpy in her merino wool skirt and sensible knee-high black boots.

Jessica glanced at the open file on Nikki's semi-messy desk. "Whatcha doin'?"

"Going over the March file. Rex had really been eager to sell the place. You know why?"

"Tiny master bath with shoddy tile?"

Nikki glanced over the desk at her friend, giving her an *I'm trying to help you here* look. "I mean, did he ever say anything about why they decided to sell? He knew the state of the market. Everyone knew Scarlett Johansson lost millions on the sale of her Spanish villa just down the street from them."

"Are you asking me if Rex and I discussed the sale of his house while we were making love?"

"No, oh gosh, no." Nikki put up both hands. "I do *not* want any of those details. I'm just . . . I'm trying to piece things together, Jess. Why would Rex fake his death?"

Jessica pressed her lips together, her eyes growing moist. "I don't know. I swear to God, I don't."

"Sorry," Nikki murmured.

"It's okay." Jessica dropped into her chair behind her desk. "You really think you're going to find the answer in there?" She exhaled and moved a stack of paperwork from one side of her desk to another. "I can go home whenever you want. Downy doesn't want me showing houses until the police are done with their nonsense questioning me. He thinks it's bad for business." She threw up her hands. "I'm thinking I might get the opportunity to show some houses, just because people want to meet me, you know, me being a murder suspect."

"Jess, that's a terrible thing to say."

She shrugged. "A girl's got to pay her AmEx bill." She glanced at the file again and frowned. "You're not going to find anything in there."

"No. I guess not." But Nikki continued to flip through the papers. There were notes on potential buyers. Copies of some estimates Nikki had gotten for Rex with the idea of making some improvements that would move the house. There was also a copy of a contract that had fallen through, and a copy of the current contract. Nothing of interest. She was scooping the papers up to drop them back into the file when a pink WHILE YOU WERE OUT slip fell to her desk. She picked it up. It documented a call from Rex a month before he supposedly died in the plane crash. For some reason, he had called the main number instead of Nikki's or Jess's cell. There was a return phone number on it that Nikki didn't recognize. This was not Rex's or Edith's cell phones or their home phone. She held up the piece of pink paper. "You recognize this?"

Jessica barely looked at it. "Nikki, that was what? Like eight months ago? I don't know what it is. And I know you don't want to hear this, but we cared for each other."

Nikki nibbled on her lower lip. "Did you return this call?"

"Nikki, I don't know. I don't remember. How many calls do we return to clients a day?" Jessica looked up at her from across her desk. "Do you think it would be okay to call the police and see if I can pick my car up from impound yet?" As expected, the police had contacted Jessica midday Tuesday, gotten the location of her car, and had it towed in to examine for evidence.

"There's no way they're going to release it this soon." Nikki held up the call memo slip. "You sure you didn't return this call, because I'm sure I didn't."

"I *don't remember.*" Jessica shrugged dramatically; she sounded like she was teetering on the edge of tears. "I think I might just go home. Of course, I *can't* go home because the police have my apartment roped off because I found a dead man in my bed. I'm just going to catch a cab." She opened her desk drawer and pulled out a cute little leather handbag that was the same burnt orange as her dress. "See you at your place later?"

"I might try to catch a bite with Jeremy tonight. Could you let Ollie and Stan out?"

"Sure," Jessica sighed; she didn't have a lot of patience for pets.

When she was gone, Nikki studied the pink slip of paper in her hand. It had Rex's name, Jess's name, and a phone number. There was something written beneath the phone number, but the pen used to write the note

Cheryl Crane

had smeared. She studied it under her desk light. It looked like the number 511.

Nikki hesitated, then picked up the phone and dialed the number.

"Good afternoon," said a man on the other end of the phone. "Sunset Tower Hotel, how may I direct your call?"

Chapter 10

It was close to five by the time Nikki reached the land-mark art deco hotel; the traffic on Sunset Boulevard was awful, even for a Friday afternoon. Nikki had given enough potential real estate buyers the canned tour of L.A. that she knew the spiel on all the hot spots by heart.

Designed by the architect Leland A. Bryant, the Sunset Tower Hotel in West Hollywood had been built in the early thirties as a luxury apartment building. It was the first quake-proof structure built in L.A. Occupants over the years had included Jean Harlow, Clark Gable, Errol Flynn, John Wayne, Marilyn Monroe, and Frank Sinatra. In the eighties, the building fell into disrepair, but was saved at the last moment from demolition by preservation laws. Truman Capote was once quoted as saying, "I am living in a very posh establishment, the Sunset Tower, which local gentry tell me is where every scandal that ever happened, happened."

Nikki didn't like to consider how many nights Victo-ria had spent in the Sunset Tower while Nikki was tucked safely in bed back in Beverly Hills. Victoria was never considered a loose woman by anyone's standards, but she managed to marry seven different men, so she had by no means been a social recluse.

Nikki pulled up to the valet parking stand in front of the hotel. "I won't be long," she told the young man who opened her car door. As she climbed out, she picked a peanut up off the seat, giving him a quick smile of apology. "Thanks," she called as she accepted the ticket, handing him a few ones instead of the peanut. As she headed for the front doors, she tossed the nut into her mouth.

The lobby of the hotel was grand, done in dark wood, mauve accents and marble floors. Unfortunately, despite the enormously expensive restoration job, Nikki got the feeling that the true ambience of the hotel was lost forever. The Tower Bar (once gangster Bugsy Siegel's apartment), where she occasionally met clients, was nice enough, but she couldn't help feeling the place was touristy. In her mind, the Sunset Tower Hotel would never be what it had once been in the Golden Age of Hollywood.

She walked up to the front desk; the clerk was busy typing into the computer, though for all she knew, he could have been bringing up YouTube clips of kittens riding unicycles. She waited patiently until the young man in the cheap suit jacket glanced up.

"May I help you?"

Nikki moved in closer, lowering her voice. "I was wondering if you can answer a couple of questions about one of your guests."

"I'm sorry, but we don't reveal the names of celebrities currently staying with us," he replied, a line he'd obviously memorized. He returned his attention to his YouTube video.

That's because no celebrities would stay here, Nikki thought, but she didn't say it. Instead, she gave him *the smile*. "This isn't exactly a celebrity. And he's . . . *was* a client of mine."

The clerk stared at her.

"Could you tell me if Rex March stayed here February 11th of this year?" She indicated the computer screen. "Would it be possible to just . . . look it up?"

"Never heard of him," the young man said.

"You've never heard of Rex March?" She reached into her handbag, pulled out a leather business card case and began to thumb through the cards. She'd been meaning for months to clean it out; the good news was that she was almost positive she still had one of Rex's cards, complete with a photo of him grinning. Bingo! She offered the business card. "You don't recognize this man?"

He barely looked at the card. "Nope."

"Do you read the newspapers?"

"Excuse me?"

"Read the papers?" she asked, trying to check her annoyance. "Watch the news? My client, Rex March, was murdered this week." Seeing no need to clutter the conversation with details, she left out the part about her friend being the main suspect.

"There's been no murders in the Sunset Tower Hotel, ma'am. Is there anything else I can do for you?"

She frowned, dropping the business card back into the abyss of her bag. "You can't just check to see if he was here that day?"

He sighed, hit a few keys on his keyboard and glanced at the computer screen. "No—what was his name, ma'am?"

She hated it when people ma'am'ed her. She wasn't old enough to be a ma'am. *Was she?* "Rex March. He did TV. Movies."

The clerk frowned. "Must have been before my time. Never heard of him. No Rex March checked in here." He looked up, his face as bland as a bowl of congealed oatmeal. "Anything else I can do for you? A dinner reservation? A spa appointment?"

She sighed, her shoulders sagging. He was already looking at the computer again. "No. Thank you. Have a good day," she added as she turned away—just in case her mother was hiding behind a potted palm. Victoria had always insisted on extreme politeness, even with the lowliest valets, key grips, or maids in restaurant bathrooms. It was a rare behavior for Hollywood royalty, and contributed to the universal adoration of her fans.

Beginning to doubt her detective skills, Nikki went back out the front door and handed her ticket to the valet.

"Be a few minutes, ma'am."

Of course, it would. Her car was probably already parked six deep. She flashed *the smile*, even though she wasn't really feeling it. As she waited, she contemplated the phone number written on the WHILE YOU WERE OUT slip and what it might mean. Nikki knew Rex well enough to know he could have been at this hotel that day on one of his many liaisons. So, did the clerk at the desk just lie about whether or not he'd been a guest that day, or had Rex given a fake name, something Hollywood stars were famous for doing? And had his hookup been with Jessica? Did it matter who the woman was?

"Miss . . . Miss Harper?"

Nikki turned to see a young man wearing a hotel name tag. "Yes?"

He tucked his hands behind his back like a child trying to keep from touching candy on a counter. "I . . . I thought that was you. I saw you in *People* magazine. That charity event you attended with your mother. You . . . you looked great."

"Thank you." Nikki didn't get a lot of recognition; there were too many real celebrities in town, but it did happen, occasionally. Always be polite, Victoria said. But watch out for crazies. Nikki glanced away in search of her Prius.

Jeremy had called her when she was stuck in traffic on Sunset. He wanted her to stop by his place on Saturday. She was looking forward to seeing him. He was always her voice of logic. He was so grounded, which was amazing, considering the fact that he had made his first million before his twelfth birthday.

"I hope you don't mind." The guy was still there. Actually, he wasn't much more than a kid. Early twenties, average height, sandy hair, attractive enough face; it was a common look in Hollywood. "But I sort of overheard you talking to the desk clerk." He lowered his voice. "About Rex March."

Nikki's ears immediately perked up. "Yes?" she said, turning to him.

He offered his hand. "I'm Julius."

"Nice to meet you, Julius." *The smile.* She shook his hand. "Do you know something about Rex being here?"

"Do you mind if we talk? . . ." He tilted his head, indicating a place on the sidewalk that wasn't visible from the lobby. "I don't want to lose my job. We're not supposed to mess with famous people."

This time her smile was genuine. She followed him. "What can you tell me about Rex?"

"I know what people say about him, but I was kind of a fan," Julius said apologetically. "I grew up watching reruns of his show." He shrugged one shoulder. "I know it was kind of cheesy and the acting was bad and all, but I grew up with him. You know?"

Nikki tried to remain patient through Julius's trip down memory lane. "I know exactly what you mean," she said, having no idea. "Did you see Rex here? In February? This is kind of important."

The young man glanced around as if he were a cast member on the set of a bad spy movie. "I saw him lots of times," he whispered.

"You did?" she whispered back, now trying to contain her enthusiasm. She didn't want to scare him off.

He nodded vigorously. "We're trained to play it cool with celebrities, you know, pretend it's no big deal, especially if they're wearing a disguise."

"A disguise?" she repeated. Not just a false name, Rex had used a *disguise?* Talk about cheesy. Images of Rex wearing a pirate's eye patch or a blackened hillbilly tooth skittered in her head.

Again, Julius glanced one way and then the other. "I'm sure he came in not long before his plane crashed. I'm comfortable enough with my masculinity to admit to you I cried when I heard he hadn't survived," he said dramatically.

"Are you, by any chance, an actor?" she asked, unable to help herself.

"I am." He beamed. "I was in a commercial for #1 Automart in East L.A. . . . I was the dancing dollar sign. And a few smaller parts."

"Ah . . . so you were saying, you saw Rex on February 11th?"

"I don't know about the date. The last time I saw him, he was wearing my favorite disguise of his: a big straw hat," he motioned, demonstrating a hat the size of a sombrero, "a flowered shirt and sunglasses. I know he had a lot of fans fooled, but not me." He winked.

She winked back. "Right . . ." She was trying to think of what else to ask him. She really needed to read some detective novels to see how this was done. "So . . . you happen to know what name he was registered under? Because the nice gentleman at the front desk said Rex March was never registered here."

"Jason?" Julius made a face. "That douche bag? He wouldn't know if Jennifer Aniston walked through his lobby. Actually, she did," he added quickly. "I know she's an older woman and all, but she's *hot*."

Nikki made a spinning motion with her hand. "Back to Rex and the name. Do you know what name he used when he checked in?"

Julius shook his head, obviously disappointed that he couldn't tell her. "But I bet I could find out," he said quickly.

"Could you?"

He nodded again. "I have to tell you, my granny, back in Idaho, she raised me and she's a big fan of your mother's. She *loves* her movies. And her eightieth birthday is coming."

"Really? Eighty years?" Nikki knew in a second where this was going. "Do . . . do you think your granny would like an autographed photo? Personalized?" That was an easy one. Her mother's part-time correspondence secretary, Cora, a woman who had been around the Hollywood block more times than most, sent out a stack of autographed photos of Nikki's mother every week. An autographed photo was *totally* doable.

"That would be great, but . . ." He glanced at her sheepishly. "This isn't like blackmail or anything, but I could lose my job, looking up stuff on the computer. And it might take me a couple of days to sneak into the office and do it, so—"

She spotted her Prius, coming their way. "What will it take, Julius?" she said, cutting to the chase. "My mother doesn't do personal appearances in Idaho."

"No, no." He put up his hands. "It's nothing like that. I was just wondering . . ."

He stalled long enough for the valet to bring up her car. "Yes?" she said, looking back at Julius.

"Is there any way she could call my granny to wish her a happy birthday?"

Nikki thought for a minute. Victoria didn't make personal phone calls often, but maybe she could be persuaded.

"It would really mean a lot to my grandmother. And to me. And if you needed to know anything else," he said quickly, "after I find out the name Rex March used, I could definitely help you out."

"Done." Nikki thrust out her hand to shake Julius's. "You get back to me on that name," she said, fishing a business card out of her bag, "and Victoria Bordeaux will call your grandmother in Idaho and offer a personal birthday wish."

Julius was still grinning when Nikki climbed into her car. All Nikki could think of was what Victoria was going to want from her in return for this favor.

"Sorry, Ms. Flaherty's gone home," the young woman with Marilyn Monroe platinum hair said from behind her desk. She was busy regluing one of her pink press-on nails. "Would you like to make an appointment? She only sees people by appointment. No drop-ins." The phone rang, but she ignored it.

"No, that won't be necessary." Nikki glanced at the ringing phone.

"After five," the secretary explained. She actually had an uncanny resemblance to Norma Jean, but there were people like her all over L.A. Marilyn Monroe look-alikes were topped only by the Elvises. Shoot, Nikki had one of *those* of her own.

Nikki nodded, trying to seem disappointed. Actually, she'd purposely stopped by late to be sure she missed Thompson Christopher's agent. J.J. Flaherty would never answer Nikki's questions . . . but the secretary might.

"I'm Nikki Harper." She decided not to shake the girl's hand, not with the nail repair going on. Glancing around, she spotted a chair and grabbed it, dragging it over in front of the desk. "You mind if I sit down? Long day," she sighed, dropping into the chair. "I'm a real estate agent with the Windsor company. You might know my mother," she went on shamelessly. "Victoria—"

"Oh, my God!" A bit of Jersey slipped out of the girl as she shot out of her chair. "Victoria Bordeaux's daughter! I love love *love* her movies. My mother and I used to watch them on Sunday afternoons." She waved her hands in excited admiration. "You were in *People* this week."

"Actually, it was a few weeks ago."

"Oh, my God!" The young woman rushed out from behind her desk. Nikki thought maybe she was coming around to shake her hand or something, but she made a beeline for the waiting area and began to pull through a stack of tired magazines. "If I can find it, can you, you know, autograph it? My girlfriends aren't going to believe this! This'll be three this week. Got it!" She spun around, clutching the said issue of *People.* "We collect autographs. Whoever gets the fewest in a week has to buy the other three a round of drinks on Saturday night." She skittered forward, balanced on high heels, her red skirt so tight Nikki could see that there were no telltale panty lines. *Commando?*

"I'd be happy to autograph the magazine," Nikki said sweetly, grabbing a pen off the desk. "Let me keep it and maybe I can get you my mother's, too."

"Oh, my God!" The girl fanned herself with the magazine. "The girls aren't going to believe this! You're sooo nice." She started to offer the magazine, then pulled it back to her boob job. "Not everyone who comes into this office is very nice." She scrunched up her pretty face.

"How about Thompson Christopher?" Nikki could see from this close that the mole was penciled in. "Is he nice?"

"Oh, yeah. Real nice." She smiled. She was actually pretty, beneath the caricature.

"What did you say your name was?" Nikki asked.

"Tawny Lion." She offered her hand, the nail appearing to now be stable. "But that's my screen name. It's Mary, actually. Mary Jones."

"Nice to meet you, Mary." Nikki shook her hand firmly. "Or would you rather I call you Tawny?"

"Oh, Mary's fine." She returned to her chair. "It's kind of nice, actually. To have someone call me by my real name, other than my mother. She lives in Secaucus. New Jersey."

Nikki leaned closer. "So you know Thompson Christopher?"

"Uh-huh. Ms. Flaherty thinks he's on the edge of making it big. She's afraid he's going to ditch her," she whispered.

As far as Nikki could tell, not only was there no one in the agent's offices, but the whole building seemed pretty empty. "You think he'd do that?"

Mary shrugged her shoulders. "Like I said, he seems nice and all, but you never know. He's almost a big star now. Stars do crazy things."

"That they do," Nikki agreed wholeheartedly. She reached across the desk. "Why don't you give me that magazine and I'll see what I can do about getting my mother to sign it? Do you happen to know if Mr. Christopher went on casting calls Monday of this week?"

Mary frowned as she relinquished the *People*. If she thought the question was odd, she didn't act like it.

"He was supposed to. Ms. Flaherty was hot with him, I'll tell you that. I could hear her yelling at him on the phone from all the way out here."

"So he didn't make his casting calls Monday?"

"It was supposed to be a big day," Mary said conspiratorially. "That's why Ms. Flaherty was so upset with him. But then Rex March turned up dead again and Ms. Flaherty calmed down. She was able to reschedule two of them. They were supposed to be for next Tuesday, but of course he's got voice on Tuesdays and nobody knows if Mrs. March is going to have another memorial service for her husband." Mary sighed. "So everything is up in the air."

Nikki tucked the magazine into her bag. "But you're sure Mr. Christopher didn't make those casting calls Monday?"

"Sure," Mary said, wide eyed, making a motion across her perky breasts. "Cross my heart and hope to die."

Chapter 11

"**D**o you think the city owes me money, keeping my car for almost a week?" Jessica applied lipstick with the aid of the mirror on the passenger-side visor. "I think they owe me." She paused. "You think they'd make a payment on my AmEx?"

Nikki flashed her an *Are you for real?* look and cruised through the intersection of Sunset and Wilcox. "You still didn't make your AmEx payment?"

"I've been under stress, Nik. The man I was in love with was found dead in my apartment six months after I cried at his memorial service. And someone is trying to frame me." She pursed her lips and slapped the visor back into place. "Jesus H., I could use a little under-standing."

Nikki did a double take, then forced herself to con-centrate on the road. "You were in love with Rex?"

Jessica exhaled. "No. Not really. Maybe. Oh, I don't know. Does it matter?"

"I suppose not."

"So back to the problem at hand," Jessica nudged. "My car? Compensation?"

Nikki kept her tone neutral, despite the fact that she was screaming inside, *No, you don't get $#@! compensation. You're lucky your pretty little derriere isn't in jail!* She took a cleansing breath, wishing she had more free time for that yoga class she'd been meaning to take. "I don't think the city owes you any money for impounding your car. After all, Rex *was* found dead in your apartment. I think you should count yourself lucky the car's being released so soon."

"You're such a Negative Nancy."

"Well then, while I'm being a Negative Nancy, can I ask you a question about you and Rex?"

Jessica hesitated. "I suppose. As long as it's not *too* personal."

"Not to worry. I want no *personal* details," she said dryly. "That phone number, the one I found in the Marches' file, it was the number to the Sunset Tower Hotel. Did . . . did you see Rex there before he died?"

"What does that have to do with any of this?"

"Nothing, probably. I'm just asking." Nikki waited a second. "So is that a yes?"

"It's a no, Nikki," Jessica said firmly. "I never met Rex at the Sunset. Okay? . . . that I can remember," she quickly added.

"That you *can remember?*"

"Nik, do you have to make me say it?" She looked at her. "I've been with a lot of men."

"At the Sunset?"

"A few," she said in a small voice. "You'd have to give me specific dates."

"Okay, okay." Jessica looked so pitiful, so contrite, that Nikki decided to let the matter slide, at least for now. What difference did it make if Jessica and Rex had met there, anyway? "So, what did the cops say about your apartment?" she asked, changing the subject completely.

"I just got a message on my cell about the car. I'm going to see what I can find out when I get inside the police station. I swear, I'm going to call my city councilman or someone if they don't let me back in my place. How do I know the cops aren't stealing my clothes?"

Nikki pulled up in front of the police station, imagining the hairy gorilla cop in Jessica's Blahnik stilettos. "They're not stealing your clothes. You want me to come in with you?"

"Nah. I've got this." She opened the door, grabbing her Alexander McQueen studded-leather bowler.

It was a nice bag, but certainly not worth a month's rent.

"Where you headed?" Jess asked.

"Beverly Hills Country Club."

Jess raised an eyebrow. "Tennis?" She glanced at Nikki's outfit with obvious disapproval. "Not dressed like that, you aren't. They'll never let you on the courts. Are those chinos, for God's sake?"

"I'm not playing tennis! I'm going under the premise of leaving some listings for Mrs. Donovan to look through. She said I should drop them off there. I'm hoping I might *bump into* Edith. I talked to the secretary in Thompson's agent's office and something isn't quite right with his alibi for Monday."

"Oh God!" Jessica groaned. "Do you think Thompson could have killed Rex and put him in my apartment? He's certainly got the muscle to do it. Maybe he's framing me."

"Why would Thompson Christopher want to frame you? Is there something between the two of you I should know about?"

"Strictly platonic. I swear." She crossed her heart as if she were in middle school. Nikki waited for the pinkie swear. "But you're going to find out where he was that day? Thompson?"

"I'm going to try," Nikki said testily, wondering what the heck was wrong with chinos on a Saturday morning.

Jess climbed out of the car, but then leaned back inside. "Sorry about the remark about your slacks. They look kind of good on you. I'm serious. You could totally do the J. Crew thing." She hesitated. "I want you to know how much I appreciate what you're doing, Nik. These bozos," she indicated the police station, "they don't know what they're doing. It's good to know I've got you on my side. That you believe in me."

Nikki smiled. "You'd do the same for me, wouldn't you? Have my back?"

"You bet. See you back at your place late this afternoon?" Jess slapped the top of the car.

"You're not going back when you're done here?"

"Retail therapy." She flashed a smile and then she was gone, all flashy long legs and three thousand dollars of leather dangling off her elbow.

Nikki wasn't a big tennis buff, nor a country club girl, for that matter, but she knew her way around the Beverly Hills CC in Cheviot Hills . . . the Beverly Hills part of the name being a bit of a misnomer. As was the country club part, if you got technical. There was no golf course, only banquet and meeting rooms, a health club and tennis courts. Over the years, Nikki had attended various meetings and charity events, and occasionally met a client at the club. It was a known trophy-wife hangout. She'd once had a crazy client shopping for a property in the fifteen million range who would only meet with Nikki while on the treadmill—and expected Nikki to be on the treadmill beside her. The sale had been nice but had given Nikki awful shin splints.

Nikki left her car with the valet and tracked down her client, who was leaving her yoga class. Then she wandered out to the tennis courts, where she spotted Edith finishing up a lesson with some hunky tennis pro with a fake-and-bake tan. Edith's swing was atrocious, but she looked nice in her tennis whites, for a middle-age woman. Trying to play it cool, Nikki walked into the women's locker room just behind Edith.

"Edith, good to see you," Nikki said, trying to look surprised she had bumped into her.

"Yes, I took my lesson!" Edith wiped the back of her neck with a small hand towel. "And if one more person says they're surprised to see me here with my husband cold on the slab in the coroner's office, I'm going to lose my religion."

Nikki smiled kindly; she, for one, felt sorry for Edith. She couldn't imagine what she had to be going through—to learn her husband had deceived her in such an awful way, and then for him to turn up truly dead in the bed of a young woman with whom he'd had an affair. *That* was enough to make a woman *lose her religion*.

"Actually," Nikki said quietly, "I was thinking how nice it was to see you here. Not all women would be so brave." All the crap people had to be saying, she knew it couldn't be easy for Edith to show her face in such a public place. "You have a right to live your life. You didn't ask for any of this. With Rex."

Edith gave a snort and then opened a locker door. "I'm not brave," she said, suddenly sounding tired. "Just worn out with Rex's crap. The bastard is still piling it on, even from the grave."

"I can understand that, too. All the more reason why you need to be out here in the sunshine hitting tennis balls." She paused. "Well, I should be going." She hooked her thumb over her shoulder. "I just had to drop something off for a client and thought I'd say hi." She turned as if to walk away, then turned back. "By the way, I ran into a friend yesterday, a casting director," she lied smoothly. "He was telling me how disappointed he was. He was supposed to see Thompson for an audition Monday, and Thompson missed his appointment. He wondered if he was sick," she pressed, certain she was going to burn in hell for this whopper. "He wasn't sick, was he? Monday?"

Edith shrugged as she pulled a toiletries bag from her locker. "No, I don't think so. Heavens, it's been such a long week, Monday seems like a year ago." She sighed. "Honestly, he's got more offers than he knows what to do with. He must have just decided to skip that audition."

"Right. Sure. Makes sense," Nikki said, thinking to herself that if Thompson didn't have an alibi for Monday, maybe *he* was the one who did Rex in. Could the solution be that simple? Her gut told her Thompson wasn't the kind of person who could murder a man, but what if her gut was wrong? "Well, you have a good day."

"You, too. And thank you for not asking if there's going to be a memorial service. There isn't. They can bury Rex in a pauper's grave, for all I care." Edith slammed the locker door.

Nikki was still smiling at Edith's spunk when she entered the women's bathroom to make a quick pit stop. She was just having a seat when a voice came from the stall next to her.

"She's blasé for a woman twice scorned, isn't she?"

"Excuse me?" Nikki murmured, unable to keep herself from lifting her eyebrows and then wrinkling her forehead. Jessica had been saying for years that she needed Botox, and Nikki knew she was making the wrinkle situation worse, but she just couldn't help herself. Sometimes bizarre situations called for some good wrinkles.

"Edith March," the voice said from the other stall. "I saw you talking to her in the locker room. She's awfully blasé, considering."

Nikki was unsure of the etiquette called for in this scenario, but she really had to go. She tried to tinkle quietly. "*Considering?*"

Her confidante on the other side of the partial wall reeled off TP like it was Christmas ribbon. "Considering the fact that Rex banged every vacant vagina in Hollywood, and now Thompson is cheating on her."

Nikki hated to sound like an echo, but she couldn't help herself. "Thompson is cheating on her?"

"That's probably why he missed his casting call. I didn't mean to listen in, I just couldn't help overhearing." The mystery woman flushed.

Nikki hurried to finish her business. She didn't want the woman to get away before she got to speak with her further. She flushed and bolted out of the stall. Then, trying to play it cool, she sidled up to the row of marble sinks, glancing at the woman next to her.

She was about Edith's age, but thin, wearing a tennis skirt that was painfully short for a woman her age. Nikki turned on the water, checking over her shoulder to be sure the other stalls were empty before she spoke. "Did you mean that Thompson was cheating on Edith on Monday when he was supposed to be at casting calls?" she whispered.

"Well . . . it's entirely possible." She began to rub her soapy hands together.

Nikki scrutinized her informant. Whoever her plastic surgeon was, he had done a nice job on her eyes. They were the eyes of a thirty-five-year-old, not droopy, but not cat-eye slanty, either. "I'm sorry. Have we met?"

The woman started to offer her hand, then realizing it was soapy, gave a little laugh and abandoned the gesture. "Carly Vonton."

"Nikki—"

"I know who you are. Nice to meet you, Nikki. Your mother and I are old friends."

"Are you?" She tried to sound like she believed her. She was always meeting people who claimed to be *old friends* with Victoria. It had been her experience that anyone who used the term *old friends* wasn't. "What makes you think Thompson Christopher was *with another woman* Monday?" Nikki asked, choosing to use a euphemism for Edith's sake. Not that it made a big difference; either he was screwing other women or he wasn't. But what a tragedy it would be if he was; Edith had put up with that crap through nearly thirty years of marriage to Rex. She didn't deserve a cheating man. As if any woman did. . . . But at least that would mean Thompson hadn't killed Rex and *that* was a plus. Wasn't it?

"Well, I'm not one to carry tales." Carly dried her hands with one of those napkin things that sort of looked like cloth but wasn't.

Nikki grabbed one of the fake towels, turning the water off with the back of her hand. She'd been a bit of a germ-a-phobe at one point in her life and still considered herself in recovery. "Of course," she murmured conspiratorially. "But, come on . . ."

"Come on." It was Carly's turn to echo. "A good-looking man like Thompson Christopher? And him being with a woman like Edith . . ." She let her voice trail off as if Nikki intuitively understood that such shenanigans were a given.

Nikki made a point of using her best gossip voice, concealing her own emotions. She'd had her own experience with cheating men in her younger years. Personally, she saw it as a crime punishable by castration . . . but that was her own little hang-up. She glanced at her newfound confidante. "So who is it? They must be pretty discreet; I haven't heard a word."

Carly squirted lotion from a dispenser into her palm. "More discreet than most, I suppose, but it's got to be true." She rubbed her hands together. "I heard it from an excellent source, a reliable friend who heard it from *her* friend."

"Ah. Reliable, for sure," Nikki said, trying not to snigger.

"Her name is Tiffany," Carly whispered. "The one he's having an affair with. She works at that diner on Sunset, the one Thompson *used* to work at, before he was discovered. Supposedly, they were *old friends.*" Carly dropped her voice to a whisper as two women entered the ladies' room. As they came in, Carly headed out, pressing a finger to her lips. "Our little secret."

Nikki didn't know which diner Thompson Christopher had worked at before he became famous, but she knew who would . . .

"Oh, God, yes. Thompson Christopher flipped tuna melts for a living at Kitty's on Santa Monica near Hancock."

"Carly said he worked on Sunset."

"Well, *Carly* needs to hire a better fact-checker. I'm telling you, he worked at Kitty's on Santa Monica. Didn't

you know that? I thought everyone knew that." Marshall
fed Stanley a tidbit of avocado from his salad.

Nikki had found him out near the pool, his favorite
spot to unwind and be himself, away from the limelight.
The housekeeper had made a big salad before leaving
for the weekend and he had insisted Nikki have lunch
with him.

"I didn't know. How *would* I know?" she asked. "And
stop feeding the dogs. You know they're not supposed
to have people food."

"But they like people food. Don't they? Yes they do,"
he crooned to Oliver as he fed him a nibble from his
salad.

"Knock it off," Nikki warned, raising her fork threat-
eningly. "You two, both of you. Off," she ordered. "Go
play." She pointed with the fork and the dogs took off,
ears flopping. "So, what do you think?" she asked, returning her attention to Marshall. "Have you heard any
gossip on Thompson Christopher?"

"I heard he has a big—"

"Marshall! Please," she groaned.

"I know. Not in front of the doggies."

"No. I mean *I* don't need those kinds of details while
I'm eating lunch." She leaned back in her chair and
wiped her mouth with her napkin. "Or any other time,
for that matter. What I meant was, have you heard anything about him cheating on Edith?"

"There hasn't been a peep of it in the papers, or on
the set."

Nikki grinned. Marshall's shoots were renowned for
being fun, because *he* was, and they were also known for
their gossip, because he *loved* gossip. "You really think
he could be seeing someone on the sly and no one has
seen him?"

He shrugged. "Anything is possible." He leaned closer

to her, his tone wistful. "What if they truly are in love, Thompson and this waitress? What did you say her name was?"

"Tiffany."

He cringed and sat up again. "Oh dear. What an unfortunate name."

"This from a man born Wilbur Sparrow Feather Jones?"

"Eat your salad. And don't taunt me. I'm in a good mood today. I have no appearances this weekend and Rob and I are going to play house. If he ever gets home. I worry about him. He works such long hours. He was supposed to be off at seven in the morning, but you know gangs on the streets of L.A. They never sleep."

Smiling, Nikki dove into her salad. As she ate, she told Marshall about her chat with Tawny/Mary in J.J. Flaherty's office.

"Oh, my God," he breathed. The dogs were back under the table again, praying for handouts. "So you thought maybe Thompson— Oh, my God, you know he wouldn't have killed Rex! He already *had* Edith. Why would he? And if he did, why would he be trying to frame Jessica for it?"

Nikki shrugged. "I don't know. Maybe he was afraid his fat meal ticket would run out of punches if Rex came back into their lives. And if he knew about Jessica's affair with Rex, she'd be an easy target to frame, I suppose."

"But if he was busy boffing Tiffany from the diner that day, that lets him off the hook, at least for the murder, if not the infidelity."

"Right." She sighed, pushing another mouthful of the tasty chopped salad into her mouth.

"But I must say," Marshall added, "I'm impressed with your investigative skills. Who thought you had it in you? If this real estate agent thing doesn't work out, you could become a P.I. I'd hire you to get all my dirt first-hand."

The dogs flew out from under the table, barking wildly, and Nikki looked up to see Rob coming out of the sliding glass doors, onto the patio. "Hey boys." He stooped to pet one spaniel and then the other.

Rob was dressed for the street in a shirt with the sleeves torn off and a belt buckle the size of Rhode Island. He had a full sleeve of tattoos on one arm and was working on the other. With his long hair pulled back and the bandana around his head and the sunglasses, he looked like a serious bad-ass. Which he was. He was also one of the kindest men Nikki had ever known.

Ollie leaped up to lick Rob's face and he gently pushed him down. "Enough, already." He walked up behind Marshall, put his arms around him and kissed his temple. "Hey, baby."

Marshall closed his eyes and leaned back. "You were supposed to be home hours ago. I was worried."

"Sorry, I got hung up." Rob massaged Marshall's shoulders. "Nik, how are you?"

"Good." She shrugged. "I guess. Considering this whole mess with Rex and Jessica."

"Well, I hope you're still good after I tell you what I heard downtown this morning."

Chapter 12

"**O**h, God. What did you hear?" Marshall turned in his chair to look at Rob. "Jessica's going to be arrested, isn't she?" He slapped his hand on the table. "I knew it! She did it."

"She didn't do it!" Nikki threw a crouton at him. It bounced off one broad shoulder and into Ollie's mouth, so then she had to find a treat for Stanley.

"Sit down, lover." Marshall patted the chair beside him. "I know you're exhausted. I'll get you some lunch and a beer, just as soon as you give us the juicy details."

Rob sank into the cushioned wrought-iron chair and pulled off his bandana, tossing it on the table. "I'm not hungry, but I could definitely use the beer."

"Not hungry? You better not be eating donuts again. You know how I feel about your cholesterol numbers."

His words seemed silly, but they came out so sweet. Nikki found it endearing that Marshall fussed over Rob the way he did. There wasn't much fussing in Nikki and Jeremy's relationship; they were both too busy and too practical.

Rob turned to Nikki. "This is not official. It's just cops talking, but chances are, Rex was not killed in Jessica's apartment."

"I think they already knew that," she said cautiously. "No weapon. No blood. Just a dead man wearing small briefs."

"I still can't get over that," Marshall groaned, feeding the dogs bits from his plate again. "Lamé? What was he thinking?"

Nikki and Rob both ignored him. "But that's good, right?" she said. "That he wasn't killed there? That takes some of the pressure off Jessica, especially since she had an alibi for Monday."

"Here's the problem," Rob explained, shifting forward in the chair and focusing his intense brown eyes on her. "He wasn't killed in her bed, but that doesn't mean Jessica couldn't have done it. Her alibi is for Monday, working hours. She could have moved the body before she arrived at her meeting. She could have done it in the middle of the night."

"But why would someone kill someone and then put the body in their own bed? It makes no sense."

"I'm not saying she did it, Nikki. I'm telling you the thought process Lutz is following. It's not beyond the realm of possibility that a clever murderer would try to point the finger at someone else by making it look like he'd been framed, to cover his tracks. The good news is that this new information allows for a greater number of suspects."

"Meaning someone actually *could* be trying to frame her."

"It's very possible. We generally start with the people closest to the decedent and work our way outward. I imagine Edith March will be interviewed if she hasn't been already. And her boyfriend, of course. After that . . ." He shrugged. "Who knows? It depends on where the investigation leads them after the interviews."

Thinking over what Rob was saying, Nikki scratched Stanley behind the ears. "No weapon was found in the apartment. What do they think was used to kill him?"

"They don't know exactly, but it was a long, thin, cylindrical-like instrument."

"Like an ice pick," Marshall breathed.

"Like an ice pick," Rob repeated. "But probably not something quite so dramatic. It went through his eye and directly into his brain." He pressed his pinkie finger to his eyelid. "There wouldn't have been much bleeding."

Marshall looked appalled and thrilled at the same time by the gruesome details. "So how do they know he wasn't killed in Jessica's bed?"

"It has something to do with the way the blood and other fluids settled in his body. Apparently, it was obvious at the scene that he'd been moved, but sometimes that can mean the body was just moved from one room to another. There was no blood—or other evidence—elsewhere in the apartment, for that matter, so the detectives have to conclude he might not have been killed there, which means he might have been killed elsewhere. Am I making sense?" he asked.

"Sure," Nikki said as Ollie pushed Stanley aside to get his own share of the loving. To further press the point, the red-and-white dog propped his front paws on Nikki's knee. She scratched and stroked as she talked. "It makes complete sense. You eliminate the possibilities as you can, adding possibilities as you need to. How long before there's an official autopsy report?"

Rob groaned. "It could be weeks. The coroner isn't going to rush to a conclusion. It's too big a case to not get it right. He'll try to get a better idea of what was used to kill Rex, maybe even an impression in the brain tissue."

"Oh, Christ." Marshall got up. "Enough gore for me! Anyone need anything? A beer, Nikki? An ice pick?"

Nikki shook her head. For an action star, Marshall was as squeamish as a seven-year-old girl.

"Be right back with that beer, baby." Marshall squeezed Rob's shoulder and walked away.

The dogs took off after him.

"Do not feed them!" Nikki called after him. "Just because you take them inside, doesn't mean I won't know. They'll tattle on you later. They always do." Knowing very well he would ignore her, she looked back at Rob. "Sorry. Go on."

Rob leaned back in his chair, pulled out the elastic holding his medium brown hair in a ponytail, and let the wind blow through it. "So far, the coroner hasn't been able to identify the time of death. He's going to have a hard time doing it."

"Why?"

He met her gaze. "The body was refrigerated, Nikki. Which adds to the conclusion that he wasn't killed in the apartment."

"Refrigerated?" Wow. She wasn't expecting that. . . . "How . . ." She stopped and then started again as she wrestled with the image of Rex being squeezed into a standard refrigerator. It would have been a tight fit, to say the least. "How does a person refrigerate a body? Is that really possible?"

He shook his head. "You wouldn't believe the things possible that human beings do to each other."

Nikki folded her hands and rested them on the table. "Why would someone do that? *Refrigerate* a body?" She found it difficult even to say.

"To throw the cops off. It's going to make it much more difficult for the coroner to determine the time of death because the refrigeration stalls the natural process."

"The natural process?" she asked, pretty certain she didn't want to hear the explanation.

"Of decomposition."

She studied the full sleeve of tattoos on his left arm, an intricate tapestry of vines, tropical leaves and slithering snakes. "Right."

"It's also practical," he continued. "You kill somebody, it's a good way to store a body until you decide how to dispose of it."

"It sounds so cold and calculating."

He raised his eyebrows.

Catching her unintentional pun, she groaned. "You know what I mean. Do you think this murder was planned?"

"It looks that way to me, but I don't have all the facts." He hesitated. "Do you know if Jessica knew he was alive? After he was declared dead in the plane crash? Because of course *that's* the true pool of suspects."

"She swears she didn't know."

Rob threaded his fingers together and stretched his arms, flexing until the snakes slithered. "You believe her?"

She thought before she answered. "Sure. Why wouldn't I?"

"Well, my bets are on the wife."

"Edith?" Nikki frowned. "If you knew her, you wouldn't say that. Edith is a good woman. Even Victoria likes her, and you know Mother. She's suspicious of everyone."

"That's because *Mother* is one smart cookie." He tapped

his temple. "She's one of those people who understands, after years in the business—a business not all that unlike my own—that no one is who they seem to be."

She sat back in her chair. "What a cynical thing to say, Rob. What about me?" She tapped her collarbone with both hands. "I'm a pretty genuine person. This is me."

He smiled kindly. "You've got your secrets. We both know that. Those secrets are sometimes what define us." He shrugged. "I'm just saying, we don't know people as well as we think we do. Ever."

Nikki wanted to argue the point further, but let it drop. Hours later, though, she was still thinking about what Rob said.

"Jeremy," Nikki said when he answered his phone. "Do you think you know me?"

"Well, hello yourself," he said. "Me? My day was fine. How was yours?"

She switched her BlackBerry from one ear to the other and reached into her bag on the car seat beside her. She was suddenly hungry; she hadn't eaten since the salad with Marshall more than seven hours before. "I'm serious," she said, digging in her bag in the hopes of finding a granola bar. "Do you think you know me? I mean, you've known me practically my whole life. Since we were kids. But do you feel like you *know* me? Do you know what I'm capable of doing? I mean the bad things."

"No, no more juice," he said.

"I don't want juice," she quipped.

"Not you," he said louder into the phone. "I'm talking to Katie. No more juice, Katie. I'm turning out the light. Good night, sweetheart." He made a kissing sound.

Nikki waited. There was nothing to eat in her purse. Not even a mint snatched off the counter at a doctor's office. Nothing. "Sorry," she said. "It's a bad time. It's bedtime. I should call later."

"Nope. It's fine," he said. "We were just saying our last good nights. She should have been asleep half an hour ago. I'm heading downstairs. I can talk."

Nikki watched the house. "You might as well leave the hall light on," she said. "Otherwise, you'll be back upstairs in five minutes."

"Where are you?" he asked as the light in the second-story window over the foyer came on again.

She chuckled. "Out front, on the street. I'm not sure the eight-foot fence does much. I can see right into your house. You need to close your front drapes."

"The fence keeps the tourists and the crazies out, Miss Stalker. Come inside," he said impatiently.

"No. I'm fine out here. We didn't have plans tonight. We agreed on the parameters and—"

"Nikki, stop already."

A second later, she saw the front door open. The white colonial, in Brentwood, was understated—at least in present-day terms of expensive houses in L.A.—but elegant. It was the house Jeremy and his wife had bought just before she got sick. Nikki had always loved the house . . . and hated it.

The front gate slid open.

Nikki started her car and purred up the drive, her Prius in battery/stealth mode. Jeremy waited for her on the front step.

"Sorry. I didn't mean to be Miss Stalker," she said when she reached the door, her bag on her shoulder. She was still wearing the chinos, which she was seriously considering donating to Goodwill.

He leaned down and kissed her on the lips. It was a

nice kiss, warm. "I'm glad you came," he said. "I missed you this week."

Inside the foyer, he hit a button that closed the front gate and then he walked toward the back of the house. "I was just cleaning up. Let me finish and we'll have a glass of wine."

The kitchen, renovated by his wife in the early stages of her cancer treatment, was very French country: a brick floor, honey yellow walls, granite countertops, distressed white cabinetry, ceramic tiles and rustic urns. Copper pots hanging from a rack over the enormous island added to the ambience. The dirty dishes in the sink, children's toys on the floor, and food on the counter did not.

She dropped her bag on the end of the counter. "Is this your mac & cheese or Maria's?" She picked up a blue plastic fork that sported a pink Disney princess handle and dug into the serving dish on the granite island.

"Mine."

"Oh, Jeremy. I adore your mac and cheese." Nikki practically moaned with pleasure. "I love the Gruyère in it. I can't believe your kids will eat this."

"I ply them with the bacon and sneak the Gruyère in," he explained. "I made dinner *and* did the art projects." He pointed to a kids' table covered with watercolor paintings. A glass of murky water with paintbrushes protruding from it still stood there.

"Impressive, you Super Daddy, you."

"Maria's gone to a wedding in Arizona. Remember? We're roughing it this week without her, hence the mess." He opened his arms, as if she hadn't already noticed it. "And my preoccupation this week. I'm really sorry that we haven't had a chance to talk about the murder." He began to collect dirty plates off the counter and rinse them in the sink before adding them to the dishwasher. "How are you? How's Jess?"

She sighed between mouthfuls of lukewarm macaroni smothered in cheese, flavored with just a hint of smoky bacon. "I'm fine. She's fine. Back to what we were talking about." She motioned with the princess fork. "Answer my question. Do you really feel like you know me? I mean, do you know me well enough to know I would never commit murder?"

"Ah, hell, what's Victoria done now?"

She laughed. Her initial starvation staved, she plucked a dried macaroni noodle off a stool, dropped it in the trash can in the middle of the floor, and sat down. "I didn't kill Mother. Not yet. Now, Mother?" She waved the fork. "I can't say for sure *she* wouldn't kill someone. You know, to protect me. Maybe some of my siblings. Not Harrison."

He cringed. "Harrison in trouble again?"

She closed her eyes. "Don't ask."

"Okay, so Victoria. Yes, she would kill, but she'd be smart enough to not get caught." He poured juice from a sippy cup into the sink.

Jeremy and Marissa's children were twelve, nine and three. Two girls and a boy. She had always wanted to ask him why a third child, once the first two were older, but she'd never figured out how to word it without sounding childless and judgmental. Marissa's breast cancer was discovered while she was pregnant with Katie. She had refused treatment until after the little girl was born. Her sacrifice had likely cost her her life. Marissa had been such a good person that Nikki felt small in her shadow, sometimes. It was a hard feeling to fight.

"But you don't think I would kill?"

He grimaced, but didn't answer.

"Jeremy, what I'm asking is, do you think that maybe

we don't *really* know people, even the people we *think* we know?"

He looked at her through half-closed, confused eyes. "I have no idea what we're talking about or why, so I'm pretty sure I'll say entirely the wrong thing here and not get to make out with you."

"There isn't a wrong answer." She licked the princess fork, choosing to ignore the making out bit, even though she liked it. This was a side of Jeremy she hadn't seen in a long time. Maybe he really *was* getting used to his new life, without Marissa. He had promised Nikki he would get there eventually, but it would take time.

"It's just that Rob was telling me today that you never know people, not inside," she explained. "He thinks any one of us could potentially kill another human being."

"Does he think Jessica had something to do with Rex March's death?"

"No. Of course not. The police are saying now that he wasn't even killed in her apartment."

"So, she hasn't been charged?"

Nikki shook her head. "I don't think they *can* charge her, even though they'd probably like to, just so they have someone to splash all over the front pages. But he wasn't killed in her apartment, they don't have a murder weapon, and Rob told me on the down low that some cops were talking this morning about how they think Rex's body was refrigerated."

"Since the plane crash?" he asked incredulously.

"No!" She thought about it for a second. That idea had never occurred to her. Surely a person couldn't keep a body refrigerated for six months? But she couldn't believe she hadn't thought to ask Rob that question. She just assumed Rex had been killed recently. "I don't think he's been dead *that* long." She got off the stool and walked around to Jeremy's side of the island, taking her fork with her. "How long can a body stay good in a refrigerator?"

He continued to load the dishwasher. "Don't ask me. I'm the tooth and gums guy."

She rinsed off her fork. "Okay, so final answer. Do you think I could kill a man?"

He took the fork from her and dropped it in the dishwasher. "Nope. You don't have a mean bone in your body." He reached out and pulled her into his arms. "But you do have some fine other parts."

She grinned, looking into his gaze. "So what's going on here?"

"What?"

She slid her arms over his shoulders, looking up at him. "You know what. This." She pressed her hips against his, hitting the bingo button just right.

It was his turn to grin. "I don't know."

She studied him carefully. "Does this mean our celibacy is coming to an end?"

After Marissa died, their relationship had gotten hot and heavy pretty quickly, but then, fearing it was based on grief and a shared love of Junior Mints, he'd insisted he and Nikki slow things down. That had translated to no sex. She'd understood completely; that didn't mean she liked the idea.

"I don't know. I guess I had a good week. Maria was gone." He let go of her and went back to filling the dishwasher. "And the house didn't cave in on us. Everyone ate, bathed, got to school on time. Almost on time." He smiled at her. "I'm feeling good."

"I'm glad." She tried not to be disappointed that he'd traded her warm, willing body for dirty dishes. "So do you think Rob's right?" She grabbed a plastic container from under the counter and began to fill it with the leftover mac and cheese. "I've been thinking there's no way Edith would have had anything to do with this. Or even Thompson, at least at first glance. Because I know them. But could anyone in Rex's life be his killer?"

"You're not serious about this, are you? You really shouldn't be getting involved."

"I'm not getting *involved*." She lowered the dirty casserole dish into the sink and turned the water on. "I'm just keeping my eye out for Jessica's best interests. Someone is obviously trying to frame her for Rex's murder and I won't let it happen."

"Well, I still think you should leave this to the police." He squirted dish soap into the running water. "But Jessica couldn't have a better person on her side."

Chapter 13

Monday morning Nikki met a potential client, taking with her a comparative market analysis. Over coffee and croissants *au chocolat,* she broke the news to the young pop diva and her assistant that if she sold her Malibu home right now, it would be at a loss, considering what she paid for it three years ago, and what the market would bear today. It had been a downer for both of them; the singer owed more on the property than Nikki could possibly list it for. She had agreed to think it over, but Nikki feared she'd just shop for a different real estate agent, searching until she found someone with fewer honesty genes.

By the time Nikki made it into the office, it was after eleven. Jessica hadn't made it in yet. Nikki tracked her down at a posh Beverly Hills spa. Jessica's reasoning was that if the bosses weren't going to let her work, what was the point in coming *to* work? Nikki reminded her about her past-due AmEx payment. Jessica conveniently found herself getting another call and had to disconnect.

Then, while on hold with the bank because of their

denial of a client's preapproved loan, Nikki found some
packing tape and boxed up the Bristol Farms gourmet
crackers that had been sitting under her desk for over a
week. Nikki didn't know how she got herself into these
things. Victoria had insisted Nikki buy the crackers to
send to her half sister, Celeste, Victoria's daughter by
her fourth husband. Nikki had argued that New York
City *had* crackers, but had given in on day three of her
mother's running monologue about *said* crackers. Nikki
had found the Bristol Farms crackers and bought them,
but then Rex had gotten himself killed a second time,
Jessica was in the process of being framed, and Nikki
had been too busy to stand in line at the post office.

With the box ready to go, Nikki snagged a bottle of
water from the break-room fridge and sat down to look
over the daily hot sheet. It was a report put out by the
Multiple Listing Service that showed new listings, status
changes, and price changes for all the properties for
sale in the L.A. area. Jessica usually just skimmed
through it. She had an amazing head for numbers and
remembered prices, and not only of the current properties, but what they had gone for the last time they
were sold. Nikki was a slower learner; she tried to make
a point of looking over the hot sheet every day.

Over the weekend, several interesting properties had
gone up for sale. There was a new listing on Benedict
Canyon Drive, and one in Beverly Hills Flats, and the
price had dropped dramatically on a celebrity's house
on the beach in Malibu. It was very important with their
clientele that celebrity buyers' and sellers' names were
kept confidential, but it was just a game. In Hollywood,
there were few secrets, including who was buying and
selling and who had lost their ass in the process.

Nikki also found on the hot sheet several new listings
for luxury condos. The first time she looked through

the list, nothing really stood out; it was business as usual. But on her second pass over the properties just reduced, something caught her eye, something she couldn't believe she missed before.

Less than a week before Rex March was murdered, a luxury corner condo on Wilshire had gone up for sale. The place on the nineteenth floor of the office-to-residential conversion on Wilshire Drive just west of downtown L.A. was a two-bedroom, two-bath, 1768-square-foot condo with amazing floor-to-ceiling windows and a gourmet kitchen. Nikki knew for a fact that the view of the city was impressive because she had once attended a cocktail party there. It belonged to Thompson Christopher.

Nikki picked up her phone and hit Jessica on her speed dial.

"Nik, I'm so glad you're there," Jessica said when she answered the phone, not giving Nikki a chance to speak. "I was just talking with Alicia, you know, Godfrey Hearst's wife, and she and her husband are in the market for something more spacious. She'd love us to come out and have a look at their place on Doheny."

Nikki could tell by the tone of Jessica's voice that she was still with Mrs. Hearst.

"We were thinking maybe tomorrow," Jessica said. "She'd like to see some properties in Holmby Hills; she likes the place near Aaron Spelling's. But she's totally open to our suggestions. Something in the eighty mil range," she added casually.

Nikki shook her head in disbelief. This was the third new client Jessica had picked up since she'd found Rex dead in her apartment a week ago. Death certainly hadn't been good for Rex, but it was doing amazing things for Jessica's client list. Shoot, at this rate, she'd be applying for a black AmEx card in no time.

"Tomorrow works. Set it up."

"You haven't got anything on your calendar tomorrow?" Jessica asked sweetly.

"Nothing that I can't change for Mrs. Hearst," Nikki answered with equal sweetness.

"Great."

Jessica must have then lowered the phone because her voice got quieter. "One o'clock will be super, Alicia. We'll bring our laptop, show you a couple of ideas we have, and then maybe go for a drive."

Nikki heard another female voice, but she couldn't make out the words.

"You too, Alicia. See you tomorrow." Jessica chuckled as her voice got louder. "And you thought I was just sitting on my duff getting a pedicure, didn't you?"

Nikki had to smile. "I don't know why Downy thinks you should ever come into the office. You should just go from spa to spa."

"*There's* an idea. I think you should bring it up next time we meet with him to discuss sales goals."

"I'll certainly bring it up." Nikki unscrewed the cap on the water bottle and eased off her pumps under her desk. "Hey, listen. Did you see that Thompson Christopher put his place on Wilshire up for sale?"

"And he didn't call us? What a prick!"

"So you didn't know?"

"I knew there was a new listing on Wilshire. That was Thompson's? The corner condo listed with Wong for $980,000?"

"The very same." Nikki sipped her water. "It went on the market October first and it was reduced this morning to 950."

"So he stood right there at the party the other night and chatted like we were his best buddies and he had already listed his place with Wong? Pretty nervy."

Nikki tapped the keyboard on her laptop and ran a search for the property. The Wong agency had a great website featuring videos of many of their properties, something Windsor was doing, but not as well yet. "Why do you think he's selling, Jess? He's owned it less than two years."

"I suppose because he's pretty much living with Edith. I know you like him, but he's got a reputation for going for the older ladies. With money. He's selling his condo so he can live off Edith's money instead of his own. Did you get lunch? I'm craving a burger. I think I'll stop at In & Out on my way to the office. I'm going to be as big as a house if I don't stop eating those things. You want something?"

"Nah. I've got to go to the post office for Mother later. I'll grab a salad while I'm out."

"You're going to the post office for her? She can't get Amondo to do that?"

Nikki sighed, wondering if she needed therapy or something. She didn't think her relationship with her mother was all that strange, but other people did. Wasn't that a sign of being truly crazy? When you thought you were normal? "Don't ask," she told Jessica, checking out the square footage and amenities listed for Thompson's condo.

"Suit yourself. I have to call Detective Lutz and check before I go over, but my apartment is supposed to be released today. I can finally go home."

"That's great news. Not that I'm not enjoying having you at my place, but . . ."

"I understand," Jessica laughed. "Slumber parties are fun, but a girl's gotta go home and wash out her undies at some point." Her voice became more serious. "I'm just glad I had a place to go. Considering the circumstances, not everyone would have welcomed me into

their home like you did, Nik. You know that means a lot
to me. You're always a good friend, even when I'm not."

"Don't be silly. You're always a good friend." Nikki
screwed the cap back on her water. "Text me Alicia's address and I'll start some preliminary work on the comps."

"I can do that when I get in."

"I'll just get started. This is what I do well, Jess. So let
me do it. Catch you later."

Nikki tossed her phone onto her desk and studied
the picture of Thompson's living room with its gorgeous view of L.A. after dark. She didn't care that much
that Thompson hadn't listed the condo with her and
Jessica. What she couldn't stop thinking about was the
coincidence that he had put his place up for sale the
same week Rex had come back from the dead, just to be
killed. Was the condo listing a coincidence, or a clue as
to who killed Rex?

Nikki was so curious about Thompson's condo that
she gave the listing agent a ring when she ran out at
lunch to do her errands. Without too much small talk,
she moved right onto business while sitting in traffic. "I
know you're not supposed to say, Chuck, but this is
Thompson Christopher's place, isn't it?"

"You know I can't say," he said, his voice bubbly with
excitement. "It's not our policy to divulge clients' names."

"It certainly wouldn't be prudent, considering the
headlines this week, would it?" Nikki asked. "Although
you might get some showings because of the buzz. We
live in a crazy world."

"I have no idea what you're talking about," he said
coyly. "But I have to say, Ms. Harper, if you have any potential clients, you should bring them by this week. I
doubt the property will last till the weekend."

Realtors were sooo full of b.s.

"Now that you've reduced the price?" Nikki watched while the light turned green, then yellow, and nary a car moved in front of her. "Why, by the way, did you reduce the price so quickly? It's been on the market less than two weeks."

"My client is eager to sell."

"Is he?" she mused. "You think I could have a look at the place? I may have the perfect client," she lied, "but I'm not comfortable showing a place I haven't seen."

"I think that can be arranged."

"Great. How about today?" A horn blew behind her. Exactly where did the guy think she was going to go? She was six inches off a Land Rover's butt. She inched forward in her Prius. "How about now?"

"Now?" Chuck asked.

"Well, when you can get there. It is empty, isn't it? The condo?"

"I could probably meet you there. Say in forty-five?"

Nikki checked the clock on the dash. "Perfect." That gave her enough time to mail off the damned crackers.

The line at the post office closest to the condo on Wilshire was long, but not any longer than midday ever was. While she stood in line, box under her arm, she checked her e-mails on her BlackBerry. Slowly, the line of customers moved forward. A text came up on her cell: *Hope you're having a good day. J*

She smiled. Her relationship with Jeremy was progressing. She was sure of it. Maybe not at the same speed she had hoped or Victoria expected, but things were moving along. The time she spent Saturday night with him, just cleaning up his kitchen and then sharing a bottle of wine on his patio made her . . . hopeful.

"Next," called a nasal voice.

Feeling as if she'd won the lottery, Nikki dropped

her phone into her trusty Prada bag and bolted forward. "Hi." She slid the package across the counter.

"How would you like to send this?" The postal worker was a small woman in her early sixties. She had an attractive white pixie-like haircut with earrings shaped like corgi dogs hanging from her ears. "Priority will be nine-fifty, two to three days. First class, seven-forty, five to seven days."

"Priority would be fine." Nikki grabbed her wallet. "Cute earrings. I love corgis."

"Not many people know them. My Buttercup is twelve years old. My husband gave me these for her birthday. We always have a little party. Doggie cake. Treat bags." She tapped her computer keyboard. "My neighbor brings her peekapoos. I'm not a big fan. Dumb as goldfish. You have corgis?"

"King Charles Spaniels. Two. Stanley and Oliver."

"Cute names." She glanced up for the first time, looked back at her computer screen, and then the moment came. Nikki saw it in her eyes. *Recognition.*

The clerk broke into a grin. "Hey, you're"—she ran her finger along the return address portion of the box and then looked at her again—"Nikki Harper."

"I am," Nikki confessed, with a nod. She offered a ten-dollar bill, but the clerk didn't take it.

"I was sorry to hear about your friend." The doggies in her ears danced.

"My friend?" she asked, thinking the postal clerk was referring to Rex.

"The real estate lady. It was in the paper today. How she was being framed by Mexican banditos. They mentioned how you were standing by her. How you refused to be intimidated by them. Good gene stock your mother gave you. Pretty blue eyes, too," she added, studying Nikki's face as she waited for the printer to spit out a label.

Ah, a tabloid story. Of course.

"Thanks. My name was mentioned?" Nikki asked, a little surprised. She led such a boring life that she rarely made the tabloids.

"Yup. Cute picture of you getting out of your little car. It's a hybrid, isn't it? Personally, I think the cops are barking up the wrong tree." She leaned on the counter, seeming to be in no hurry, despite the ever-lengthening line of people. She lowered her voice. "Pretty girl like that. She would never kill a man. They ought to be looking at that young actor. Thompson Christopher."

Nikki's ears perked up. "Should they?"

"Comes in here once in a while. Mother lives in Idaho, Iowa, one of those states where there's a lot of corn." She waggled her finger and then pulled the label off the printer. "I don't like his eyes. Gotta close look at them the other day. Took his passport picture right back there." She pointed over her shoulder.

Nikki caught her breath, certain there was significance in what the clerk had just said, just not sure what it was. "Thompson Christopher applied for his passport here? Last week?"

She nodded. "He had a birth certificate and everything, with his real name on it; we have to check the documents, but he had changed his name legally. Can't remember what it used to be, but it was something silly. I can tell you that."

Nikki leaned across the counter, pushing her ten-dollar bill toward the clerk. "But you're certain it was him?" she whispered, not entirely sure why she was whispering.

The woman made change, the Corgis in her ears

dancing as she turned back to Nikki. "Positive." She handed Nikki what was left of the ten. "You have a fine day, Miss Harper. It was nice to meet you."

Nikki grinned and offered her hand over the counter. "It was nice to meet you, too."

Before Nikki reached her car, she was on her cell. She had to talk to someone, but she didn't want to call Jess, and Marshall was on a set. She barely hesitated before she called Victoria, who answered the phone herself.

"Mother."

"Daughter," Victoria echoed. "Autism Foundation Gala next month. Tickets. Include Jeremy, or no?"

Nikki groaned. She and Jeremy didn't go out in public often, but this was one cause he felt strongly about. "Give me the date and I'll check with him. Listen, I want your opinion on something. Does this sound odd to you? I just found out that Thompson Christopher put his condo up for sale the week before Rex died."

"*This* time?" Victoria asked.

Nikki was beginning to feel like she was caught in some kind of sick comedy routine. "When he died this time, yes."

"Just clarifying. Go on."

"Okay, so he put his condo up for sale two weeks ago, then reduces it this week."

"You're listing it?"

"No, Mother. He didn't ask me."

"Well, I can see why. Edith never would have stood for it. Not with her knowing about Jessica and Rex."

"Mother, that's not the point of this conversation." She unlocked her car door and got inside. "My point is that I think it's odd that Thompson put his condo up for sale so suddenly."

"Well, how would you know it was suddenly? He's

been Edith's bunky for months. Maybe they decided that since she'd sold the house, he might as well sell his place."

Nikki pulled on her seat belt. Her mother had a point. "He also just applied for a passport."

There was silence on the other end of the phone.

"Mother, did you hear what I said? Two weeks ago Thompson puts his place up for sale, then Rex comes up dead again, then Thompson applies for a passport and drops the price of his condo. What does that sound like to you?"

Victoria sniffed. "Sounds to me as if Edith is going to be single again."

Chapter 14

Nikki took a quick tour of the condo, which was, indeed, Thompson's. She didn't know what she was hoping to find there, but she came up with a big fat nothing. At least nothing that would help Jessica's case, like maybe a bloodstained carpet with the killer's name scrawled in the gore. It was a nice place, though, decently priced, so who knew, maybe she would sell it.

After saying good-bye to Chuck, the listing Realtor, inside the parking garage, Nikki got into her car, but she didn't pull out of the parking space right away. It was relatively quiet in the garage. A good place to pause and think for a second. Her life was always so hectic; it never seemed like she got enough time to just think.

She mulled over the sale of the condo, the skipped auditions, and the application for a passport . . . could this mean Thompson was preparing to skip town? Possibly. But why would he? His career was going well. He had the première of his latest movie in a few months. What would make him flee the country?

A murder charge?

Then she considered the fact that Edith had been purposely vague about where she was going once the house in Outpost Estates sold. Over the months, she'd talked about New York, but she'd also joked about sandy beaches and umbrella drinks. What if there had been a plan to kill Rex and flee? There were countries in the world where she and Thompson could go, where there would be no extradition. Look at Polanski; he'd lived his whole life in plain sight without ever being extradited to the U.S.

Had Edith discovered that Rex had faked his death and convinced Thompson to kill him? If the body had been moved as the police suggested, it was ridiculous to think that Jessica or Edith could have done it. But maybe Thompson killed Rex *for* Edith. With Thompson's reputation for romancing older women for their money, Edith's husband returning from the dead might put a serious kink in his plans. Maybe he decided it was time he found a *permanent* meal ticket. If he killed the *widow's* husband, she would forever be indebted to him. . . . And Edith clearly had motive for trying to frame Jessica. What better payback for screwing her husband than life in prison?

It was all *possible*, but deep down, Nikki just couldn't see Thompson killing someone. He was such a good guy. Such a gentleman, and he really seemed to care about Edith.

But what about the affair with the waitress? If he cared about Edith the way he said he did, the way he *acted*, there was no way he was cheating on her.

Nikki's eyes widened. But what if he *had* cheated on her? What if Edith found out about Thompson's affair with the waitress and threatened to kick him out of the house if he didn't rid her of her pesky husband?

Was that even plausible?

More plausible than Jessica killing Rex and then transporting his bloated body to her own apartment . . .

Nikki started her car and purred down the ramp. This whole Thompson-having-an-affair-with-a-waitress thing was bugging her. She couldn't decide if she wanted it to be true or not. Of course, there was only one way to find out. Go to the source.

Two-fifteen; the diner would be quiet. She pulled onto Wilshire and headed for the diner on Santa Monica Boulevard.

Nikki sat in a booth in Kitty's Diner and studied the laminated menu. Only a few of the booths were taken. She'd been by the place many, many times, but never inside. Decorated in the style of diners of the fifties and sixties, it was nice enough. The bench seats at the booths were covered in red vinyl, but they were clean. The Formica tables sported individual jukeboxes.

A waitress in a pink uniform dress and a white cap that looked something like an old-style nurse's cap walked past Nikki. "Be right there to take your order," she said, carrying a plate with a monstrous burger and a heap of fries in each hand.

It was no wonder Americans were overweight. There was enough beef on those plates to feed a small village. "Thanks."

A bell rang when the door opened and Nikki looked up to see Elvis walk in. Her first impulse was to hold the menu up in front of her face. *Childish.*

She casually lifted the menu higher.

"Darlin'?" he crooned as he approached.

Nikki groaned and dropped the menu on the table.

Several patrons were looking their way. A teenager in an Ohio high school band t-shirt held up her cell phone to take a picture and Elvis posed for her.

He slid into Nikki's booth, across the table from her. He looked good. The way he had in his early days before the booze, women and drugs caught up with him. He was sporting a perfect pompadour that was his own inky hair, not a wig.

"E." She smiled for old times' sake.

"Nikki." He met her gaze, the right side of his upper lip slightly upturned, then he looked away. "Hey, little lady," he called to the waitress who was two tables over. "Can you get us some coffees?"

"Water for me," Nikki corrected. She didn't need the caffeine; she was hyper enough as it was. She looked back at her half-brother seated across the table. "You look good." She nodded, indicating the gold suit. "*King Creole*, right?"

He snapped his fingers, giving her that familiar Elvis smile that was so spot-on, it was eerie. "Oh, you're good. It takes most people a few tries to get this one right. They all like the white jumpsuits. I hate the jumpsuits."

She shrugged. "We know our movies, don't we?" She pushed the menu toward him. "Hungry? How have you been? I see you on Sunset sometimes. Business seems to be good." He lived mostly on the street, though once in a while he would hit a shelter for a shower and a cot. He made his *living* posing on street corners with tourists for tips.

"Better than you, apparently." He picked up the menu and glanced at it, then put it down. "You made the tabloids. She must be horrified."

He always referred to their mother as *she*. Elvis, a.k.a. James Mattroni, Jr., had had a falling out with Victoria years ago and they didn't speak. Their mother maintained it was because her son refused to seek help for his mental illness, help she was willing to pay for. Jimmy, who refused to answer to any name but Elvis, insisted it was because she was jealous of his talent. Nikki tried to remain neutral; it was hard for her to see him ill. She just wished he would take his meds regularly.

His father, James, had also been schizophrenic and had committed suicide when Jimmy was a freshman in college. Jimmy had never forgiven Victoria for not fighting harder to get custody of him when she and his father had split up, when he was a toddler. If it was any consolation, even though Victoria rarely spoke of the matter, she'd never forgiven herself, either.

"So, you've taken to befriending murderesses, have you?" He smirked.

"I'm not having this conversation with you." Nikki sat back as the waitress set down a glass of ice water and a mug of coffee on the table.

"What would you like?" she asked Nikki, pen poised over a notepad.

"The Caesar salad."

She scribbled. "Chicken with that?"

"No." Nikki glanced at her name tag. She was Mary, with an i. *Mari!* her name tag read. Or was it pronounced *Maury*? Either way, she wasn't Tiffany. "Dressing on the side, please."

"Mr. Presley?"

The getup didn't faze her. It probably didn't faze anyone who lived in Hollywood. Elvises were a dime a dozen, although she had to give him credit where credit was due—he did an excellent impression. At least until he tried to sing. Jimmy couldn't carry a tune. Never could, which was why his stint in Las Vegas years ago had been so short.

"You buying?" he asked, looking at Nikki.

"Anything you want." She opened her arms. She'd learned the hard way to never give him money outright, but she was always happy to buy him a meal. Take him to the doctor if he got sick. She'd have put a roof over his head if he'd let her, but he said he liked living the way he did. It made him feel closer to his dead mother, Gladys.

"Well, little lady . . ." he said in his best Presley voice, "I'll have the big beef burger with bacon, a double order of fries, and a chocolate malt. And maybe a slice of that pie on the counter." He winked at her. "You make that pie, Sugar?"

"Yup," she said. "Came in early just to make you that pie." She grabbed the menus.

"I thought you were a vegetarian," Nikki said as the waitress walked away.

"You're avoiding the subject." He drew his hand down the lapel of his gold suit jacket.

Some of his costumes were pretty cheap, but this one was nice. She wondered where he'd gotten it.

"So where was Rex March all this time when his fans thought he was dead?" He folded his hands and leaned over the table.

He smelled better from a distance. Nikki leaned back. "I have no idea. That's up to the police to find out."

He laughed. "It's all a conspiracy, you know. Rex's disappearance, D.B. Cooper's. Obama's trying to hide the truth from the taxpayers."

She nodded. It was always this way with Jimmy. At first glance, he seemed perfectly sane, but it never took long for the fruit to spill out of the bowl. "Seriously. How are you doing? You need anything? You keeping your appointments at the clinic?"

"You want to hear my theory?" he asked in complete earnestness.

So, apparently, they were not going to talk about him. "Sure."

"I think Ginger did it. The redhead. She killed Rex March."

Nikki had no idea who he was talking about. "Ginger?" she asked.

"The movie star," he sang. "She'll try to make it look like the Professor or Mary Ann did it, but the truth will come out."

"Ah," Nikki said, her synapses finally firing. "From *Gilligan's Island*." She sipped her water and then reached for the straw, taking her time ripping the paper off. "Rex was on *Shipwrecked Vacation*. Different show."

Elvis frowned. "This is why we can't talk, Nikki. You blatantly disregard my opinions just because you don't like my lifestyle choices."

"I disagree with your choice to be homeless when you don't have to."

He crossed his arms over his chest. "I'm trying to have a serious conversation with you. If your friend Jessica didn't kill Rex March, who did? Clearly, the logical answer is Ginger."

"Clearly." She nodded. "I didn't know you were a Rex March fan."

"I wasn't, but he didn't deserve to die in a fiery plane crash."

"Which, apparently, he *didn't*," she pointed out.

The waitress brought the burger and fries and salad to the table. "Be right back with your pie and shake." She looked at Jimmy. "You want ketchup, Mr. Presley?"

"If it's not too much trouble, darlin'," he crooned. He popped a fry into his mouth. "So if Rex didn't die in the crash, where was he all this time?"

Nikki was afraid she might jump onto the same merry-go-round again, so she tried a different tack. "I don't know. Where do *you* think he could have been?"

"Somewhere nice. Nicer than here. When I filmed *Blue Hawaii*, I seriously considered moving to Hawaii. Not the Big Island, but maybe Molokai or Kauai. But I could never leave Graceland permanently. Thank you, darlin'," he said to the waitress as she walked by their booth, dropping off a bottle of Heinz, the milkshake and pie.

"So you think Rex was on Kauai all these months, while his widow was settling his affairs, selling the house, and getting cozy with her boyfriend?" Nikki said, just throwing out random conversation at this point.

"It's very possible. The important question is," he waved a French fry, his eyes narrowing with concentration, "who knew Rex wasn't dead? You can't kill a man you don't know is alive." He bit the fry in half. "Was it his wife? His girlfriend? His mother?" He gasped. "Maybe *she* killed him. No one ever looks at the mother. We always assume it's the jaded wife or girlfriend, the cheated business partner. But *she* could have done it. *She* had motive and opportunity."

The way he said it made Nikki think he meant *she,* as in Victoria, which was an interesting turn. Of all the people popping up on the radar as suspects, she doubted the police had considered Victoria Bordeaux.

The crazy thing was, part of what Jimmy was saying wasn't entirely crazy. He was absolutely right. Whoever killed Rex had to know he was alive. Or found out and decided to remedy the problem.

While Nikki ate her salad with a sparing amount of Caesar dressing and Jimmy consumed a couple of hundred grams of fat, they chatted about several subjects:

the new baby orca born at Sea World, the pothole on Hollywood near Vine, and the president's plan to send illegal immigrants into space to cultivate rice fields.

By the time Nikki hugged Jimmy good-bye and asked for the check, she was feeling oddly humbled. He always did that to her. He made her feel so thankful for the life she had—her mother, Jeremy, Stanley and Oliver, her friends, a good job. And that gratitude made her all the more determined to make sure that nothing bad happened to Jessica over this whole Rex thing. Maybe the investigation wasn't her business, but she wasn't going to sit by and allow mistakes to be made that could ruin her friend's life.

Nikki waited for Jimmy to go before waving the waitress over. "Do I pay for this at the counter?" she asked. "Or do I give you my card?"

"Either way."

"Is it Mary or Maury?" Nikki indicated her name tag and then dug into her wallet.

"Actually, it's Marie. They left the 'e' off when they printed the name tag." She was cute, with a brunette bob and green eyes. "Whatever."

Nikki smiled. "Listen, Marie, I was looking for an old friend who works here. Tiffany?" she said hopefully.

The waitress screwed up her little bow mouth. "No Tiffany here."

"No?" Nikki couldn't help but feel disappointed. How had Carly gotten *all* the details of her gossip wrong? Wrong diner, no waitress named Tiffany. That made the whole "Thompson cheating on Edith" thing doubtful. "You're sure?"

"Pretty positive. I work all the shifts. My roommate, Deliah, moved out, leaving me with the whole rent until I can find someone else. She went home to Poughkeepsie. Her stepdad sent her the plane fare. She's going to community college now. Thinks she wants to be a kindergarten teacher."

Nikki nodded as if she were interested in the turn of events for Deliah. "So you don't know Tiffany? Maybe she used to work here?"

She thought for a second. "No, but Thompson Christopher used to work here," she said, her face lighting up.

"I heard that. In fact, I think they were friends, Thompson and Tiffany."

Marie shrugged. "Kelly might know. She's the cashier. Or Joe." She pointed with her Bic. "He's the cook. But he might not remember her. He's high a lot," she whispered, then sniffed with one nostril and then another.

"But *Kelly* might know if Tiffany used to work here?" Nikki slid out of the booth, grabbing a ten from her wallet along with her credit card. She handed the waitress the money. "Thanks, you've been helpful."

Marie looked at the money. "This is way too much," she said, looking thrilled.

"Keep it. You did a nice job waiting our table." Nikki headed for the cashier behind the counter.

"Well, thanks." Marie tucked the ten into the pocket of her apron. "I better get back to work."

At the counter, Nikki handed the girl behind the cash register the ticket Marie had written up, but not her credit card.

"How was everything?" She punched in the price of each item, not leaving Marie's addition skills up to chance.

"Everything was good. Marie was great. Listen . . . Kelly . . ."

The cashier looked up.

"I was wondering. Did a Tiffany work here?"

"Tiffany Mathews? Used to." She went back to her adding machine. "She just got a new job. That'll be thirty-one sixty-eight."

"But she *did* work here?" Nikki tried not to get too excited. "Recently?"

"Oh, yeah, for years. She started a new job a couple of months ago, though." Kelly peered over the cash register. She was wearing the same pink dress as Marie, only she'd added a big pink button with the cancer research slogan, SAVE THE TA-TAS. "Hey, do I know you?"

"I don't think so."

"Yes, I do." She thought for a moment and then pointed. "I knew it! Victoria Bordeaux's daughter. You're a lot prettier in person. Wait!" She jumped off her stool. "I've got the paper here." She slid a tabloid newspaper across the counter, flipping through the pages. "You're in the paper! Nikki Harper. You sell real estate, too. I've seen your picture in the ads. Me and my boyfriend, we like to see what's for sale in the Hills, you know, for when we make it big someday."

Nikki leaned over the counter and glanced at the grainy photograph Kelly was pointing to. Page three. It was a pretty innocuous photo of her getting out of her car on a palm tree–lined street. She couldn't tell where it had been taken or even if it had been taken recently. Sometimes the paparazzi dug deep to make a few bucks. Fortunately, she'd had makeup and Spanx on when the shot had been taken. She didn't look half bad, and there were no banditos in sight from what she could see.

"The article is stupid, I know." Kelly pointed out. "But it's a good picture."

The picture of Jessica was better. She was leaving her apartment building, looking hot even in shorts and a sports tank, carrying her gym bag. Nikki wondered how old *that* photo was.

The cashier bit down on her lower lip. "You think you could autograph it for me?"

Nikki sighed and offered a quick smile. "Sure." She started to dig for a pen. "So Tiffany . . . she worked here for a long time? When Thompson Christopher worked here?"

"Uh huh."

"So they were friends?" Nikki came up with a pen from her Prada pit and plucked a piece of tissue off the clip. "Good friends?"

"People ask me about him all the time. Everyone's disappointed to hear that he was a nice guy. Did his work, kept his hands to himself. That was back when he was in the middle of changing his name. He's really Albert Klineberger, you know. He was never checking out my ass like some of the other pigs that have worked in the kitchen. Even after he started getting parts and stopped working here, he was always nice to us. He used to stop by sometimes late at night just to have a Coke and a burger. You know, like normal people."

Nikki leaned over to sign her name on the corner of the photo.

"Hey, he's dating Edith March, isn't he? Rex March's widow." Kelly gave a little laugh. "Now, that's crazy. What's that thing, Seven Degrees of—"

"Six Degrees of Kevin Bacon," Nikki finished for her. "Thompson Christopher *is* dating Edith March," she said, thinking there was no harm in saying that. It was all over the papers in all the stories about Rex. "So were he and Tiffany . . . are they, you know, *an item?*"

Kelly looked at her quizzically, making Nikki feel older than her years. "Were they . . . are they *dating?*" Nikki asked.

Kelly laughed, picking up the newspaper to check out Nikki's signature. "Thompson Christopher and

Tiffany? No way. He's way too big a name to date a girl like Tiffany." She leaned forward. "She had a bad boob job. One's bigger than the other."

Why did complete strangers tell her these intimate details she didn't want to know? What was it about her that made people think they should tell her these things? Nikki tried to focus. She wasn't sure what Tiffany's lopsided breasts had to do with dating the actor, but she tried to go with the flow. "So they aren't dating. Never were?"

Kelly wrinkled her pretty forehead. "No way. But, oh, my God, that Seven Degrees thing." She flapped her hands excitedly.

Nikki waited with Victoria Bordeaux's attentive patience.

"Tiffany . . . she and the husband used to hook up all the time."

Nikki blinked. "The husband?"

"The fat dead guy. Edith March's ex-husband." She pointed at the paper. "The one your friend killed."

"Wait a minute," Nikki said, trying to process. Did this mean the gossip in the bathroom at the country club had gotten all of her information wrong, but there had been truth somewhere in the telling? It was like a bad game of telephone. And maybe a lucky break. "You're saying that this Tiffany was friends with Thompson—"

"Back when he was Albert," Kelly interrupted.

"Albert." Nikki stood corrected. "But it was Rex March who had an affair with Tiffany?"

"He used to come in here all the time wearing fake mustaches and stuff. A lot of celebrities do. Come in. Not wear fake mustaches. Tiffany thought it was funny. He bought her stuff, sometimes, clothes and shoes."

Nikki nodded, just letting Kelly ramble.

"She was really broke up when he died in the plane crash." Kelly grimaced. "She said they were in love. She used to go on all the time about how he was going to divorce his wife and they were going to get married and go to some tropical island. She bought a straw hat once—to start packing to go."

"Wait a minute, so this wasn't just a fling?"

Kelly shrugged. "Didn't sound like it to me. Tiffany cried and cried the night it was on the news—about how he'd died in that plane crash, burnt so bad to a crisp that there wasn't even a body." She made a face. "You wonder how someone could make a mistake like that. Think it was one person and really it was another. I don't know who died in that plane, but obviously it wasn't Rex."

Nikki handed her her credit card. Nikki didn't know how Tiffany and Thompson played into Rex's death, but she knew there had to be some significance to this latest twist. "Do you think you could tell me where I could find Tiffany Mathews?"

"Sure." She smiled slyly as she slid Nikki's card through the TeleCheck. "You think I could have another autograph?"

Chapter 15

"Jess, you're not going to believe this," Nikki said, using the Prius speakerphone as she eased onto Santa Monica. Luckily, Tiffany's new place of employment was only a few blocks from the diner. She'd moved up in the world and was now a waitress at Barney's Beanery. "Rex was having an affair with a waitress from the diner where Thompson used to work. Right before he died, *the first time*. How crazy a coincidence is that?"

When Nikki didn't hear anything, she tapped the volume on her touch screen. "Jess?"

"Yeah, I'm here," she said.

Nikki closed her eyes for a second. She was an idiot. Jessica had admitted she was seeing Rex at the time of his death. "You didn't know he was dating other people," she said with a groan. "Sorry, I didn't mean to be so insensitive."

"I knew. Or at least I guessed," Jess said in a small voice.

Nikki braked as the light ahead turned yellow. "I'm

going to talk to her now, if I can find her." She heard a male voice in the background. "Where are you?"

"Um . . . at my place. The police said I could go in. It's a total wreck."

Nikki furrowed her brow, Botox-bound for sure. "Who's with you?"

"My neighbor. Pete. He just came by to see if I needed anything."

"Oh. Okay. Well, I'll let you go. Do we have an appointment with Mrs. Hearst tomorrow?"

"One o'clock."

"Great. I'm going to stop by Mother's later, then head home. I'll get some stuff ready for our appointment with Mrs. Hearst tomorrow. You take the evening off, get settled back in, and I'll be totally set for tomorrow."

Spotting the iconic Barney's Beanery, she signaled. "You need me for anything, anything at all, you call me. Okay?"

"Sure. Thanks. And . . . if you find out anything from this waitress . . . let me know." Jessica hesitated. "He wasn't very nice to me at the station, Nik. Detective Lutz. I swear to God, he still thinks I did it. Like I could have carried Rex anywhere. Really."

"He doesn't think you did it. He knows the evidence is to the contrary."

"Yeah, but if he doesn't come up with any other suspects, is he going to charge me, just to cover his ass?"

"Don't worry," Nikki assured her, turning into the parking lot of the sports bar. "I'm going to figure out who did this." She hesitated. "I was serious when I said I would get a lawyer for you. And pay for it."

"How many times do I have to say 'I don't want a lawyer,' Nikki? It makes me look like I have something to hide."

"I don't think—"

"Let's just wait and see if I'm charged. Okay?"

"Okay. Sure," Nikki said. She hesitated as she pulled into a parking space. "You didn't know he was alive, right? Rex."

"Let me say it again. I didn't know he was alive, Nik. How could I have known?" Suddenly, Jessica sounded teary. "I can't believe you're asking me this after—"

"It's okay. I'm sorry." She hit the ignition button, cutting the engine off, feeling like a complete jerk. "I'm just clarifying details. You going to be okay? You want me to come over when I'm done here? Bring you a burger?"

"No, it's okay. I'm fine. I'm going to clean up. You wouldn't believe the mess the cops made with their fingerprint dust. Then I'm going to take a hot bath and watch something completely mindless on Bravo."

"Sounds good," Nikki said. "Talk to you later."

Entering the famous watering hole a minute later, Nikki was surprised by how busy it was at four in the afternoon. She'd been in many times over the years and knew the West Hollywood location had been built in the twenties as a destination for travelers westbound on Route 66. As she walked in, her senses were assaulted by the music, multicolored booths and abundant memorabilia on the wall.

"Just one?" the hostess asked. She had a tattoo of spots on both her temples, resembling a creature from the Star Trek Federation. The crazy thing was, she somehow pulled it off. Maybe it was the severe asymmetrical haircut. Or her winning smile.

"Actually, I was wondering if you could tell me if Tiffany Mathews works here?" Nikki said hopefully. She couldn't stomach the thought of eating another meal right now, or possibly bumping into another half-sibling.

"Cute? Blond? Accent?" the hostess asked.

"Yup, that's her," Nikki agreed.

The hostess made a face. "You might have missed her. She got off at four."

"Would you mind checking?" Nikki flashed *the smile*. "It's important."

The young woman shrugged. "Sure. Lemme check."

While Nikki waited, she picked up a newspaperlike menu. It was pure American: chili, burgers, fries and nearly a hundred choices of beer. She and Jeremy rarely went out, but as she took in the ambience, it occurred to her that this would be a fun place to come, with or without the children.

The hostess returned. "You just missed her. Some-one in the back said she just clocked out." She gathered menus for the group who had just come in behind Nikki. "You might be able to catch her in the parking lot," she suggested.

Nikki didn't want to confess she didn't actually know what Tiffany looked like. Instead, she thanked the host-ess and excuse-me'd her way out the door. So how was she going to recognize Tiffany? All she knew was that she was fairly young, blond . . . and was the unfortunate recipient of a botched boob job.

Thankfully, Nikki didn't have to check out anyone's chest too closely. As she walked around the rear of the restaurant, a young woman with long white-blond hair was just exiting a rear door.

"Tiffany?"

The girl looked up. When she spotted Nikki, and likely realized she didn't know her, her face grew guarded. "*Yays?*"

Nikki approached her slowly, thrilled to have tracked

her down, but realizing that in L.A. you had to be careful not to look like a stalker. "Hi, Tiffany. I'm Nikki Harper. We have a mutual friend. Albert . . . Thompson Christopher," she said, deciding to start with the live one first.

"Albert! How is *hey*?"

She had a pretty smile and a serious southern accent. And if her breasts weren't perfect, Nikki couldn't tell through the Barney's t-shirt.

"I *mayne* Thompson." She arched her eyebrows with amusement as if to say *I knew him when*.

"He's good. Well . . . considering the week he's had."

"The week *hey's* had?" she asked, slipping a tube of lip balm from her jeans pocket.

"With Rex March being found. Dead. Thompson and Mrs. March are . . . a couple," Nikki explained delicately.

The young woman's pretty face changed at once. "*Reyx*," she said, as if suddenly deflating.

"I . . . understand you knew Rex?"

"Who *sayd* that?" she asked, her guard up again. She slipped the lip balm back into her pocket without putting it on her lips. "Who *dayd* ya say ya were?"

Nikki took a step back. She didn't want to scare the girl. And God knows there were plenty of scary people in this town. "My name is Nikki Harper and my friend, Jessica, is one of the suspects in Rex's death."

"Oh my." The young woman pressed her hand to her mouth. "*Ah rayd* about her in the *pay-per*. They found *Reyx dayd* in her apartment."

"They did," Nikki conceded. "But she didn't kill him, Tiffany. I'm trying to find out who did."

Tiffany looked at her as if trying to decide if she was going to talk to Nikki or run. "*Yah're* talking to people about *Reyx*? Like a *day-tective* or somethin'?"

The accent was somehow endearing. And a little unsettling for Nikki. The girl seemed too young to have been working at the diner for years, as Kelly had said. She looked too young to be living on her own anywhere but a college dorm.

"I'm not a detective," Nikki answered. "I'm a real estate agent. But I'm trying to help my friend."

Tiffany put her chapped lips together. "Were y'all *frens* with *Reyx*, too?"

"I knew Rex. And I worked for him. Selling his house."

Tiffany swung the canvas bag on her shoulder forward, resting her hand on it. "*Ah* was real sorry to hear that *Reyx* was *dayd*. Both times." She started to walk away. "*Ah* need to go. *Ah* . . . *Ah* have somewhere *Ah* have to be."

Nikki followed her at a non-stalker distance. "I have a few questions, Tiffany. Please. Can I talk to you? I won't get you in any trouble. I swear I won't."

She stopped. "Why would *Ah* be in trouble?"

Nikki took the opportunity offered. "Tiffany, I know you dated. You and Rex."

She glanced around the parking lot. "Ya sure *yah're* not a cop? I didn't do nuthin' wrong. *Ah* didn't even know he was married. *Besaydes*, he's *dayd*. *Ah* can't get in no trouble if he's *dayd*, can *Ah*?"

A car came toward them in the parking lot and both had to move to keep from being run over. Nikki tried to take advantage of the moment of camaraderie. "I just need to ask you about your relationship with Rex . . . and Thompson. Did . . . did you date Thompson?"

She laughed, seeming almost flattered. "Oh, no. Albert and me, we never *dayted*. *Ah* knew he was goin' ta be a *stah.*" She smiled. "*Ah* use' to *allahs* tell him *hey* was gonna make it big. He was so handsome. And *hey* was *nahce.* Ya know. *Nahce* like not many *main* are."

"I know exactly what you mean." Nikki looked into Tiffany's eyes, hoping she'd be able to tell if she was lying. "So you and Albert . . . never dated? You *aren't* dating?"

"Nooo. Never *deid.*"

"But you and Rex did?"

Tiffany looked away, her eyes suddenly tearing over. "Who tol' you?"

"I went to Kitty's," Nikki confessed.

"*Ah* never took no money from him," she said stubbornly. "Not really. Not much." She chewed on her bottom lip. She looked like she was about to burst into tears.

"I'm sorry, Tiffany." Nikki moved closer to her. "I don't mean to upset you. I really don't, but this is important. It could mean the difference between finding out who killed Rex or my friend going to jail for something she didn't do."

Tiffany sniffed. "*Ah* don' know who *kielled Reyx* if tha's *whatcher* askin' me."

"I understand. I just need to be clear as to your relationship with him. Were you having an affair with him?"

"*Ah* wouldn't say that." She looked down at her feet. She was wearing sneakers. She sighed and looked around the parking lot again. "*Ah* did take money from *hiem*, okay? *Fur . . . fur* companionship."

"You mean for . . . sex?" Nikki said as nonjudgmentally as she could. And, honestly, she didn't feel judgmental. The poor girl looked barely old enough to have graduated college. An opportunity Nikki doubted had been available to her. "Okay," Nikki said slowly, thinking about what Kelly had said about them running away together. "So . . . you . . . you had a business arrangement, but you weren't, like, in love with him?"

Tiffany shook her head, her gaze on the pavement again. "*Hey* was nice to me's all. He *payd* for my actin' classes. He was gonna pay for a new augmentation." She looked down at her breasts and tears began to slip down her cheeks. "And then *hey* was *dayd*. The plane crash." She wiped at her eyes with the back of her hand. "It was awful. *Reyx wadn't* the kind of person to *dah* like that, ya know?" she said in her sweet southern drawl. "*Ah* remember *thanking* there was somethin' not *raht* there. *Ah* thought it was his lawyer."

"You thought it was his lawyer?"

Tiffany started to walk again. Fast. Luckily, Nikki was wearing her sensible shoes.

"What do you mean, you thought it was his lawyer, Tiffany?"

She stopped beside a beat-up blue sedan. An old BMW. "*Ah* thought Alex sab-o-taged the *playne*, or somethin'. You know, people can do that. Do somethin' *tuh* the engine so's it bursts *intuh* flames. I thought Alex killed him. Okay?"

"By Alex, you mean Alex Ramirez?"

Tiffany nodded, looking away. She was leaning against the driver's side door. Nikki sensed she might bolt at any moment.

"How did you know Alex Ramirez, Tiffany?"

She shrugged one slender shoulder. "Met him a couple 'a times with *Reyx*. *Ah* didn' *lahk* him much. Ya know?" She dared a peek at Nikki. "The way *hey* looked at me . . . *lahk* he coulda jus' eat me *raht* up."

"So what made you think Alex had something to do with Rex's death . . . when he supposedly went down in the plane crash?"

Again, the pretty shrug. But then she met Nikki's

gaze and there was an honesty in her eyes that held Nikki's attention.

"Somethin' 'bout him a body jest couldn' trust," she explained. "Somethin' in his beady eyes."

The words that came out of Tiffany's mouth sounded like a line from a bad western, but Nikki knew exactly what the girl meant. She knew Alex Ramirez and she had never cared for him. She'd always thought he and Rex were perfect for each other.

"*Ah* gotta go," Tiffany said, slipping her key into the door.

"Sure." Nikki backed up a step so Tiffany could swing open the door. "Just one more question, Tiffany, and then I'll let you go." Nikki made eye contact with her, her hand on the car door. "Did you know that Rex didn't die in that plane crash? Did you know, at any point after the crash, that he wasn't dead?"

She didn't try to look away this time. "*Ah swayre* to God, *Ah deidn't* know."

Chapter 16

When Nikki walked into Victoria's bedroom suite, her mother was seated on the couch, looking stylish as always, today in a black jogging suit, with her pearls. She wore no makeup (apparently, no public appearances today) but she had such a flawless complexion that, even at her age, she was beautiful without a hint of foundation or a stroke of mascara.

She was on the phone, so Nikki sat down on the other end of the couch and shuffled through the stack of magazines on an end table. Her mother always had an eclectic choice of reading materials: *Variety*, *Ladies' Home Journal*, *The New Yorker*, *People*, *The Economist*, *Soap Opera Digest*, and the *Boston Review*. She flipped through the latest *New Yorker*, half-listening to her mother on the phone.

"No, no, I can't say that I make potato salad often. You should e-mail me the recipe, though, so I can give it to my housekeeper." Victoria paused, then chuckled. "I agree, even girls our age need to watch our figures, but

it doesn't hurt to treat ourselves occasionally, does it?"
Another chuckle.

Nikki felt herself frowning. Who the heck was her
mother talking to? Never in her entire life had she
heard Victoria exchange recipes with someone.

"Well, do send me that recipe. And I'll have Ina jot
down that shrimp salad recipe." Pause. "No, she speaks
English. When she wants to," Victoria added with a bit
of *tone.*

Nikki met her mother's gaze and mouthed, *Who are
you talking to?*

Ellie, Victoria mouthed back. Then, "It is quite a
privilege, and I thank God every day for my good fortune."

Ellie? Who's Ellie? Nikki mouthed.

Victoria motioned as if placing a crown on her head.

The queen? Victoria was speaking to Queen Eliza-
beth? Nothing would surprise her . . .

Frowning, Nikki got up and went to a small refrigerator, choosing a bottle of sparkling water. Her mother
was still going on about Ina and the shrimp salad.

Nikki unscrewed the cap and took a drink. The bub-
bles tickled her nose. She was thinking about the
houses her company currently had for sale in the price
range and area Mrs. Hearst was interested in. There
were plenty of houses on the market, but they always
tried to show Windsor properties first, for obvious reasons.

Victoria was laughing again, and Nikki was intrigued.
Who could her mother be talking to? Nikki didn't know
anyone named Ellie. Though Victoria had a large circle
of *acquaintances,* she had a small group of *friends,* and her
mother had never been one for chatting on the phone.

"Yes, yes, but we'll talk again," Victoria said. "Send
me that recipe and you have a wonderful birthday.

Enjoy that cake and have a slice for me." She was still chuckling as she hit the off button on the cordless phone and dropped it on the couch beside her.

"Who was that?" Nikki asked.

"You never were good at lipreading, Nicolette. I told you. It was Ellie."

"Ellie who? Queen Ellie?"

"Queen Ellie of what country? Who said she was a queen?" Victoria tucked her feet up beneath her. She was wearing the sheepskin boots Nikki had given her two Christmases before. They looked cute on her, and very hip with the jogging suit.

"I don't know what country, Mother. *You* were the one saying she was a queen." Nikki imitated her mother's hand gestures, pulling an imaginary crown over her own head.

Victoria scowled. "She was the birthday girl, not the queen! That was my birthday girl mime. Remind me not to play charades with you."

"What birthday girl?" Then Nikki realized who she was talking about. Julius the bellhop's grandmother in Idaho. *Her* name was Eleanor. "Oh my gosh! You called her? You actually called Eleanor in Idaho to wish her a happy birthday?"

Victoria reached for a pack of cigarettes on the coffee table, but seeing Nikki's frown, left them where they were. "Of course I called her. I told you I would, didn't I? You called and asked me and I said I would, so I did. Her birthday isn't until Sunday. I may call her again on Sunday," she thought aloud. "Make her day."

"I can't believe you called her." Nikki was smiling as she sat on the edge of the couch beside her mother and gave her a big hug. "That was so nice of you."

"My fans are important to me. Are you saying I'm not nice?"

"Not at all. I'm saying you are." Nikki took a sip of water. "I wouldn't have blamed you a bit if you didn't want to call. It's got to be awkward."

"It wasn't awkward. Ellie was very pleasant. Spunky for eighty years old. She still drives; she has an F150, whatever that is. I told you I would help you with your investigation. I was helping."

Nikki's recollection was that her mother had been *against* any involvement in Jessica's case, but she knew better than to bring up that little tidbit. "I appreciate your help," she said, meaning it. "I'll give her grandson a call in a day or two, if I haven't heard from him. See if he found out what name Rex was using at the Sunset."

"What are you going to do with the information?"

"I don't know." She took another sip of water. "But I'm learning that it's smart to just keep asking questions. And listen. I just have to keep in mind that everything I hear isn't necessarily the truth. Guess what I found out today?"

Her mother eyed the cigarettes. "I can't imagine."

"Rex was cheating on Edith with a girl who worked at a diner on Santa Monica."

"I imagine he was cheating on Edith with many waitresses from many diners."

The way Victoria said it, the way she fluttered her lashes, made Nikki want to laugh.

"Did *she* kill him?" Victoria asked.

"Who? Edith? I don't think so."

Victoria motioned impatiently. "The waitress. Try to keep up, Nicolette."

"I don't see how she could have. She was a little bitty thing. Seemed like a nice girl. Too nice to be wrapped up with Rex March."

"Anything short of a snake would be too good to get wrapped up with Rex," Victoria said with a sniff. "I don't think you can discount her, though. Edith or the waitress."

"Mother, how can you say such a thing about Edith? You like her."

"The fact that I like her has absolutely nothing to do with whether or not Edith could have killed her husband. In fact, the fact that I *am* fond of her makes it *more* likely she put an end to her own misery. I like a woman who can take charge of her own life."

"The police are saying the body was moved." She put her knee on the couch so she was facing her mother. "After Rex was dead, someone picked him up, transported him somehow, and put him in Jessica's bed. Edith could never have carried Rex."

"Where there's a will, there's a way. If you're going to seriously look into this matter, you have to keep an open mind. Do you remember *Curiously Dead*?" she said, naming a who-done-it she'd done in the seventies. "No one suspected the mild-mannered neighbor. She was a small woman and Alex was a tall man. Not as heavy as Rex, though, and his breath wasn't as bad."

"Wasn't that Gregory Peck who played Alex?"

Victoria smiled. "He was *such* a gentleman. Handsome. God rest his soul." She reached out to pat Nikki's hand. "Now tell me what else you've found out."

"Well, I was actually following a lead I was given in the bathroom at the Beverly Hills Country Club. Don't ask. But I found out the lead was just gossip. Sort of. I'd been told Thompson Christopher was having an affair with the waitress, which I was half hoping was true because he missed several appointments the day Rex was found in Jessica's bed. And he is big enough to have moved Rex."

"Well, what did Thompson say? Where was he Monday?"

"I didn't ask yet. He wasn't all that receptive when I tried to talk with him the other day." She took another sip of the water. "When I was talking to Tiffany the waitress, who did *not* have an affair with Thompson, but *did* with Rex," Nikki clarified, "she said something very interesting. She said that when Rex's plane crashed—"

"Which he wasn't on," Victoria interrupted.

"Right." Nikki nodded. "Anyway, she said that at the time, she suspected Alex Ramirez had sabotaged the plane, causing the crash and his death."

"Which wasn't true either."

"No," Nikki conceded. "But the point is that she seemed to think Ramirez had something to do with Rex's death. Don't you think it's odd that this waitress would even know Ramirez's name?" She shrugged. "I'm not saying Ramirez did anything so convoluted as causing a plane crash, but what if, like the rumor I heard in the bathroom, there's some truth buried in there somewhere? Ramirez was Rex's lawyer *and* his agent. What if—"

"Nicolette, I have to put my foot down here. I don't want you anywhere near Alex Ramirez. He has *connections.*"

"Connections?" Nikki waited for her mother to elaborate but all Victoria did was nod solemnly. "What kind of connections, Mother?"

"Mafia. Las Vegas."

Nikki stared at her. "Is there even such a thing as *Las Vegas Mafia*?" She paused. "By the way, speaking of Vegas, I saw my brother today. He was wearing the suit from *King Creole.* The gold one."

Victoria rose and went to her dressing table, picking up a little glass jar of moisturizer.

"He seemed good," Nikki added.

"On his meds?" Victoria asked, her tone painfully neutral.

"I think so. Maybe." Nikki exhaled, leaning back on the couch and stretching out. "Who knows? But he looked healthy. At least he's eating."

"Did he say anything about coming home?"

"He didn't." She decided not to bring up Jimmy's suggestion that perhaps Victoria had been the one who killed Rex. "He came into the diner while I was looking for Tiffany. Who, actually, no longer works in the diner. She's at Barney's Beanery on Santa Monica now. I tracked her down there."

Victoria rubbed moisturizer into her cheeks in a circular motion. "I'm sure her mother's proud. So what are we going to do about speaking with Ramirez?"

Apparently there would be no more discussion of Jimmy. At least not today.

"We?" Nikki glanced at her mother. "I don't know what I would even say to him. I don't have any information that would suggest he had anything to do with Rex's disappearance or death, except that Tiffany said she didn't trust him or his *beady eyes.*"

"Those, he has." Victoria screwed the lid on the moisturizer and placed it on her dressing table. She then walked back to the couch where she picked up the phone and dialed 411. She cleared her throat as she waited for the automated message. "Offices of Alex Ramirez, West Hollywood, California, spelled R-A-M-I-R-E-Z, please."

Nikki sat up on the couch. "Mother, what are you doing?"

"What's it sound like I'm doing? I'm making an appointment with Alex Ramirez. We're going to see if he had anything to do with this mess with Rex March."

"Under what pretense are we making this appointment?" Nikki asked in disbelief.

"Thank you," Victoria said into the phone, then to Nikki, "I'm considering looking for a new agent." She was doing the arched eyebrow thing.

"You're retired."

"Maybe I'm coming out of retirement." She smiled and turned her back to Nikki as she ramped up the charm. "Good afternoon, this is Victoria Bordeaux and I'd like to make an appointment as soon as possible with Mr. Ramirez. Yes, I'll hold. Thank you."

"Mother," Nikki said in a stage whisper. "You shouldn't be doing this. You just told me he might be dangerous."

Victoria glanced at Nikki as she put her hand on the phone. "Not to a woman like me. Now Victoria Bordeaux, *she's* dangerous."

The following afternoon, Nikki drove her mother to Ramirez's office on Sunset Plaza Drive. She parked in the large parking lot behind the building and they walked together across the parking lot.

"Now, let me do the talking," Victoria instructed. She wore a blue-and-green watercolor-print Roberto Cavalli dress and cute Italian flats. The subtle Vuitton bag on her elbow made the outfit and just for a second, Nikki was envious of her mother's fashion sense. "You're here to listen. I'm here to draw him out."

Nikki tried not to grin as she opened the door to the lobby for her mother. The building was small, with only a few offices. Ramirez's was on the second floor. "I'm starting to feel a little silly. We're here on the say-so of a waitress who doesn't like the man's beady eyes."

Victoria took the steps with the same sense of presence with which she tackled a movie première. (She never took the elevator when she had a choice.) "I don't like his beady eyes, either."

Nikki hurried to catch up with her mother. She'd made no attempt to compete with Victoria's sense of style and was wearing a three-quarter-sleeve vintage dress, tights, and knee-high black boots. With a sensible heel, of course.

On the second floor, they halted in front of a glass door with Ramirez's name written on it in gold lettering. "Are you ready?" Victoria asked.

Nikki wasn't nervous anymore. Mostly she was curious, curious as to how her mother would play this appointment and even more curious as to what Ramirez would have to say. "Ready."

Victoria then surprised her by reaching out and touching Nikki's face in a rare show of affection. "You look pretty today. I like your hair longer, like this." She gave a nod. "It suits you, Nicolette." She was still looking up at her. "I was always a little jealous, you know. Of your red hair."

Nikki was still smiling when Ramirez's secretary escorted her and her mother into his inner office. It was nicer than the outside of the building suggested: paneled walls, cherry bookcases and conference table, a leather couch and chairs, and a massive antique desk.

There was the usual hand-shaking and offers of refreshment, but Victoria took command of the situation at once, not giving anyone the opportunity to exchange too many pleasantries.

"I missed you at the party at Edith March's," Victoria said, sitting in the massive leather armchair that Nikki was pretty certain was the chair Ramirez normally sat in. That left Nikki with one end of the oxblood leather couch and him with the other.

He was an attractive enough man, despite the beady eyes: fifty years old maybe, Hispanic, fit, with a well-defined jaw. His short-cropped hair was nicely styled, as was his goatee. A diamond band glittered on his left ring finger. Married.

"Um, yes, I was sorry I couldn't make it. Scheduling conflict." He unbuttoned his suit jacket before he sat.

Nikki didn't know a lot about men's fashion, but she could tell by the fabric that he'd laid out several thousand dollars for the boring blue suit.

"My niece's engagement party," he went on when Victoria made no comment. "I'd hoped to make Edith's party afterward, but . . ." He opened his arms and chuckled.

Victoria smiled. "But?" she asked sweetly.

"But . . . I wasn't able to make it in time."

Victoria nodded. "Where did your niece have her engagement party?"

"Um . . . at Osteria Mozza. On Melrose."

"I know it well. What a lovely choice. It's one of my favorite places to dine. Not that I go out all that often anymore, but when we do go there to eat, I like the veal breast stracotto."

He spun his diamond ring, looking a little uncomfortable. Victoria had a way of doing that to people. "So . . . I understand you're considering a new agent?"

"This meeting is just to see how we get along," Victoria explained. "We've met, but never really talked. You don't mind just talking today"—the eyebrows—"do you, Mr. Ramirez?"

"Please, call me Alex."

"I certainly will, Alex."

Taking note that Victoria did not offer to have Ramirez call her by her first name, Nikki had to stifle a chuckle. She looked away, her gaze drifting over to his desk. There was a family photo of Ramirez with a boy and a girl and a woman, who was obviously his wife. She noted with interest that the woman looked to be only in her thirties, and was in a wheelchair.

"I have to tell you how sad I was to learn of Rex March's death," Victoria was saying. "How tragic to lose the same client twice."

"Yes, tragic. I was very fond of Rex."

"Well, that club was small."

Nikki glanced at her mother reprovingly, fighting the urge to shake her head. "I . . . I'm sure you were as shocked as we were, to hear that he had been murdered," Nikki said awkwardly, thinking she needed to take control of this interview before it went too far awry. "Who could have imagined Rex would fake his death, putting Edith through that pain?"

Ramirez was spinning the diamond ring a little faster, his beady eyes darting now.

"Well, obviously he didn't know he was going to be murdered, did he?" Victoria pointed out.

"I can't imagine the legal ramifications. I suppose it will take you months to sort out the details." Nikki tried to meet his gaze, but he wouldn't look her way.

"I can't really discuss Rex March, ladies. There's an ongoing investigation into his death right now. Which I'm sure you're aware of." He finally glanced at Nikki with something akin to intimidation.

Nikki offered a quick smile, boring her Bordeaux blues into him. "You . . . you didn't know he was still alive, did you, Mr. Ramirez?"

Ramirez surprised Nikki by coming to his feet. "You've obviously not come to discuss my firm representing you, Ms. Bordeaux, so I'm afraid I'm going to have to ask both of you to go." He started to move toward the door. "As Mr. March's lawyer, it would be inappropriate for me to discuss any matter pertaining to him, and therefore, I think it best we end this appointment before anything inappropriate is said. Especially considering the fact that Ms. Harper's good friend is the chief suspect in my client's murder."

Victoria looked at Nikki as if to say, *The audacity!*

Nikki rose from the couch, grabbing her handbag. She didn't know what was going on here, but something told her that Ramirez was worried about more than the integrity of his client–attorney relationship. He knew something about Rex's faked death, even if he knew nothing about the subsequent murder. She could see it in his beady eyes and his ring-twisting. "Mother?"

Victoria took her time rising from Ramirez's chair and walking past him through the open door. He said nothing more, and neither did they. It wasn't until they were in the parking lot that Victoria spun to face Nikki, excitement on her face.

"I don't think I've had that much fun in years. Imagine, me, at my age, getting kicked out of someone's office!" She laughed, starting for the car again, her flats tapping on the blacktop. "I hadn't imagined P.I. work could be so much fun. He knows something, of course, you know that, don't you?" She waited at the passenger door of the Prius. "Someone obviously needs to speak to Edith." She looked up at Nikki, her amazing blue eyes dancing. "Do you want to do it or should I?"

Chapter 17

"I just need your signature on this inspection report," Nikki said, taking a seat in front of Edith's desk in her gaudy nineteenth-century French-inspired office. "And then I'll be out of here." *As soon as you answer a few questions about Ramirez,* she thought.

It hadn't been easy for Nikki to convince her mother that *she* should be the one to talk to Edith. After the visit to Ramirez's office, Victoria was pretty gung-ho about investigating Rex's murder. Not so much because she cared who killed him, or if Jessica was being framed, but because she'd enjoyed herself immensely. Nikki and Victoria had gotten into something close to an argument last night at movie night (*The Maltese Falcon*, one of Nikki's all-time favorites) over who would go see Edith. In the end, Nikki had won only because she honestly needed Edith's signature (though it could have waited a day or two) and Victoria had a charity luncheon to attend that she couldn't get out of.

"I'm glad you came," Edith said from across the ornate desk. "You'll have to excuse the mess. My assistant,

Anita, is out of town for a few weeks. Her daughter's having a baby." The desk, piled with paperwork, was a monstrous reproduction in the gilded asymmetrical Rococo design popular during Louis XV's reign.

Edith looked more relaxed today than when Nikki saw her at the country club. She'd had her hair done a little differently this week; it was attractive. Edith reminded Nikki of the TV chef Paula Deen.

Dressed in slacks and a pretty floral blouse appropriate for her age and size, she appeared rested today. Calm . . . almost content. Why? Her life was in complete upheaval again, thanks to Rex. Had she relaxed because the police investigation of Rex's murder was basically stalled, meaning Edith wasn't a suspect? Nikki hated to consider the possibility, but she was trying to keep an open mind.

"I was going to call you." Edith folded her plump hands, looking down at them, then back up at Nikki. "To apologize for my behavior when you came by last week. And at the country club, too."

"It's fine, Edith." Nikki heard her cell vibrate in her handbag, but ignored it. "I understand—"

"No, no, it *wasn't* fine," she interrupted. "I was rude. Yes, I was in shock. Here I thought I had survived Rex's death in that plane crash, I was getting on with my life, actually finding happiness, and then I find out he faked it all? And *then* he gets himself murdered?" she said with a hint of bitterness in her voice. "But that's no excuse for rudeness. You've been nothing but kind to me, both you and your mother. That night at the party, when Victoria Bordeaux came as my guest, it was one of my shining moments." She leaned over the desk, meeting Nikki's gaze with a genuine sincerity. "You know, one of those moments you'll remember forever."

Nikki smiled, knowing exactly what she meant.

"And then I repaid you with rudeness. You came here last week out of kindness, to offer your condolences, which was particularly kind since I know very well that you know what a prick my husband was."

Nikki pressed her lips together, making an event of settling a manila folder on her lap. This was precisely why she liked Edith, because she called a spade a spade. And this was why she desperately wanted to believe that Edith had nothing to do with Rex's death.

"I know you had nothing to do with Jessica's affair with my husband," Edith said softly.

"I didn't," she admitted, her heart aching for Edith. Her phone began to vibrate again. "I would never have allowed it." She made herself look at Edith. "It was a complete breach of ethics."

The older woman gave a wave. "All in the past. And now, of no consequence." She paused. "Thompson asked that I extend an apology for him as well. For his behavior last week. He's at his voice lesson. That day, he was only following my lead. I was upset, so he was upset. I wouldn't want you to think poorly of him. He's a good man. A good man," she repeated firmly, leaning back in her white leather office chair. "And I love him."

"I understand completely." Nikki opened the folder she'd pulled from her briefcase, thinking back to her chat with J.J. Flaherty's secretary. For some bizarre reason, Elvis's "Suspicious Minds" played in her head. Was Jimmy's craziness rubbing off on her?

"I . . . I didn't realize Thompson took voice lessons," she lied. "Does he go every Thursday?" Her mother got away all the time with asking questions that weren't her business. Maybe she could, too.

"Tuesdays and Thursdays. He's very devoted to his craft."

Nikki nodded. J.J. Flaherty's secretary had been very

specific. Thompson's voice *lesson,* as in singular, was on Tuesdays. *Interesting.* She glanced up at Edith, exhaled, and decided to just plow forward, hoping the older woman's apology was heartfelt enough that she'd be willing to answer Nikki's questions.

"Edith . . ." she began. "Mother and I ran into Alex Ramirez the other day, and I have to tell you, his behavior was odd."

"Odd, how? Can I get you something to drink?" She reached for a bottle of diet soda on a coaster on her desk.

Nikki shook her head. Her phone was vibrating, yet again. Who the heck was calling her over and over? She had an idea who. "I brought up Rex's name," she continued, "offering my condolences, and he became very abrupt and, well, evasive." She looked at her across the desk. "So much so that his behavior seemed . . . suspicious. He got very nervous when I asked him if he'd known Rex was still alive after the plane crash."

"I doubt Rex was ever even in that plane," Edith snorted. "You know that a body was never recovered. The FAA investigators said at the time that either his burned remains were dragged off by coyotes, or he survived the crash, wandered off and died." She made a sound of derision. "He was always a liar and a cheat. With me, with his business partners, with his fans. I don't know why anyone who knew him would be surprised by the thought that he staged his death."

"Edith . . . I hope this isn't too forward." She scooted toward the edge of the white leather armless chair. "But do you think Ramirez could have had anything to do with all this? Maybe even with Rex's murder?"

Edith rose from her desk and turned her back to Nikki to look out the window onto the gardens. There was a young man vacuuming the pool. "You're asking because?"

"I'm not trying to invade your privacy, but I'm very concerned about Jessica. With no leads, the police may arrest her. I know it was wrong for her to have an affair with your husband, but that makes her immoral, not a murderer."

"No, I don't suppose she would have killed him, would she? Obviously, she had feelings for him." Edith sighed. "So, to answer your question about my husband's agent, the more I think about it, the more I believe he might be the one who killed Rex."

Nikki's eyes widened, but she kept her voice calm. "What would make you say that, Edith? Mr. Ramirez represented Rex for years."

"Exactly. Giving Rex time to cheat him out of every penny he could . . . or maybe vice versa. I can't tell you how many times Rex fired Alex, only to rehire him a few weeks or months later. The two of them had a volatile relationship."

"Have you spoken to the police about this?"

"No, and I'd ask that you not say anything to them, either." She shook her head, her back still to Nikki. "I'm keeping my mouth shut about Ramirez. Until we meet in court, at least."

Nikki set the file on Edith's desk. "In court?"

"I don't think I'll have a pool again. Too much work. I want to simplify my life. Do you think that's odd? After all this?" She opened her arms, turning to face Nikki.

Nikki waited.

"Did you know that Alex Ramirez was involved in a car accident a few years ago that left his wife paralyzed from the waist down?"

Nikki recalled the family photo on his desk. "I knew

she was in a wheelchair," she said carefully. "But I didn't know why."

"He was driving while intoxicated on Laurel Canyon Road. He lost control of his vehicle and went off an embankment. He was uninjured, but her spine was damaged. In the end, he walked away without even a traffic citation and she's never walked again. That's the kind of man Alex Ramirez is."

Nikki didn't know what to say, so she said nothing.

"I'm suing the bastard. Or at least I was, before Rex turned up dead again. Now I don't know where we are with the lawsuit. My lawyers have been calling, but I just haven't had the energy to meet with them yet. I imagine it will take years to sort this mess out now."

"You're suing him? For what?" Nikki asked.

"Well, when I initiated the lawsuit, I thought he was stealing from me. A few weeks ago, I was talking with a studio executive who had worked on *Shipwrecked Vacation* with Rex. Long story short, I discovered that the show has been throwing off more residuals than I was aware of . . . or being paid for. It's doing a lot better overseas than I knew."

"You think Ramirez was stealing from you?"

"I'm sure he was. The question now is whether he was stealing from me for himself, or for Rex. Obviously Rex had been living somewhere between the time his plane crashed in the Mojave, and when he turned up dead in your partner's apartment."

"So if Ramirez was funneling money to Rex, that would mean . . . he *knew* Rex was alive," Nikki said, thinking out loud.

"Or maybe he didn't know, maybe he wasn't sending money to Rex, and he was just stealing from me. It's hard to say at this point, isn't it?" Edith pressed her hand to her forehead. "Anyway," she continued, "that's why I was eager to see Ramirez at my party that night. I wanted to tell him myself that he was about to be served."

Nikki's head was spinning now. "Well, do *you* think Ramirez knew Rex was alive?"

"I have no idea, and honestly, I don't care. I just want *my* money. I want my money, I want Thompson, and I want to be happy." She sat down in her leather chair again. "Is that so wrong?"

"No, it's not." Nikki opened the manila folder she'd brought along with her. As she searched for the inspection report, her gaze drifted to a WHILE YOU WERE OUT pink slip of paper on Edith's desk. It was the date that caught her eye: Monday, October 4th, the day Rex's body was found in Jess's apartment.

She rose to hand Edith the report to sign and as she did, she tried to read, upside down, what the pink slip said. It was from Star Security. Nikki recognized the name because her mother used the same security company. The note was hard to decipher, but apparently there had been a question of an old access code used at the front gate.

Nikki's heart was suddenly pounding. She had no idea what the message might mean, or if it had anything to do with Rex's murder, but she intended to find out.

"I just need you to sign here, and then initial a couple of places. Here and here," Nikki said, standing up to lean over the desk, "and then I'll get out of your hair."

Out of her hair and into someone else's . . .

In the driveway, Nikki checked her cell phone. Three missed calls in the twenty minutes she was with Edith.

Her guess had been correct. She hit the TALK button on her dash. "Call Mother."

"I tried to call you," Victoria said as soon as she picked up. She was *definitely* put out.

"I know. I was in the meeting with Edith. I thought you were at a luncheon."

"I ate fast. I needed to talk to you."

"Is something wrong?"

"There are all sorts of things wrong, Nicolette. You just have to look at the Middle East to see that."

Nikki smiled, unsure if she wanted to laugh or cry. "I mean, is something wrong with *you?* Did you call me three times because *you* have an emergency, Mother?" The gate slid open, allowing Nikki to pull out of the driveway and onto the street.

"I went for a manicure this morning, before lunch."

Nikki waited.

"Desiree did a nice job. She wanted to give me French tips, but I said no."

"You called me three times while I was meeting with a client to tell you decided *against* the French tips? That was your emergency?"

"I don't appreciate your sarcasm, Nicolette. I would never call you three times to tell you I didn't get French tips." She hesitated. "Although I might have, had I decided to get them."

"Mother, why did you call?"

"I can call you later if you're busy. I don't like to disturb you while you're working. Not that you really need to work. The trust fund your father left you would be more than adequate to live on. To live well on."

"I'm not busy now," Nikki said, not taking the bait. "That's why I called you back." Nikki rolled to a stop and waited for a Benz to go through the intersection. The driver waved. Nikki smiled and waved. She had no idea who she was waving at. "I was busy, but now I'm not. Tell me about your manicure."

"Why would I tell you about my manicure, Nicolette? You say the most ridiculous things. I called you to tell you what Desiree said about Edith."

"Edith March?"

"Yes, Edith March." Victoria's voice was full of *tone*, now. "Desiree is Edith's manicurist and she went to Edith's that Saturday afternoon of the party, to do her nails. Only she didn't do her nails."

Nikki frowned. "Okay . . . ?"

"She showed up right on time, got as far as Edith's sitting room off her bedroom, but was turned away by someone on Edith's staff."

Nikki was all ears now. "Go on," she said, recalling Jessica pointing out at the party that Edith's nails were chipped and that she needed a manicure. "Why was she sent away?"

"The maid said Edith didn't have time. Paid her and sent her packing. But Desiree told me she doesn't think that's why she was sent home."

"Why does *Desiree* think she was sent away?" Nikki asked, having no clue where the conversation was going, but intensely curious. Reaching the end of Outpost Drive, she turned onto Franklin.

"Because she was having a knock-down, drag-out shouting match with a man and didn't want to be disturbed."

"With Thompson?"

"I asked Desiree that. She said she couldn't hear what was being said, but it didn't sound like Thompson to her. She does his nails, too."

Nikki gripped the wheel, thinking aloud. "Edith's maid told me Edith and Thompson had an argument the afternoon of the party and that he left on his motorcycle. So, Desiree must have heard them arguing." She paused. "What did Desiree mean when she said it didn't sound like Thompson?"

"I don't know. She just said it didn't sound like him. She heard Edith arguing with a man, but it didn't sound like Thompson."

"Interesting. Did you ask her what time of day this happened?"

"Of course I asked her what time!" Victoria gave an indignant snort. "What kind of detective wouldn't ask the time of an event that could be key?"

Nikki was smiling again. "What time, Detective Bordeaux?"

"Her appointment was for three o'clock. She said she waited less than ten minutes before the maid came with the money and sent her away," Victoria said triumphantly; then, with less confidence, "What does it mean?"

"I don't know," Nikki said, thinking back to the message on Edith's desk. "But I'm going to find out."

Back at the office, Nikki was disappointed to find that Jessica wasn't in. She was eager to tell her what Edith had had to say about Ramirez and about what the manicurist told Victoria. After making a couple of phone calls (her P.I. work was certainly cutting into her day job) she looked up the number of Star Security and dialed. Leaning back in her squeaky desk chair, she identified herself as Anita, Edith March's assistant, and provided the address of her residence. She explained that she was calling on behalf of Mrs. March, and was put on hold. A few seconds of nervous anticipation and the phone clicked.

"Star Security, this is Dave, how may I help you?"

Nikki again identified herself as Anita, using a slightly nasal tone of voice—she had no idea where that came from.

"How can I help you, Anita?"

"One of the house staff took the message last Monday," Nikki said, trying to sound aggravated, "and it makes no sense whatsoever. Something about an old security code was used to enter the front gate?"

"I'm sorry . . . who am I speaking to?"

"This is Anita." She cringed, not knowing Anita's last name. "Mrs. March's assistant."

"Could I have the password, Anita, to access the information?"

Shoot . . . Nikki tried not to panic. She didn't know the password! "I'm not asking you for the security code, Dave. I'm simply asking you to translate the message left on October 4th at . . ." She paused. "Nine twenty-five a.m. I'm not privy to the password. Mrs. March is funny about her security codes, which I imagine you would understand, especially in light of what happened last week," she said, taking on the tone Victoria used when she was trying to gently bully someone into doing something for her.

"Ummm . . ."

"The message was that the security code used . . ." she prompted.

"On Saturday the 2nd. Ummm, it was expired."

Her phone beeped. Another call was coming in. Mother again? She ignored it. "Expired?"

"According to our records, the code was changed March 27th of this year. Mrs. March called it in herself."

"Oh, that's right," she said, having an *ah-ha!* moment. "That would have been after Mr. March's death. His *first* death," she clarified. "So the code used was the previous code?"

"That's correct," Dave said. "Access was denied. Then we received a phone call . . . from a man," he said, obviously reading notes out loud. Then, "Shit."

"Yes?"

"The caller provided the password and the last four digits of Mr. and Mrs. March's social security numbers."

Her phone beeped again and she lowered it for a second to see who was calling. It was Jessica. Nikki spoke into the phone again, using her Anita voice. "What time of day?"

"It's logged in here. Two-ten p.m. He . . . he provided the password. I . . . I'm terribly sorry for the . . . um . . . error. Was . . . was there a security problem?"

"Let's hope not, for your sake, Dave. Have a good day." Nikki's hand was shaking as she set her cell phone on her desk.

So who had called into Star Security and demanded access to the Marches' Outpost Estates home? Had it been Rex? A boyfriend of one of Rex's hussies? Maybe, but not likely. Thompson, trying to create a lie? Who else would have had access to the information? Ramirez? Probably. The only information the security company had was that a male with the required information had called. What if this was some sort of setup leading to Rex's death? Thompson, Rex, Ramirez? Or was it really Rex? And where did Edith, who supposedly didn't know Rex was alive, fit into all this?

Nikki's BlackBerry rang, startling her, and she picked it up. It was Jessica again. "Sorry, Jess, I was just going to call you—"

"Oh, sweet Jesus, Nikki. You're not going to believe this. The coroner released some kind of preliminary report and he's determined when Rex was killed."

Nikki switched gears. "And?"

"Saturday night. The night of the party." She sounded like she was close to hysterical.

"Well, that's good, Jess. You were at Edith's party that night. You have more than a hundred witnesses."

"No, you don't understand, Nik. He was killed *after* I left the party. Now I don't have an alibi . . ."

Chapter 18

The next day, Nikki eyed Edith's gate from half a block away and returned her attention to the comp sheets on her lap. She'd taken a chance driving up to Outpost Estates when she had an eleven-thirty staff meeting back at the office, but she wanted to catch Thompson alone. She'd thought about phoning him, but decided it would be better to catch him off guard. Obviously, he wasn't being honest with Edith concerning his whereabouts. Who knew what kind of mischief she might catch him in?

When her cell rang at 9:45, Nikki grabbed it off the seat. "Chessy?"

"Eagle One done left the building," Chessy stage whispered.

"What?"

Chessy cackled. "Eagle One, the president. That's the kind of thing the Secret Service say when the president leaves. You asked me to tell you when Mr. Christopher left this morning. I'm tellin' you, he's leavin'."

"Oh." She laughed. "I get it now. Thanks, Chessy. Thanks so much."

As Nikki hung up, she looked up to see the gate at the end of Edith's driveway open and heard the loud sound of an engine. A moment later, a black Ninja motorcycle flew onto the street. Thompson was in the full getup: black helmet, black boots, black leather jacket.

Nikki grabbed her sunglasses off the dash, and practically laid rubber pulling away from the curb. She tried to stay off his tail as she followed him through the neighborhood. Then he hit Franklin Avenue and headed west. There was more traffic on Franklin, so she put a couple of cars between them. When he turned left on North Vista, she had to cut off a white SUV to make the light.

Thompson suddenly gunned his engine, passed a red convertible illegally on the right and made a sharp right onto Hollywood Boulevard. Had he seen her, or was he just being yet another jackass on a crotch-rocket?

She followed Thompson for a couple of blocks, changing lanes when he changed lanes. When he suddenly darted into the right-hand lane near Courtney Avenue, she had to let two cars go by before she could move over. Then someone cut in front of her and she had to hit the brakes. By the time she made the next right turn onto a residential street, Thompson was nowhere to be seen.

Shoot! She hit her steering wheel with her hand in frustration. She hadn't realized how hard it was to follow someone and not be—

Thompson stepped out into the street from the far side of a panel van, helmet under his arm. He didn't look at all happy. Nikki braked hard. She looked at him, he looked at her, and a car behind her blew its horn. She pulled over behind his bike.

Thompson took his time getting out of the way of the car. Nikki shut off the engine, put down her window and waited, feeling a little bit like she'd been caught with her hand in the cookie jar.

"You're following me," Thompson said.

It seemed pointless to argue, so Nikki didn't say anything.

"Nikki, why the hell are you following me?"

Still, she didn't answer.

"Edith told me you were at the house yesterday asking questions. About Rex and Alex Ramirez. Look, I'm sorry your friend is in hot water over this whole Rex thing. I get you wanting justice and all that, but you can't involve me," he said angrily. "And you can't involve Edith!"

"Seems like you're kind of already involved," Nikki said quietly. She glanced up at Thompson. He looked pretty pissed, but he still didn't look to her like a killer. He was *so* stinkin' cute.

"*I'm* not involved," he said bitterly. "*We're* not, and if you don't knock it the hell off, all of it, I'm going to call the cops. I don't think they'll appreciate the fact that you're playing private eye in the middle of Rex's case."

"I'm not playing. This is serious, Thompson. They think Jessica killed him."

"Well, I'm sorry about that, but that doesn't change my situation, or me wanting to protect Edith." A car passed on the street and he had to move closer to Nikki's car.

He was a little intimidating, standing so close. Nikki nibbled on her lower lip. "Can I ask you where you're going?" she said in a small voice.

"No, you may not." Taking his helmet from under his arm, he gestured toward her with it. "I want you to leave us alone. Do you understand?" There was emotion in his voice that she couldn't identify. "You have to leave us alone before you *ruin everything.*"

"And that was it? That was all he said?" Victoria was sitting up in bed in a pretty cotton robe, a book beside her.

After Nikki's strange conversation with Thompson, she'd barely had time the rest of the day to think about where she was on the case. The sales meeting had gone on forever, then she'd had to show two houses, then she'd been on the phone tussling with an attorney's office about a client's escrow account. After that, she'd met with a potential new client moving to L.A. from New York. By the time she'd picked up her dry cleaning, stopped for dog food, and gone home to feed her starving boys, it was eight o'clock.

Nikki sat on the edge of Victoria's bed. All the information she'd gleaned about Rex and the potential *players* seemed like a jumble to her in her head. She needed someone to bounce ideas off. Jeremy was entertaining his in-laws this weekend; she intended to stay far away from that. Besides, she didn't want to get Jeremy involved.

And Jessica . . . She didn't dare talk to Jessica right now about anything pertaining to her case. It had taken Nikki an hour the day before to talk Jessica down after Detective Lutz had called to say that Rex had died Saturday night and that she needed to come downtown to be reinterviewed. Nikki hadn't heard how it had gone and was half-afraid to call Jessica to ask.

According to Detective Lutz, Rex's time of death had

been narrowed down to between nine p.m. Saturday night and three a.m. Sunday, the night of Edith's party. So now Nikki had to adjust her timeline. She needed to know where all her suspects were during that time frame.

"Nicolette?"

Nikki turned to her mother. "I'm sorry." She shook her head. "Long day." She reached down to stroke Ollie's head, then Stanley's. Both lay at her feet. Actually, Ollie was lying *on* her foot, looking up at her with those big brown eyes. She'd been neglecting them these last two weeks and they had no qualms about letting her know it. "Yes, Thompson told me that if I didn't leave him and Edith alone, I would *ruin* everything. He was semi-rude again."

"Can you blame him?" Victoria smoothed her pink and white bedspread.

Nikki spotted the shape of a pack of cigarettes under the bedspread and the faint scent of air freshener. She imagined there was an ashtray somewhere. But she only had so much fight in her and tonight she was running on reserves. She let it go.

"Still, Edith needs to work on his manners," Victoria continued. "Imagine, not even being at the party to greet the guest of honor Saturday night."

"He wasn't there Saturday *afternoon*." She was getting such a kink in her neck leaning over to pet the dogs that she got off the bed and sat down on the floor. "I told you that."

"What are you doing on the floor, Nicolette? I'm trying to talk to you."

"They miss me," Nikki crooned to Ollie. "They've had more attention from Sabrina this week than from me."

"Who's Sabrina?"

Nikki rubbed Stanley's back and he rolled over so she could rub his belly. He made sweet little grunting dog sounds as she rubbed vigorously. "My dog walker. She takes them out midday for me."

"Get back up here where I can see you." Victoria patted the bed. "Them, too."

Nikki looked at her mother. In Nikki's house, there was nowhere that wasn't fair game for the dogs, except maybe the refrigerator. They had full reign of the house: beds, couches, lawn chairs. They had their own chair in the family room. Victoria did not allow dogs on beds. "You serious?" she asked her mother.

Victoria batted her eyelashes. "Hurry up. Put them up here before I change my mind."

Nikki scooped up Oliver and dropped him on the bed. He immediately sashayed up to Victoria and plopped down on the pillow beside her. Stanley made the decision to stay near Nikki once she was seated on the bed again. He lay down and rested his muzzle on her thigh.

"Anyway," Victoria said. "Christopher . . . Thompson, whatever his name is, was not there to greet me. Can you imagine the gall? Edith was positively mortified. Rightly so."

"Okay, go back," Nikki said. "What do you mean, Thompson wasn't there? I saw him. I spoke to him."

"Apparently he was called away." She scratched Oliver beneath the chin. "Edith apologized profusely. Maybe he had a *waitress emergency?*"

Nikki shook her head. "That rumor wasn't true. I told you that. Tiffany was dating Rex, not Thompson."

"Dating?" Victoria arched one perfect eyebrow. "Is that what you call it these days?"

Nikki rolled her eyes and then went on. "Mother, this is a big deal. Don't you see? Rex was killed the night of the party. Now we know Thompson wasn't there for the entire thing." She narrowed her eyes. "You sure he wasn't there? He didn't just go upstairs or something?"

"Are you asking me if he was intentionally avoiding me? I don't think so, Nicolette. He likes me. He thinks I'm funny." She scratched Oliver behind the ears. "You think he ran off to kill Rex?"

"I don't know. But we have to consider the possibility, don't we?" Nikki sighed, trying to think clearly. "Do you know what time he left the party?"

"How would I know that?" Oliver had inched his way across the pillow and was now resting his head on Victoria's lap. "He simply wasn't there when I asked Edith where he was."

"I wonder who would know for sure if he left that night and if so, when?" Nikki thought aloud.

"What about her housekeeper? Ina certainly knows more about the comings and goings in this house than I do."

Nikki turned to her mother with a smile. "You're brilliant. You know that?"

Victoria stroked Oliver. "So I've been told."

On the way home, Nikki called Jessica. She didn't pick up, but she called right back.

"Hey," Nikki said, lowering her headlight beams as a car approached. "How'd the interview with Detective Lutz go?"

"Fine," Jessica sighed. "He asked me all the same questions, just about Saturday instead of Monday."

Nikki thought she heard a man's voice in the background. "You out?"

"No, I'm home."

"Someone there?"

"Just Pete from next door. We were having a glass of wine. So, anyway, the interview was fine."

"What did you tell him?"

"What do you mean, what did I tell him? I told him the truth. I went to Edith's party, then I went to In & Out and got a burger, and then I went home to eat it. I used my credit card to pay at In & Out and Pete can verify what time I got home."

"Wait a minute." Nikki stopped at a stop sign. There were no cars behind her so she sat there for a minute. "What about you saying yesterday that you didn't have an alibi?"

"Yeah, I was kind of a mess yesterday. I didn't mean to flip out like that. PMS." She gave a little laugh. "Sorry. After I talked to you, I remembered seeing Pete in the hall that night. He already talked to Detective Lutz."

"So you're no longer a suspect?"

Jessica sighed. "I'm still *a person of interest*. You know, because he was dead in my apartment."

Nikki heard the male voice again. Pete. "Well, I'll let you go." She glanced into her rearview mirror to see that the dogs were sitting nicely in their kennel, and then pulled through the intersection. "Enjoy your wine. I'll talk to you tomorrow."

"Thanks!"

And then Nikki was alone, just her and her boys.

Saturday morning, Nikki pulled up to Edith's gate five minutes after Edith left for her tennis lesson. She called the house and Chessy opened the gate for her. When Nikki walked into the kitchen, she was greeted with the heavenly smell of chicken and potatoes. Chessy was standing at one of the counters, rolling out dough.

"Smells great, Chessy."

"Chicken potpie. My grandmama's recipe. I got extra. You want me to whip up one for you and Miss Victoria?" She was wearing a flowered apron right out of the 1940s. "Your mama says I'm the best cook in Hollywood, better than any of those chefs in them fancy restaurants."

"That's nice of you, Chessy, but it's not necessary."

" 'Course it's not necessary. It's what nice folk do for each other. And your mama, she's nice folk." Chessy continued to roll out the pie crust with a big wooden rolling pin. "You know what your mama did the night of the party? She come back here to the kitchen to thank me for them hors d'oeuvres we served. I tol' her, most I didn't make. It was all the caterers done that, but she said she wanted to thank me anyway because she knew it was a big job, servin' all them people at the party and keepin' everything straight."

"She came back here? My mother?" Nikki leaned on the opposite side of the counter.

"Sure did. She does things like that. My cousin Ida's friend JoJo said she was once workin' some party at a hotel downtown and Ms. Victoria Bordeaux come into the bathroom, told JoJo she looked like she was tired, and said they should both sit down. Right there in the bathroom. On them little stools they got." Chessy threw a pinch of flour on the dough. "It was years ago, but people don't forget them things."

Nikki smiled, imagining Victoria and a ladies' room attendant taking a load off in a bathroom at some $2,500 a plate benefit dinner. It sounded like something Victoria would do. "The party was actually what I wanted to talk to you about. Edith's party."

"You didn't come to peel shrimp?"

Nikki shook her head with a laugh. "No, but I'll peel them if you need me to."

"I'm just messin' with you, Nikki. Shrimp don't go in chicken potpie. You don't cook much, do you?"

"Back to the party, Chessy. Do you know if Mr. Christopher left during the party?"

She wrinkled up her nose. "How would I know that? You know how many people I had runnin' in and out of my kitchen that night? It's a wonder I know if I was here!" She cut her eyes at Nikki. "Why you askin'?"

"I talked with Mr. Christopher early on in the evening. Shortly after my mother arrived, I left. Mother said she never spoke with Thompson. That Edith said he'd been called away."

"Called away where?" Chessy harrumphed as she lifted the perfect circle of dough and laid it in a glass pie plate. "I don't think they got emergencies on the toothpaste commercial set on Saturday nights, do you?"

Nikki laughed. "Some people say he's on the edge of making it big."

"Some people'll say just about anything. Don't make it true."

"Don't you like Thompson, Chessy?"

"I like him all right." She started rolling out another circle of dough. "He's nice to me. He treats my Shondra good. I like him. It's just natural, a woman like me distrusts a man like him."

"Because he's good-looking?"

"That and because he says he loves Miss Edith."

"And you don't think a man like Thompson Christopher could love a woman like Edith?"

Chessy sniffed. " 'Spose anything is possible."

Nikki gazed around the kitchen. "I don't suppose you know anything about Rex being here the weekend of the party."

"Dead or alive?" Chessy lifted a dark eyebrow.

Nikki opened her arms. "Either."

"Nope."

"How about an argument between Edith and Thompson . . . or anyone else?"

"I was in the kitchen supervisin' the makin' of food for two hundred of Miss Edith's closest friends. I didn't have time for listenin' in through peepholes."

Nikki watched Chessy roll the dough again for a minute. "Can you think of who might know if Mr. Christopher left the party early?"

Chessy stopped rolling to think. Grimaced. "You could check with my sister's boy, Marquette."

"Marquette would know?"

"Might. He was parkin' cars here that night. Works for Numero Uno Valet Service. Downtown. It's a good job. Pays good. He's a smart boy, my nephew Marquette. Goin' to UCLA." She nodded proudly.

Nikki watched Chessy retrieve an identical pie plate from under the counter and lay the pie crust inside. Apparently, Nikki was getting a potpie whether she wanted one or not. "I don't suppose you have a number for Marquette?"

"I can do better'n that. He's comin' to my place for dinner tonight. Him and his mama. If you stop by 'bout dessert time, you could talk to Marquette and have one of Chessy's famous apple dumplin's." She winked. " 'Less you got somethin' better to do."

"No, no, actually I don't," Nikki said, thinking of the in-laws at Jeremy's. "I told Mother I'd stop by, but other than that—"

"Good. You can bring her, too." She began to pour the fragrant filling into one of the pie shells. "And she can tell me what she thinks of my potpie."

Chapter 19

When Nikki invited her mother to go to Chessy's that evening, she was sure she'd decline. It sometimes took Victoria hours to prepare for an outing. But when Nikki warned her that she had to leave in half an hour, Victoria beat Nikki to the door. After some discussion, Nikki had managed to convince her mother that it wouldn't do to have Amondo drive them in the Bentley. Chessy lived in such a poor neighborhood that Nikki thought it would be just plain rude to arrive in a chauffeured car that cost more than their hostess's home.

"How do I look?" Victoria asked, tugging at the hem of a pale peach tunic.

Standing at Chessy's front door, Nikki glanced at her mother. Victoria looked casual and comfortable in the brown slacks, peach tunic, and patent-leather brown ballerina flats. She was completely out of place in the poor neighborhood, but had movie star trying-not-to-look-it chic going on. "Quite appropriate for a movie star paying a call to a run-down house in East L.A."

"You're poking fun. Don't poke fun, Nicolette. This

is quite exciting for me. I'm not often invited to people's
houses. Homes." She glanced up at the tired-looking
single-story bungalow that couldn't have been more than
eight hundred square feet. "Not people like Chessy.
She's a smart cookie, Chessy."

"She said the same thing about you."

"Did she?" Victoria looked up at Nikki, beaming. "Do
you have the house gift?"

"I do." Nikki held up a gold gift bag. "But I really
don't think it was necessary, Mother. She told me to just
stop by. Shalini perfume is a little over the top."

"What, you think just because she's a housekeeper,
she can't appreciate good perfume? Nonsense. Every
woman appreciates good perfume. Ring the doorbell,
Nicolette."

Nikki glanced at the door. There wasn't a doorbell.

"Oh, for heaven's sake!" Victoria reached around
Nikki and rapped the door with the knuckles of her
ringed fingers.

A dog barked and a moment later Chessy was standing in the open doorway, grinning for all she was worth.
"You came."

"I told you I would," Nikki said.

"Miss Victoria, so nice of you to come. I got fresh-
baked apple dumplin's." Chessy stepped back to let
them in.

As Victoria stepped into the tiny, neat-as-a-pin living
room, a shaggy mutt rushed across the room, barreling
into her.

"Down, Duke!" Chessy shouted. "Marquette! Come
get this dog before I make him into a dog pie!"

"It's all right," Victoria insisted as the dog licked her
hand. "Dogs like me. Don't they, Nicolette?" She petted
the big dog affectionately, paying no attention to the
drool.

"Marquette!" Chessy shouted as she closed the front door behind Nikki.

"Coming, Aunt Chessy!" a young man hollered from the back.

"Nicolette." Victoria nodded to the gift bag Nikki was holding.

"Something for you," Nikki said, feeling a little embarrassed. "Mother likes to bring house gifts."

"That's 'cause your mama, she got good manners." Chessy chuckled as she accepted the bag. "Oh my!" she exclaimed as she pulled the perfume box from the bag. "Shalini!" She was blushing, she was so excited. "How did you know I always wanted to try this?"

"You know Shalini?" Nikki asked.

Chessy looked up indignantly from reading the box. "A delightful scent of sandalwood, musk and tuberose," she mimicked haughtily from something she'd seen or read. " 'Course I know Shalini," she snapped in her own voice. "Miss Edith got some on her dresser. I like it way better than that Hermes stuff." She turned to Victoria, who was still petting the slobbering, boisterous dog. "You shouldn't have done this, Miss Victoria."

"Oh, please, Chessy. Call me Victoria. You're not on my staff! And you know very well I didn't pay for it. Someone gave it to me." She raised a finger almost beneath Chessy's nose and smiled. "But I *knew* you would enjoy it. And it's never been opened."

Nikki groaned but knew better than to speak. Instead, she tried to lure the dog off her mother.

"Well, come on back to the kitchen." Chessy waved them along. "I just pulled the dumplin's outta the oven. Marquette! You comin' to put this dog out or not?"

Chessy's kitchen, like the living room, was covered with worn linoleum and furnished with old, battered furniture, but it was so clean it sparkled. And the heavenly scent of cinnamon-baked apples was practically making *Nikki* drool.

"Shondra's workin' late. Overtime. She'll be sorry she missed you." Chessy stopped at the table and indicated a large black woman that could have been her twin. "This is my sister, Sissy. Sissy, Victoria Bordeaux and Nikki Harper. Friends of mine." She beamed.

The rotund woman stood, not seeming to be in the least bit intimidated by Victoria's fame. "Pleasure to meet you both," she said, shaking Victoria's hand, then Nikki's.

"And that's my nephew, Marquette. He's the one that parked the cars at Miss Edith's that night."

A handsome young man turned from the sink, grabbing a towel to dry his hands. He'd been washing the dinner dishes. "It's nice to meet you both," he said, offering his hand. "Sorry about the dog." He tossed the towel on the counter and clapped his hands. "Come on, Duke. Come on, boy." They disappeared down a dark hallway.

"Sit yourself, Victoria, and I'll get them dumplin's. Look what Victoria brought me, Sissy." She slid the gift bag with the perfume inside across the scarred Formica table. "Take a sniff, if you want."

Chessy turned to Nikki. "He's just gone out back to let the dog out. You go talk to him in private." She lowered her voice. Not that it was necessary. Sissy and Victoria were busy chatting about the wonders of Shalini perfume. "His mama don't need to hear nuthin' 'bout no murders. Lost her oldest son on the streets few years back. Marquette, he's all she got."

Nikki dropped her bag over the back of the nearest wooden kitchen chair and followed Marquette and the dog. Off the hallway was a tiny laundry room. There was an old washer, but not a dryer; wooden drying racks held rows of large items of clothing. The door to the backyard was open. "Marquette?"

"Right here," he called from just outside the door. "Sorry, light's shorted out again."

Nikki stepped out onto a small wooden stoop. "Pretty night," she said, looking out into the postage stamp–size fenced-in yard. Duke was running the parameters of the chain-link fence, much the same way her dogs ran the parameters of her mother's eight-foot-high privacy fence. "I guess your aunt told you," she said awkwardly, "that I had some questions about the night you worked Edith March's party."

"I was parking cars. Had a good night. Good tips. Watch your step." He pointed to a cracked board on the stoop.

Nikki stayed where she was, in the doorway. She could hear the three women in the kitchen chattering. It amazed her; despite the lifestyle Victoria had been accustomed to most of her life, she could still fit in with anyone. *Nicolette, people are people,* she often said.

"I was wondering, do you know if Thompson Christopher left the party that night? While guests were still there?"

"Sure did. Get away from there!" he hollered to the dog, who was sniffing at the corner of the fence.

"Hole in the fence. He goes under it sometimes," Marquette explained.

Nikki nodded, totally able to relate. Stanley had once dug a hole under Victoria's fence and escaped. Nikki had been scared to death for the minutes it took her to run out the front gate and down Roxbury. Stanley had, fortunately, been waiting patiently for her on the next corner.

"So, Mr. Christopher *did* leave the party?"

"Yup. Super-cool Ninja bike. 1000 cc's. He tore off down the street; I bet he was going a hundred."

"Do you know about what time that was?"

He exhaled. "Phew. Can't say for sure."

"It's important, Marquette. I'm sure your aunt told you that Rex March's body was found in my good friend's apartment. She didn't kill him, but right now she's the number one suspect. Their only suspect, apparently."

He looked at her. "Ten, maybe ten-thirty?"

"But you were sure it was him?"

"It was his bike, for sure. I've seen him on it before. I was parking cars in Holmby Hills last month and he came in on it. Mrs. March was on the back." He chuckled. "Everyone was talking about it."

It certainly sounded like Thompson had left the party, but she was trying to take her mother's advice and keep an open mind. "But you didn't actually *see* him."

"Well, no. Not his face. He was wearing a black helmet. But it was a guy wearing a white dinner jacket on *his* bike."

"You know where he went?"

"No idea. Come on, Duke," he called. "Let's go, boy." He looked to Nikki. "We better get inside before the ladies eat all the apple dumplings. My Aunt Chessy's apple dumplings are bangin'." He shrugged. "Sorry I wasn't more help."

"No, no, that's fine. I'd heard he left; I just wanted to confirm it with someone I could trust. Your aunt says you're a student at UCLA. She's pretty proud of you."

"I'm an accounting major." He hooked his thumbs in his jeans pockets. "Kinda boring, but I'm good with numbers and there's plenty of jobs for CPAs."

"Good for you." The dog bounded up the steps and Nikki turned to go inside, then turned back to Marquette. "Did . . . did you see anything else?" she asked, on impulse, wondering if maybe Rex could have been there that night, or something equally crazy. "Anything else out of the ordinary?"

"Nope. Inside, boy!"

The dog bounded past Nikki into the laundry room.

"Oh, wait! There was something," Marquette said.

Nikki turned around.

"There was this woman . . . this blond chick that pulled up in front of the house. She kinda looked like a, well, a hooker," he said hesitantly. "Her dress was really short and she had a lot of makeup on. And she didn't have an invitation, so Duran wouldn't park her car. He told her she had to leave. He was the one in charge."

"Did she say who she was?"

He shook his head. "No, she didn't give her name, but she had this accent."

"An accent?"

"Like she was out of the Deep South. I recognized it because I have a friend from Georgia and we give him a hard time about it."

Nikki immediately thought of Tiffany. Could Tiffany have been trying to crash the party? If so, why? "Did this happen before Mr. Christopher left or after?"

"Definitely before. Around nine-thirty."

That had been about the time Victoria had been arriving and Nikki had been leaving.

"Marquette, you better get this dog of yours outta my kitchen before he gets a spatula across his nose," Chessy hollered from the kitchen.

Nikki met Marquette's gaze in the semidarkness of

the laundry room. She smelled fabric softener. "And she didn't say what she wanted, or why she was there?"

"Nope. Duran was polite to her. He just told her she couldn't go in because she wasn't invited. She said okay and took off in this old blue BMW."

"Marquette!"

"Excuse me," he said, stepping in front of her. "I better rescue Duke."

Nikki stepped aside to let him go by. An old blue BMW. A blonde with a southern accent. It *had* to be Tiffany. Were she and Thompson more than she'd led Nikki to believe? So . . . when she was turned away at the party, did she call Thompson? Was that why he left in such a hurry? Did that mean it was Tiffany and Thompson who were involved in Rex's murder, rather than Edith and Thompson?

"Nicolette?" Victoria beckoned.

"Coming." Nikki walked into the bright light of the kitchen, once again with more questions than answers.

Sunday morning, Jessica called and invited Nikki for brunch at her place. Just a thank-you, she had said. Nikki had still been in her silk PJs, sitting out on the patio, reading the Sunday paper when she rang, and had seriously consider turning down the invitation. It was a beautiful day and she wanted to take the boys up to the dog park in Laurel Canyon. In the end, Jessica had begged and Nikki decided to go have brunch, then take the dogs for an afternoon run. It would also give her an opportunity to stop and say hello to Mrs. McCauley. Just in case she now remembered seeing someone carry Rex's dead body into Jessica's apartment. It was a long shot, but Nikki had always been an optimist.

As Nikki was taking the stairs in Jessica's apartment

building, she ran into Pete, coming down. He was in gym shorts and a t-shirt, with a gym bag in his hand. The odd thing was, he already looked sweaty, his hair rumpled.

"Hey," he said, meeting her on the landing between the second and third floors.

"Hey." Nikki stopped.

"Going up to see Jessica?"

She nodded. "Brunch."

"Cool." He slipped his gym bag over his shoulder. But he didn't head down the steps. He just stood there. "So . . . it's looking pretty good for Jess, right? I mean, with the murder investigation?"

"I think so," Nikki said, noncommittally.

"Because, like, there's no way she could have hauled that lard-ass around, right? And . . . because of what time she came home that Saturday night?"

Nikki waited, thinking the whole conversation was a little odd. She barely knew this guy. Why was he chatting her up?

"Because, I guess she told you, I saw her. I ran into her that night. We talked in the hall. I gave the police a statement. I'll really be glad when this is over. She's too nice to have something like this happen to her."

"Right . . ." Nikki looked at him, finally getting it. Pete Toro, like half the guys in L.A., had the hots for Jessica. That was what this was about. "I don't think the police care if she's nice or not, but they don't have any evidence."

"Right. No evidence. This is the United States. Innocent until proven guilty."

"Exactly."

"Well, I gotta run. Hit the gym." He passed Nikki and headed down the stairs. "You have a good day."

"You, too," she called after him.

At Jessica's door, Nikki rang the bell. When Jessica didn't answer, she rang again, wondering where she was. She was certainly expecting her; she'd invited her.

"Keep ringin'."

Nikki looked up to see—actually she *heard* her first—Mrs. McCauley with her walker, tooling toward her. She was dressed, maybe for church, in a pink silk Easter bonnet, a white fluffy sweater, bike shorts and yellow Crocs. There were colored Christmas lights looped around her walker. Not plugged in, fortunately.

"Keep ringin'. She's a busy woman."

Nikki smiled. "How are you this morning, Mrs. McCauley?"

"How do I look?" She halted in front of Nikki and leaned forward on her walker.

Nikki was afraid she'd be forced to answer. Luckily, Mrs. McCauley went on. "Got arthritis in my back, my left ear's ringing, and I got dry skin. Like an alligator. How do you think I am?"

"Pretty bonnet," Nikki remarked.

"Thank you." She grinned. "You have a nice day." She started to roll by.

Nikki turned to her. "Mrs. McCauley, I was wondering. The Saturday night before Rex March's body was found, do you happen to remember seeing Jessica when she came home? Somewhere around ten, probably?"

"Ten o'clock at night? I'm in bed! Not that I was asleep. That was the night they had the dog circus in the courtyard. You wouldn't believe the racket dogs'll make flying around on a trapeze and such."

"Right. And . . . you don't remember anything unusual you saw that *Monday* that Mr. March was found in Jessica's apartment? Other than Captain Picard," she reminded, feeling silly even saying it.

"Glad you asked." She slowly turned the walker around so that she was facing Nikki again. "I did. I thought I should give you a call, but that Jessica, she wouldn't give me your number. She thinks I'm a bother. Do you think I'm a bother?"

"No, not at all." Again, Nikki smiled, just as she'd been taught. "You were saying you remembered something from that Monday?"

"Yup. A washing machine."

"Pardon?" Nikki leaned closer . . . as if that were going to aid in interpreting the conversation.

"There was a washing machine. The hula dancer tried to deliver it but I told him he had the wrong apartment. Last week I got a girlie magazine in the mail. Wrong mailbox." She steered her walker around in a circle and started for the elevator again.

At that moment, Jessica opened the door. She was in her robe, her wet hair up in a towel. "Sorry. In the shower."

"Have a good day, Nikki Harper," Mrs. McCauley threw over her shoulder as she rolled away. "I'll let you know next time those dogs are back. It's quite a sight, really, dogs on a tightrope."

"Have a good day," Nikki called after her cheerfully. Then she looked at Jessica as she darted into the apartment. "You don't want to know . . ."

Chapter 20

"**I** brought bagels and that strawberry cream cheese you like," Nikki said, walking into Jessica's apartment. She held up the paper bag. It was the first time she'd been inside since *that* night. She tried not to think about it. "Lox and plain cream cheese for me."

"And I've got champagne and OJ in the fridge." Jessica took the bag and left it on the kitchen counter. "Come on back while I get dressed; we'll sit on the balcony and eat."

As Jessica walked down the short hall to the master bedroom, Nikki noticed that she was wearing high-heeled slippers. The kind with the powder-puff bunny tail glued on them. Nikki was fascinated. They looked like something her mother would have worn in one of her early movies.

Nikki left her handbag on the white couch and followed Jessica to the back. She avoided looking at the bed. Even though the sheets and comforter were different than the ones on the bed that night, she couldn't stop thinking about Rex lying there dead, that black hole where his eye had been. She wondered how Jessica could stand to sleep in the same bed where a dead man had lain.

"I was organizing my clothes. They're a mess." Jessica motioned to the mirror-doored closet that appeared to run the entire length of the wall.

It was actually a row of closets, rather than one long one. Jessica had spent several thousand dollars adding shelves for shoes and clear boxes for handbags. Nikki, who mostly kept her clothes in dry-cleaning bags flung over a chair and in the clean clothes basket in her laundry room, had always been fascinated by Jessica's meticulous care and organization of her clothing. Fascinated, and maybe just a little frightened that anyone would spend that much time, effort, and money for the sake of fashion . . . or organization.

Nikki sat down on a white damask–covered chair just inside the door. Jessica went to the far right, where she kept casual clothing, and began to pick through a row of neatly pressed blue jeans.

"I ran into Pete Toro on the stairs," Nikki said conversationally. She wanted to talk to Jessica a little bit about what she'd learned last night from Marquette, just so she was up to speed, but she wanted to ease into that conversation. Maybe after Jessica had had a couple of glasses of champagne.

"Did you?" Jessica murmured, her back to Nikki.

"He said he talked to the police. About when you got home the night of the party." Nikki stared at the closet on the far left where the shoes and handbags were stored. There were little labels attached to each bin that looked like they had been made with one of those label makers Nikki used in the office to mark her files. She slid forward on the chair, squinting. "Are those labels on your shoes?"

"Mm-hmm." Jessica pulled a pair of jeans from the closet and held them up to look at them. "It was nice of Pete to call Detective Lutz. He's a good neighbor."

"Mrs. McCauley said there was a dog circus in your courtyard the night of Edith's party." She was still staring at the labels on the shoes and handbags. "Three letters? What are the three letters on the labels?"

Jessica returned the pair of jeans to the closet and grabbed another pair. "It's a code. So I know what bag goes with which shoes." She kicked off her slippers and slipped out of her robe. She was wearing a matching pink bra and lace panties.

"A code? You have a *code?* You've got to be kidding me!" Nikki slid back in the chair and watched Jessica step into the jeans. It had occurred to her this morning that she'd never tracked down the bellhop at the Sunset Tower again and she made a mental note to call today to see if he was working. Nikki had held up her end of the bargain—Victoria had called his grandmother for her birthday. At this point, the fact that Rex was seeing women at the hotel didn't really seem to matter to her investigation, but she didn't want to leave any potential leads dangling out there, just in case one became a real lead. Besides, a deal was a deal.

Nikki crossed her arms, still staring at the boxes of shoes and bags. They were kind of like little plastic coffins . . . "Pete said he was going to the gym, but he looked like he'd already been there. Weird."

"Hmm," Jessica responded, not really paying attention. She pulled two white t-shirts from the closet. "Which one?" She held up both.

They looked identical to Nikki. "One on the left."

"Good choice." She put the other back, tossed the wet towel from her hair on the floor, and slipped the shirt over her head. "How long do you think the police investigation will take?"

"I don't know. As long as it takes, I suppose."

"Can they do that?" She stepped back into the slippers. "I don't see how they can." She grabbed the towel and strode to the bathroom. "I mean, I can't remain a suspect permanently, right? I have that trip to Cancun for Christmas. I should be able to leave the country by then, shouldn't I?"

"I don't know. That would be something you could ask *a lawyer.*"

Jessica threw her a look as she went into the bathroom.

"I know," Nikki groaned. "You don't want a lawyer. But I think you're being foolish not to at least talk to one." She watched Jessica in the reflection in the mirror as she combed out her gorgeous blond hair. Self-consciously, she tugged on her own rather hastily done ponytail.

"I've heard that the more time that passes after a murder, the less chance police have of catching the killer. They said that on that show on TV, *First 48.* You ever watch it?" Jessica rubbed some kind of goop into her hair. "They show how real cops catch the bad guys. What they do in the first forty-eight hours of the investigation."

"You never gave any guys a key to your place, did you?" Nikki asked.

"No. You sound like Detective *Duntz* now. Why would you even ask me such a thing? I'm not stupid. I'm just promiscuous."

Nikki smiled to herself, glad to see that Jessica was keeping her sense of humor about this. "I just keep wondering how on earth whoever killed Rex got him

THE BAD ALWAYS DIE TWICE   227

into your apartment. The police said there was no forced entry."

Jessica flipped off the bathroom light and walked into the bedroom, twisting her wet hair up on her head. She was holding a plastic clip in her mouth, so her speech was garbled. "Obviously, he used one of those lock pick thingies; I sure as hell didn't let him in." She took the clip from her mouth and clipped it into her hair. "My brother had one when we were in high school. He used it to get into my bedroom and read my diary. You hungry?" She walked past Nikki and out of the bedroom.

"Starved." Nikki popped up out of the chair. "I need to make a quick phone call," she said, thinking about the bellhop again. "Then I'll meet you on the balcony. I've got some stuff to tell you about the case."

"Oh, goody," Jessica replied, without much enthusiasm. "Good thing there's alcohol."

Nikki caught Julius at work. He told her he couldn't talk, but he was off at seven. At seven-fifteen, she was waiting for him in a coffee shop on Sunset, not far from the hotel.

"I was afraid you weren't going to call," Julius said, slipping into the chair across from her. He'd changed into street clothes and was wearing a ball cap. If she hadn't heard his voice, she might not have recognized him. "I left a message at your office last week. When you didn't call, I was afraid you were blowing me off."

"You're kidding. I never got the message." She smirked. "I thought you were blowing *me* off, Julius."

He looked one way and then the other, then met her gaze. "What do you think?"

She raised one eyebrow, just the way her mother did when she thought Nikki had said something ridiculous. "Of?" Now she was *sounding* like her mother. It was *the tone*. It was all about *the tone*.

"My disguise," he whispered loudly. "In memory of Rex."

Nikki pressed her lips together. The kid was completely serious. She cleared her throat. "It's good. So, what did you find out? Would you like some coffee? Something to eat?" She pushed the menu across the table to him.

Again, he looked left, then right. There were about a dozen people scattered in the coffee shop, none of whom was in the least bit interested in Nikki *or* her undercover bellhop. "You're not going to believe what I found out," he said excitedly. Then he lowered his gaze and fiddled with the fork and knife in front of him. "I was wondering . . . my granny is coming out to visit sometime this winter and it would be absolutely amazing if she could meet Victoria Bordeaux in person." He sneaked a peek at her.

Fortunately, the waitress came to the table, giving Nikki a second to consider her reply. She ordered a caramel latte, decaf, and a piece of lemon icebox pie. He got a Coke and the apple pie à la mode.

Nikki waited until the waitress walked away. "I can't make you any promises like that, Julius. Still, I hope you have some real information so we can catch the killer of one of your childhood heroes," she said. "A hero to a lot of people." She knew the childhood hero part was laying it on pretty thick, but it was worth a try.

He made a face. "Sorry. I didn't mean to sound like I was trying to . . . blackmail you or anything."

She leaned back, amused. "Which is a good thing, because you don't have any information on *me* that you can't share with anyone and everyone. I'm the world's worst blackmail target." The things in her past that might have been blackmail-worthy had played out publicly in the papers long ago, but she didn't bring that up. No need to muddy Julius's waters.

"It's just that having your mom call Granny, it was like the most exciting thing that's ever happened to her. To her whole town."

"I'm glad." Nikki folded her hands on the table and leaned forward. "So, what did you find out?"

"He *was* there the day you asked about! In February."

"I knew it!" She slapped the table in celebration of her finely honed detective skills.

"Mr. Atlas." Julius sat back and grinned.

"Pardon?"

"Mr. Atlas. That's the name he uses . . . *used*," he corrected. He looked sad for a moment, then perked up again, obviously pleased with his own detective skills. "Whenever Mr. March checked in, he used the name Mr. Atlas. I checked the hotel's records. I'm not allowed to do that."

"I understand. But I'm so glad you did." Nikki pressed both palms on the table. She didn't know how this affected the case, but it was just too good. Mr. Atlas? It was *sooo* Rex, there was no doubt in her mind that Julius had the right hotel guest.

"It gets better," Julius said, adjusting his ball cap.

"It does?"

Again, Julius glanced around.

"It's okay," Nikki whispered. "We're not being watched."

The waitress showed up again, this time with their order, and Nikki had to wait until she walked away. "So, you were saying?"

"You're not going to believe this!" He popped his

straw out of the wrapper, dropped it into his drink, and took a long sip, so long that Nikki was tempted to take the straw out of his mouth.

"He was there. Mr. March."

Nikki waited.

"That weekend!" Julius said excitedly. "The weekend before he was found dead in that woman's apartment. He was at our hotel Friday and Saturday."

Nikki felt like she'd stepped off a cliff. Her mouth was so dry, she took a sip of her latte. "You're positive?" she said as she ripped off the corners of two packets of sugar. She was so excited that her hands were shaking.

"Positive."

"You saw him?"

He shook his head and stuffed a fork full of pie into his mouth. "No, I was off both nights. If he'd been there, I'd have known it was him. No matter what he was wearing: fake beard, a wig, whatever. I always recognized Rex. Me being such a big fan and all."

Nikki noticed that "Mr. March" had become "Rex," as if Julius and Rex had been best buds. "So how do you know Rex was there, if you didn't see him?"

"I checked the computer. It's all in there. You just have to know *where to look*. He checked in on Friday. He never checked out."

She squinted at him half suspiciously, wondering if he would lie just to get her to get Victoria to meet his granny. "But *you* didn't see him?" She stirred her latte.

"No, but my girlfriend did. She works in the kitchen. Delivers room service."

This was like being on a roller coaster. "You've got to be kidding me." It made sense. Rex never checked out of the hotel because he didn't get a chance. Because he *really* checked out.

He shook his head, grinning. "She saw him Friday around seven. She delivered steaks."

"As in plural?" Nikki asked.

He put another forkful of pie in his mouth. "Sorry?"

"You said your girlfriend said she delivered *steaks* to Rex March's room. Was there someone else with him?"

"That's the funny part." He laughed.

She waited.

"Laura said—she's my girlfriend—she said he had this girl in the room. She looked just like Julia Roberts in *Pretty Woman*. When she's wearing the blond wig. Have you seen it?"

Nikki nodded, wondering if there was anyone who hadn't. "Mm-hmm," she said.

"The dress, with the big hat." He motioned. "But by then, in the movie, she had red hair. Not the girl in the hotel room. Julia Roberts. I like red hair." He smiled.

Nikki had been fiddling with her hair. She dropped her hand, trying to make sense of what he was saying. "Rex's lady friend was wearing a big hat in the hotel room?"

Julius shrugged. "You see a lot of crazy things in my work."

She couldn't help but smile, but refrained from saying *mine, too,* for fear he'd get off the subject again. "Did this *Pretty Woman* have a name?"

"Laura didn't hear a name." He sipped his Coke. "Oh, but she said she had a southern accent."

Nikki practically fell out of her chair. "You're kidding? A blonde with a southern accent?" It had to be Tiffany . . .

He nodded excitedly. "Guess what else I found out? . . . From Laura's friend Macy, who works the front desk?"

Nikki had fully intended to buy Julius's meal. She

was wondering if she could offer to put him through
college. "What?"

"He got a call Friday night. A Mrs. Atlas for Mr.
Atlas." He lifted one brow, nodding as if he were a rap-
per. "Only the woman who called, she was older. She was
not the Pretty Woman."

Chapter 21

The next day, Nikki sat in her car in the rear parking lot of Barney's Beanery and checked her vintage art deco–style Benrus wristwatch for the third time. It was 10:45. Tiffany would be pulling up at any minute.

After meeting with Julius, Nikki had decided she would talk to Tiffany before she confronted Edith about her call to the Sunset Tower the night before Rex died, or the fact that she had lied about knowing Rex was alive. Nikki had gone straight to the Barney's Beanery on Santa Monica. Tiffany wasn't working, but Nikki had exchanged a gift card for a thirty-day gym membership to a place in West Hollywood for information on when Tiffany was working that week. With the freebie in his back pocket, the muscle-bound dishwasher having a smoke behind the restaurant had been happy to check the work schedule to see when Tiffany would next be in.

At the time Victoria had forced the gift card on her, Nikki had tried not to take it, arguing she had her *own* gym membership, which she didn't use. Walking away from Barney's the previous night, she'd been glad she'd had it to bargain with. She'd have to keep that in mind the next time Victoria was stuffing things in her handbag as she went out the door.

At exactly 10:51, Nikki spotted Tiffany pulling into the parking lot in her old blue BMW. Nikki was out of her car before Tiffany, in shorts and a Barney's t-shirt, was halfway across the parking lot.

"Tiffany!" Nikki left her bag in the car and just took her keys and BlackBerry. "Tiffany?"

The minute the young woman spotted Nikki, she walked faster, headed for the employees' entrance in the rear of the restaurant.

"Tiffany, please. Can I talk to you?"

"*Ah haf* to be at work."

"I know. I'll only keep you a minute." Nikki stepped in front of her, blocking her path. "I wouldn't be bothering you if this wasn't really important."

"Oh," Tiffany groaned, letting her hand, which was gripping a canvas bag, fall to her side. She looked away, not making eye contact with Nikki. She knew she was busted.

"I talked to someone at the Sunset Tower Hotel, Tiffany. Why didn't you tell me you saw Rex a couple of weekends ago? The weekend he died. You told me you didn't know he was still alive."

To Nikki's surprise, Tiffany's eyes welled with tears. She glanced at Nikki and then off into the parking lot again. "*Ah'm* sorry. *Ah* didn't *main* to *lye* to you." A fat tear ran down one cheek.

Nikki felt like a total jerk. Either this girl really could be a movie star, or she was genuinely upset. "It might be easier to tell me than to tell the police," she suggested softly. "You saw Rex Friday night, the weekend he died. In the hotel."

Tiffany nodded and sniffed.

Nikki wished she had tissues to give the girl. "Tell me why you went to the Sunset that night."

She pressed her lips together. "Ya already know *whya.*"

Nikki felt her cheeks grow warm. "To have sex with Rex. Right. I understand." She gave a wave. "I don't care about that, Tiffany. I really don't. What I need to know is how you came to be there that night. Did Rex call you and ask you to come to the Sunset Tower?"

She nodded. "*Hey* tol' me *tuh* wear the dress and that *haht hey* bought me." She sniffed. "*Hey* liked the big *haht.*"

A young woman in a Barney's tee stepped out the employees' entrance. "You okay, Tiffany?" the girl asked.

Tiffany nodded. "*Ah'm* fixin' to come in in *jest* a minute. Could you punch my card for me, *Ai-mee?*"

The young girl glared at Nikki, making Nikki feel like an even bigger heel. She'd made Tiffany cry.

"Come sit in my car," Nikki suggested.

"*Ah cain't. Ah* got *tuh* get *tuh* work. *Ah* need the money."

"I understand." Nikki found herself reaching out to rub the young woman's arm. "Just tell me what happened, Tiffany. Tell me everything. You said Rex called you. Where had he been all this time? What did he say when he called? He knew you thought he was dead."

Tiffany rubbed her nose with the back of her hand. "*Hey* called me that Frahday. At first, *Ah* thought it was some kinda joke. *Hey* tol' me how sorry he was that he made me think he was *deid.*" Fresh tears filled her eyes. "He *sayd* he came back for me because he missed me so much. He *sayd* he couldn't live without me."

"He came back from *where* to get you?" Nikki asked, certain what Tiffany was saying was true.

"*Ah* don' know. *Hey* didn' say."

"Did he say *where* he was taking you?"

She shook her head. "No. *Hey* just *sayd* we were goin'
tuh a place where *Ah* could order umbrella *drainks* all
the day long." She smiled through her tears. "Rex knew
how much *Ah* like those frozen *drainks.*"

"Did Rex tell you why he'd disappeared?"

"He *sayd* he ran away from home."

"Meaning he faked his death?"

"*Hey* didn' say how *hey* did it. The plan and all. *Ah* was
just so glad *hey* wasn't *deid* that *Ah* didn't care."

"Did he say *why* he faked his death?"

"*Ah* asked him why *hey lyde* to me. *Tuh* the whole
world. His fans and all. *Hey* . . . *hey sayd* something about
hey didn' *wanna fayde* away." She looked at Nikki, her
pretty face blotchy with tears. "*Ah* didn't really understand what *hey meynt. Ah* was so happy to hear his voice."

Nikki ignored a car that pulled into the lot and
parked next to hers. "But he said he came for you?"

She nodded. "*Ah* went *tuh* the hotel. We had dinner
in the room. It was very romantic. He tol' me *hey* had a
business meetin' Saturday night, but that we would go
on Sunday. *Hey sayd hey* already had the plane tickets.
First class." Fresh tears rolled down her pretty face.

Nikki's thoughts were going a mile a minute. A business meeting? He met someone on Saturday night? Was
it his killer?

"What business meeting? With who?"

Tiffany shook her head. "*Hey* didn't say. But he *lyde.*
Rex *lyde* to me again. *Ah* looked in his bag when *hey* was
in the shower. *Hey* had a first class *playne* ticket, all right.
But only one. *Hey* wasn't takin' me. *Hey* jest called me
up and fed me that *lahne* so *Ah'd* go to the hotel in the
stupid hat and have sex with *hym.*"

Nikki covered her mouth with her hand to keep
from laughing. It wasn't funny. It was sad. How could

this poor girl be so naïve? And so hurt by the truth? She felt so bad for Tiffany that she wanted to give her a hug.

"Listen, Tiffany. I know you have to get in to work, but I just have a few more questions. Where was he going? What did the plane ticket say?"

"It *sayd hey* was goin' to Pa-pete." She scrunched up her face. "*Ah* don' know where that is."

Pa-pete? Pa-pete? Where the heck was Pa-pete?

"You're sure it said Pa-pete?" Nikki asked Tiffany.

"That's what it *sayd.*"

Pa-pete. Nikki tried to think. Then it suddenly occurred to her what the ticket must have said. "Was he going to *Papeete?* In Tahiti? It's spelled P-A-P-E-E-T-E."

"That was it," she said.

"Okay, so what happened after Rex got out of the shower, after you found out that he'd lied about taking you with him?"

"*Ah* don' know."

"You don't know?"

Tiffany slung her canvas bag on her shoulder and looked longingly at the employees' entrance. "Because *Ah* left. Last *Ah* saw Rex, *hey* was in the shower. He was singin'." She smiled sadly. "It was the theme song *tuh* his TV show."

"And then what did you do?" Nikki prompted.

"*Ah* did what any girl would do. *Ah* went home and cried. Then *Ah* ate a half a gallon of Rocky Road ice cream."

"But that wasn't the end of it?" Nikki pressed. "Was it? What happened Saturday night?"

"*Ah* went *tuh* Mrs. March's house. *Ah* was so mad, *Ah* was gonna tell her what a *li'r* Rex was. *Hey lyde tuh* me and *hey lyde tuh* her. About *bein' deid.*"

"But Mrs. March was having a party and the parking attendant wouldn't let you in."

Tiffany's eyes grew wide. "How *deid* you know that?"

"Tiffany, let me tell you something I learned the hard way many years ago. Nothing happens in this town, ever, that everyone doesn't eventually find out about." She squeezed the young woman's shoulder. "Why don't you give me your cell number and then go on into work? I'll call you if I have any more questions." She entered Tiffany's name in her BlackBerry.

"Well, okay," Tiffany said hesitantly. "But *Ah* don't have too many minutes left on my plan this month. So if ya don't mind, we could just meet or somethin' if we need *tuh* talk more than a minute or two?"

Nikki knew she couldn't discount anything, but Tiffany certainly didn't sound like a killer. Nikki put Tiffany's number into her phone and said good-bye. Walking to her car, she hit her speed dial. There was no answer. Victoria's cell phone was still MIA, apparently. She called the house and got Ina. Amondo picked up next and Nikki finally got Victoria.

"Can you meet me for lunch?" she asked, not giving her mother a chance to speak. "We need to talk about the case."

"Can't do lunch, Nicolette. The girls are coming for lunch."

The girls Victoria referred to were a group of older women who had been friends forever. All had been in the business in one form or another; Hollywood had been built around them.

"That's okay. I really should do some work. You want me to come over or would you like to go out for dinner? We haven't been out in a while."

"Let's go out."

"Where? You name it."

"I'll have Amondo make us a reservation for Osteria Mozza," Victoria said, obviously delighted.

Nikki grimaced and got into her car. "Mother, we won't be able to get in there tonight."

"Nonsense. I know the hostess. Nice girl. I'll call her myself if I have to. Seven-thirty? Maybe that nice Mr. Batali will even be there."

Nikki knew better than to argue any further. "See you there," she said with a grin.

At precisely seven-thirty, Nikki and Victoria were seated at Osteria Mozza on Melrose and Highland. There were certainly more expensive places to dine in L.A., but since it had opened a few years ago, it had been Victoria's favorite place to dine. She and *the girls* came here all the time.

"It's so nice to have you with us, Ms. Bordeaux," the hostess said, handing Victoria a menu.

"Lorena, this is my daughter, Nikki Harper."

"Nice to meet you."

"Lorena has a little girl," Victoria told Nikki from across the table. "Tabitha. Isn't that a sweet name?"

"Sweet." Nikki opened the menu, eager to make her selection. Every time she came, she chose something different. Her plan was to eat her way through the entire menu.

"Raúl will be your waiter," Lorena was saying. "But let me know if there's anything I can do for you, Ms. Bordeaux."

"Thank you, dear." Victoria smiled *the smile*, flashing those Bordeaux blues.

"I don't know how you do it," Nikki said, reaching for her water glass as the hostess walked away.

Victoria was removing her reading glasses from a silk pouch. "What's that, Nicolette?"

"Remember people's names." She was glancing at

the antipasti list. Should she get the Ribollita "Da Delfina," or the grilled Santa Barbara prawns? "I'm so bad at that. And you, you remember the hostess's daughter's name?"

"It's only polite, dear, to know the names of the people who provide you with services."

Nikki's gaze strayed to the list of items available on the mozzarella bar. She'd need to go to the gym by the time she finished this meal. "Okay, so I need you to help me think through everything I've learned in the last day." She glanced up. Her mother looked gorgeous as usual with just the right amount of makeup and perky lip stain. "Are you going to have a cocktail?"

Victoria lifted one perfect eyebrow.

Nikki smiled. "Cocktails it is. So here's what I know so far."

By the time they had placed their order for appetizers and entrées, Nikki had gone over everything Julius, Marquette, and Tiffany had told her and their cocktails had arrived. Nikki ordered a Sicilian Etna Rosso, and Victoria a margarita with specific instructions on how she liked it made. Victoria was a good listener and didn't interrupt, for once, while Nikki talked.

"So, let's see our timeline," Victoria reviewed. "Rex checked into the Sunset Tower on Friday, probably flew in that day. He calls his bimbo—"

"Mother, she's not a bimbo. She's really a nice girl. I just think she's struggling to keep from being eaten alive by the big bad world."

Victoria sipped her margarita. "So the *nice girl* goes to see him Friday night, they dine and . . . do what *nice girls* do with men who buy them steaks in hotel rooms, and then she finds out he isn't really taking her to Tahiti." She relaxed in her chair. "But the *nice girl* actually saw the plane ticket. Rex really was going to Tahiti?"

"That's what she said. But obviously *she* wasn't."

"So, Saturday night the *nice girl* goes to Edith's to tattle on Rex. The whole woman scorned thing . . . but she's turned away at the door."

"Right. Meanwhile, Rex went to this *business* meeting."

"We can't assume anything. Maybe he lied to her. Maybe she lied to you. That aside, business meetings don't usually take place in the evening, unless someone's doing something shady."

"Or doesn't want to be seen," Nikki pointed out. "Obviously Rex didn't want to be discovered: checking in under the false name, eating in his room." The wine was excellent, earthy with a hint of dark cherries, reminding her of a burgundy.

Victoria slid forward in her chair and leaned over the table. "*Ramirez,*" she whispered.

"Ramirez?"

"*That's* who he was meeting. His agent. If Rex ran away before he faded away, the only reason he would come back and risk discovery would be because of money."

Nikki smiled mischievously. All day she'd tried not to think about Rex and what had happened, hoping that if she let it sit on a back burner, it would all make sense. What she should have done was just told Victoria and let her make sense of it all.

"Edith said that she thought Ramirez was stealing from her. What if he was in on Rex faking his death and was supposed to be sending Rex money—"

"But Ramirez was stealing from Rex, too? That's exactly what happened in *Kiss Me Once*, remember?" Victoria said. She had starred in *Kiss Me Once*. "There were two brothers bickering over their father's fortune and, meantime, the sister, Emiline, was stealing from them both."

As Nikki recalled, things had not gone well for Emiline. In the end, she lost everything: her brothers' love, her husband, her fortune. It had been one of Victoria's finest death scenes. "Wait." Nikki took another sip of wine. "So you think that Rex and Ramirez had some sort of deal where Ramirez would funnel money off what was due Edith for Rex's residuals and send it to Rex in Tahiti?"

"But Ramirez was taking a cut for himself. A big enough cut to bring Rex back to L.A." Victoria met Nikki's gaze, her Bordeaux blues intense. "If Rex intended to live his life out in Tahiti, he would need that money to live." She smiled. "And Ramirez was not at Edith's party that night."

Nikki's mouth fell. "Oh, my gosh, you're right. But . . . he said he went to his niece's engagement party. *Here.*"

"Why do you think we're here?" Victoria smiled.

Nikki smiled back. "So, you're saying that maybe Ramirez met with Rex and then killed him . . . and then put him in Jess's apartment?" It sounded far-fetched to Nikki.

"Or maybe it was the *nice girl* who killed him before he ever made it to the meeting with Ramirez. Maybe she didn't leave Rex *singing in the shower.*" Again the eyebrow.

"But how would Tiffany get Rex's body out of the hotel? Rex was huge and Tiffany is tiny."

"You're so naïve, Nicolette. *Nice girls* have friends. Big, brawny male friends."

The waiter approached and Nikki was quiet while her prawns were served. She thought about the big guy who was a dishwasher at Barney's.

Nikki just didn't want to believe that Tiffany could

have killed Rex. Maybe she *could* have, but Nikki was
pretty sure she hadn't. Her emotions had been too genuine that morning.

"Raúl," Victoria said as the waiter started to walk
away. "Could you get Lorena for me?"

A moment later, the hostess was tableside.

"I've a delicate question for you, dear." Victoria
waved Lorena closer. "Saturday, the second, did you
have a private party? An engagement party?"

Lorena looked at her, obviously unsure where the
conversation was going. "We did."

"Alex Ramirez. The agent. Do you know him? I know
you do," she went on, not giving the hostess a chance to
respond. "I've seen him here with clients. I've spoken to
him."

Nikki wasn't certain if that was true, but from the
look on Lorena's face, the young woman believed her.

"Was Alex Ramirez here that night?" Victoria asked.
"Did he attend the private engagement party?"

"Mr. Ramirez's brother made the arrangements,"
Lorena said uneasily.

"Of course he did. It was his daughter's engagement.
But did Mr. *Alex* Ramirez attend the engagement party?"

"I'm not sure, but I don't believe he did," Lorena
whispered.

Nikki could tell by the look on the hostess's face that
she knew she shouldn't be giving out information about
clientele, but she seemed more afraid of Victoria than of
Ramirez. Wisely so.

"I didn't think so," Victoria said, looking like a queen
holding court in the busy restaurant. "That was all I
needed, dear." She patted Lorena's hand, which rested
on the table.

Lorena hurried away before she was seduced by the
Bordeaux blues to reveal more state secrets.

"Oh, my gosh," Nikki whispered, licking her fingers. The prawns were amazing. "If Ramirez wasn't here, maybe he *was* meeting Rex."

"More than likely," Victoria agreed.

"So, what do I do?" Nikki whispered, thinking surely Jessica was safe from prosecution now. "Do I go to the police?"

"Whatever for? For all you know, Ramirez is completely innocent of everything but being a conceited jackanape. Maybe *he* was at the Sunset Tower with some *nice girl.*"

"Mother!"

"It happens," Victoria pointed out diplomatically. "And men like Ramirez are just the kind of men who cheat on their wives in wheelchairs. And then there's the matter of Mrs. Atlas calling for Mr. Atlas at the hotel Friday night. An older woman? It *had* to be Edith, which means Edith *knew* he was alive Saturday night. The man who crashed the gate earlier in the day was most likely Rex. Did Edith make plans for a business meeting with Rex for after the party, and kill him? Did she send her beau off to the meeting to kill him while she entertained her guests? We don't know that that young man with the silly name *got a phone call* calling him away. All we know is that Edith told us he got a call."

Nikki was almost to the bottom of her glass. She wondered if she was going to need another. "Okay, so what *do* I do now?"

"You eat your wild boar ragu, of course," Victoria said, sipping her margarita. She was obviously pleased with herself. "And then we pay a call on the grieving widow."

Chapter 22

Edith received Nikki and Victoria on her back patio the next afternoon. When Nikki called to say that Victoria wanted to stop by and express her condolences, Nikki could tell Edith was torn between not wanting to be questioned further by Nikki, and wanting to be able to say that Victoria Bordeaux had paid her a personal call. In the end, Edith went with the bragging rights.

Shondra showed them onto the patio. The sun was shining and it was another incredible day in Southern California. "Ms. Victoria Bordeaux and Nikki Harper," she announced.

Nikki gave her a wink as Shondra walked away.

"Edith, dear." Victoria opened her arms.

Victoria was dressed in a calf-length black skirt, amazing knee-high boots that looked like they had come out of the riding ring, and a pearl-gray short-sleeve sweater; pearls around her neck, of course, and big Jackie O sunglasses that were absolutely adorable on her petite face.

"It seems foolish, in these circumstances, to say I'm sorry." Victoria kissed both of Edith's cheeks as she embraced her. Real kisses, not air kisses. "But I am." She stepped back. "For all of it. The whole darned mess."

"Thank you so much." Edith pressed her lips together. "Please, sit down and join me. Thompson couldn't be with us."

"Voice lesson?" Nikki piped in.

"Voice lesson." Edith indicated that they should have a seat at the table. "I've got lemonade, but we can have something stronger, if you prefer."

"Lemonade is perfect." Victoria took a seat first, Edith and Nikki followed.

"From our own lemon trees," Edith added, nervously. She lifted a glass pitcher and began to pour lemonade into glasses of ice.

"Thank you so much." Victoria took a dainty sip. "Divine," she declared. She took another sip and then pushed the glass away.

Nikki could tell by the look on her mother's face that she was about to launch into some sort of speech. Nikki had asked to let her question Edith herself, but she knew in her heart of hearts that there was little chance of that.

"I truly did come to offer my condolences, Edith. And I genuinely am sorry for what Rex has done to your life. Before and after his death. Both of them," she added. "But in truth, I came because I'm concerned for *you*, now that I've learned some details of Rex's death. And I understand he really is dead this time. My Nicolette saw his body herself."

Nikki saw no need for that detail, but it was too late now. She took a gulp of lemonade.

"You're concerned for me?" Edith asked. She didn't

even try her lemonade. She knew she was in the hot seat.

"I am." Victoria nodded her regal chin. "Because, honestly, it doesn't look good, Edith. We all know that chit Jessica didn't kill him. She had no motive. And if you kill a man, you don't drag him into your own apartment and then call the police. You dispose of the body. Or you set up someone else to take the fall."

Edith just sat there looking at Victoria. Victoria kept talking. "The police *always* look at the wife, dear. In the end, it's nearly always the wife who's done the bastard in. Pardon my French. You saw *Twice Shy*, didn't you?" she asked. "I played the widow, Melissa."

Edith nodded.

"And look what happened to her."

"Mother, there are no firing squads anymore," Nikki said, feeling compelled at that point to interrupt. "We execute humanely, by lethal injection."

"Untrue, Nicolette." Victoria turned to her, indignantly. "Utah still gives its citizens the right to death by firing squad. Ronnie Lee Gardner."

Nikki wondered where on earth her mother gleaned information like that. Somewhere in all the magazines, she imagined. "I'm sorry for interrupting," she apologized. "Go on with what you were saying to Edith."

"Yes." Victoria turned in her chair. "As I was saying, I'm concerned. And that's why I came to you. I know that you knew that Rex was still alive." She held up a finger, indicating Edith was not to speak. "You called the Sunset Tower Hotel on Friday, October first, and left a message for him. For 'Mr. Atlas.' You knew he was alive, Edith."

"How did you—" Edith looked at Nikki, then back at Victoria. "So what if I did know? I didn't kill him, Victoria."

"No, but you lied to the police. You told them you didn't know he was still alive." She moved closer to Edith. "Not that anyone would blame you." She looked right at her, big sunglasses to big sunglasses. "So if you didn't kill him, you need to come clean with me and tell me exactly what happened that weekend. And then, perhaps, I can help you out of this mess." She sat back, folding her hands neatly in her lap.

Edith looked at Nikki, then back at Victoria. "I don't understand how this is any of your business," she said, sounding as if she might burst into tears.

"It's my business, dear, because my daughter has made it her business, for whatever reason." She fluttered her hand. "The reason doesn't matter, at this point. What does matter, dear, is why you lied."

Edith hung her head. "Why do I feel so awful? I didn't do anything wrong. I didn't create this mess."

Victoria patted Edith's hand. "There, there. Give yourself a moment." She pushed Edith's untouched glass toward her. "Have a drink of your lemonade. Should I have Chessy or Shondra bring us some vodka?"

Edith took a drink of the lemonade and slowly set down her glass. She removed her sunglasses and rubbed her red eyes. "You don't know what it was like being married to him, Victoria. The lies, the cheating. It was an embarrassment. And what could I do? Divorce him? I've never been anything *but* Rex March's wife." She was quiet for a moment. "So, was I glad when that plane went down and the police told me he was dead? I'm ashamed to say I was. For the first time in my adult life, I was going to do what *I* wanted. I was going to live for me. And then Thompson came along . . ." She smiled bittersweetly. "I know you think it's ridiculous, a woman my age with a man like him, but I love him."

"You don't have to tell me about a ridiculous love,"

Victoria said. "I've been married nine times, Edith. But we'll save that for another conversation."

Nikki couldn't resist a smile. How her mother could be so compassionate and at the same time so . . . *Victoria,* she didn't know. She had this way about relating everything to her own experiences; the crazy thing was that it usually made sense.

"Did Rex call you when he arrived in town?" Nikki asked.

"Of course not." Edith ran her finger along the rim of her glass. "I was always suspicious of the plane crash because there was no proof, you know. No body. He always said he wanted to go out with a bang." She gave a humorless laugh. "Like everything else, his bang was fake." She exhaled. "But I didn't know for certain that he was still alive. He never contacted me after the plane went down. Then . . ." She hesitated.

"Spit it out, dear," Victoria suggested. "You'll sleep better tonight."

Edith exhaled again. "Friday, the day before the party, I got a call that my credit card had been used to rent a car at the airport. You know, it was one of those automated calls from the credit card company. There was nothing wrong with the card, but they were just checking to be sure I had used it. My assistant, Anita, took the call. When she asked me about it, I told her I would take care of it." She made a fist. "I just *knew* in my gut when she said it was a rental car that it was Rex."

"So Rex rented a car at LAX Friday, October first." Nikki wanted to be sure she had all the facts straight. She'd be checking on this whole car rental thing.

Edith nodded. "He thought he was being clever. Rex always thought he was clever, but he wasn't. He rented the car at a kiosk, but I closed his credit card accounts when he was supposedly killed. So instead of using cash, the cheap bastard put it on my credit card. He thought no one would ever check." She shrugged. She was wearing a pretty lavender tunic and gray slacks with pearls à la Victoria around her neck. She'd dressed for the visit. "He probably would have been right if it hadn't been for the random call from the credit card company."

"So how did you find him?" Nikki asked.

"I just guessed where he would stay. He always took his chippies to the Sunset Tower Hotel. Girls. Young girls. The ones barely of legal age. Never adult women. Women like me." Her voice broke.

"Put your sunglasses on, dear." Victoria handed them to her. "The sun is bad for crow's feet."

Edith gave a little chuckle as she slipped on her glasses.

"So you called the Sunset on a hunch," Nikki said.

"Yes. I asked for Mr. Atlas's room. He always checked in as Mr. Atlas." She glanced at Nikki. "A tribute to his overinflated ego."

Nikki nodded, but didn't speak.

"So I asked for Mr. Atlas and, lo and behold, I find that he *has* checked in. Probably wearing one of those stupid disguises he used to use. He didn't answer the phone. Who knows who he had in his room with him," she said bitterly.

Edith took another drink of lemonade before she continued. "I suppose Rex eventually got the message that Mrs. Atlas had called. He didn't call me back, but the next day, Saturday, the day of the party, he let himself in at the front gate."

"He tried to use an old security code," Nikki injected. "The one you were using at the time of the plane crash."

Edith looked at Nikki. "How did you know—"

"Not important, Edith," Victoria interrupted. "Go on with your story."

Edith hesitated, then surrendered and continued. "I didn't know how he got in until Monday, when the security company called. At that point, it no longer mattered. Rex just showed up in my bedroom suite the afternoon of the party. I was alone. Thompson was in his own suite. Rex startled me half to death. I don't know how he got in without any of the staff seeing him. There was a lot of confusion that day, because of the party."

"So you argued?" Nikki asked.

"Yes, we argued! He tried to sweet talk me, but I wouldn't let him touch me. I was just praying Thompson wouldn't come in and do something crazy, like kill him."

Victoria looked at Nikki and raised her eyebrow.

"Thompson didn't kill him, Victoria," Edith said firmly. "It's not that I wanted Rex dead. I just wanted him out of my life. Permanently. And I told him that. He said he hadn't meant for me to ever know he was alive. He came back to see Ramirez. Apparently, there *were* money issues."

Victoria looked at Nikki. Nikki kept quiet.

"Rex said he was leaving the next day and that I would never see him again, if I would just wire him some money every few months." She looked up at them. "Honestly, I was willing to do that to get rid of him. I couldn't risk losing Thompson. Not for Rex." She folded her hands in her lap. "Rex asked me to wait a month and then fire Ramirez and find a new lawyer. Of my own choosing. I was to get all the residuals and then just send him half. It seemed fair enough. And then, of course, he asked that I not tell anyone, not even Thompson, that he'd been there. Or that he was alive."

Nikki thought about what her mother's manicurist had said about overhearing an argument with a man that was not Thompson. But Shondra had said Edith had argued with Thompson and that he'd left in a huff and not come back until the party. Nikki decided to follow a hunch. "But Thompson saw him."

"Yes. As Rex was leaving. I kept Thompson from going after him, but we had a terrible fight." There were tears in her eyes again. "I was so afraid when he left on his motorcycle like that, that he was going after Rex. That he would do something terrible." Realizing suddenly what she had said, Edith pressed both hands on the table. "Thompson did *not* kill Rex. He would never kill a man. Not even for me," she murmured.

Victoria looked directly at Edith. "Be entirely honest," she said. "Did you follow Rex? Did you kill him?"

Edith surprised Nikki by laughing out loud. "No, I didn't kill him. There was no need. He didn't want anyone to know he was alive. He was too pleased with all the publicity his *death* had created. He was too proud to ever want his fans to know that he duped them. No," she said with what seemed like complete honesty. "As long as I sent the money to his love shack in Tahiti, I was certain I would never hear from him again." She opened her arms. "So there it is. My confession. Please tell me you believe me, Victoria. I need to know that you know that I'm not a killer."

Victoria took one of Edith's hands in both of hers and smiled her gorgeous smile. "Believe me when I say I hope you didn't do it."

Chapter 23

Back at her real estate-turned-P.I.-office, Nikki learned that getting the information on the car Rex rented at LAX was far easier than she expected. Calling as Edith's assistant—who was still enjoying her new grandbaby in Tulsa—she learned that Rex had rented a white Mercedes 350 SL on that Friday. The creepy thing was, it was returned to the airport on Sunday. On time. There was no record of who returned it, but the guy she talked to assured her it was clean, with no belongings left inside. Surely he would have mentioned it if there had been blood on the seats. He didn't say anything about the police. Just to be sure she hadn't missed anything, Nikki got the name of the attendant who had received the car that Sunday. *Ray* had called in sick, but Nikki made a note in her BlackBerry to call him on Wednesday.

Nikki also found out from a call to Julius, whose number was now in her cell, that even though Rex didn't check out, he left no suitcase or articles of clothing in the room . . . except for a large lady's hat. Julius dug it out of lost-and-found and his girlfriend identified the chapeau as the one that the Pretty Woman had worn the night she served Mr. Atlas.

Seeing a note she'd jotted down about the autopsy report, Nikki next called Rob and left him a cryptic message, asking "Detective Bastone" if he could get a copy of the "paperwork" they had discussed. She wasn't sure if there would be anything in the autopsy report that would help her, or what she was going to do with the information, but it just made sense for her to know if there were any interesting details.

Her last call before going out to show two homes was to Jeremy. He was at work, but she wanted to leave him a message. She had a little surprise for him. The night before, when she'd been riding home with Mother (Victoria had insisted Amondo drive them in the Bentley), Victoria had handed her an envelope with two courtside tickets to see the Lakers Saturday night. It was a pre-season game, but Jeremy loved basketball. Victoria thought it would be a fun date and even went so far as to offer to find an "overnight babysitter."

As Jeremy's phone rang, Nikki dug for a power bar in the top drawer of her desk. It was already three and the only thing she'd eaten today was some whole wheat toast she'd shared with Oliver and Stanley at seven a.m., after their morning walk, and the lemonade at Edith's. Her stomach was growling.

"Hey."

"Jeremy!" Nikki pulled a slightly flattened bar from her drawer. "I wasn't expecting you to pick up." She laughed, a little flustered.

"Well, it *is* my cell phone, hon."

"But you're working. You never answer your phone when you're working."

"My three o'clock crown prep cancelled. I'm running down to the bookstore to get a book on science fair projects."

"Science fair projects! I love science fair projects."

"Good. I'll put you in charge. Our first one is due November first."

She could hear traffic in the background.

"What's up?" he asked. "It's not like you to call in the middle of the day."

"I wanted to see if there was any way you could get away Saturday night . . . for a date."

"With you?" he teased.

"Very funny."

"I don't know. I'll have to check the kids'—"

"To see the Lakers," she interrupted. "Courtside."

"You're kidding! Let me guess, Victoria got tickets?"

"Who else?" She laughed. "You don't think *I* have those kinds of connections, do you? Apparently, she was shopping in La Perla for camis and ran into one of the owners of the Sacramento Kings."

"Only your mother can make that kind of connection over underwear," Jeremy said.

"Only my mother. So the Kings are playing the Lakers and I've got tickets. Can you go?"

"Definitely, maybe." He groaned. "I hope. This is really nice, Nikki. Of you *and* Victoria. I'm almost sure I can make it happen. Can I let you know?" he said hopefully.

"Sure. And if you can't make it, I'm sure one of my newfound friends, like the bellhop at the Sunset Tower Hotel, can."

"What?"

She laughed. "Never mind. Go buy your book on science fair projects. Call me tonight after you put the kids to bed."

"Will do."

Nikki grabbed her Prada and the power bar and ran for the door.

Both showings were a bust. She showed the first client an opulent home in Bel Air built in the style of an eighteenth-century French palace with two-story columns, gilded moldings and striking chandeliers. The client didn't realize that a French palace (a style she said she adored) would be ornate. She was looking for a contemporary home—something she had not told Nikki when they'd spent an hour discussing her likes and dislikes. The second client didn't like anything about the Italian villa in Beverly Park. With nine bedrooms, fifteen bathrooms, and twenty-six thousand square feet, the client was afraid the home wouldn't be large enough for her four-member family.

Making appointments to show both clients additional houses over the next three days, Nikki finished her day job and then headed for Ramirez's office. It would be seven by the time she arrived, but she wasn't looking for Ramirez. Not yet. She was hoping she might bump into someone in the building working late, maybe a security cop or a janitor. She needed to find someone who had seen Ramirez, or Rex, or better yet, both together, the night Rex was murdered.

Nikki walked up and down the street in front of Ramirez's office building and the one next door. The buildings were unusual for L.A.; they actually had their own parking lots. Most office buildings had gone to parking garages ages ago. By this time of evening, the lots were almost empty. Nikki walked into the lobby of Ramirez's building. There was no security desk—too small a building, probably. According to the directory, there were only seven offices in the building. Nikki was standing near the elevator, considering going up to Ramirez's floor just to snoop around, when she heard someone coming down the hall. She turned around to see who approached.

"Can I help you?" asked a man in his late twenties with shaggy, dark hair and a mustache. He was wearing khaki pants and a matching shirt and carrying a black bag of garbage. "Everyone's gone home for the day."

"Mr. Ramirez's office staff gone, too?"

He spun the garbage bag and tied it with a twisty-tie. He reminded Nikki a little of Johnny Depp. "Just me and the dust bunnies."

"Ah." She smiled *the smile*. "So, you provide custodial services?"

He smirked. "I'm the janitor. But it's not a bad job. Pays good and I pretty much work on my own. I do three buildings on this street. Five till one. As long as I do my job, my boss stays off my case."

Nikki took a step toward him. "Do you work weekends?"

"Just Saturday."

"Every Saturday?" she asked.

"Every Saturday."

"Do . . . do people here in the building work on weekends?"

"They work all kinds of crazy hours. I like it better when they don't." He lifted his shoulders in a shrug. "I'm kind of a loner."

"What did you say your name was?"

"I didn't," he said slyly. Then, "Teddy. Teddy Cruz."

"Nikki Harper." She offered her hand and he dropped the bag of garbage to shake it.

"So why are you snooping around here, Nikki Harper?"

"Snooping?" she asked, surprised by his forthrightness. "I wasn't snooping."

"I saw you when you pulled into the parking lot. You walked up and down the street, then all the way around the building. You checked out the cars in the parking lot and you spent a couple of minutes checking out the directory. You didn't need to ask about Mr. Ramirez's staff. You already knew the place was empty."

She half-smiled. "Maybe I was snooping, Teddy. Well, not so much *snooping*, as . . . having a look around. Were you working three weekends ago on a Saturday night?"

"I work every Saturday night, five to one. I told you that." He looked her over more closely. "You a cop?"

"No."

"I didn't think so. P.I.?"

"Sort of." She spun her finger. "So back to that Saturday night. It was October second."

"I'll take your word on it."

"Was Mr. Ramirez working?"

"He *works* a lot of nights," he said, an odd tone in his voice. "He's got a lot of different assistants, if you know what I mean." He winked.

Nikki lifted a brow. If it worked for Victoria, it could work for her. "Was Mr. Ramirez, um, working *that* night?"

"Did his wife send you? Did she, like, hire you to follow her husband? Catch him cheating on her so she can divorce him and take him to the cleaners in the settlement? That's why I'm never getting married. Not that I have anything for anyone to take from me at the cleaners." He chuckled at his own joke. "My girlfriend keeps talking about getting married. But no way."

"I wasn't hired by Mrs. Ramirez. But this is important, Teddy. Do you know if Ramirez was working that night?"

He pushed the trash bag with the toe of his brown work boot. "Mmm. Don't know. His car wasn't here." He shrugged again. "But that doesn't mean he wasn't. Sometimes he parks down the street and walks over."

"Why would he do that?"

"I guess so if his wife sends a P.I. after him, it won't be so obvious that he's dicking around."

She nodded. "So . . . you don't know if he was working that night."

He shook his head. "No."

"Can't remember or don't want to say?"

He gave her a shy smile. "Can't say. That Saturday night, I was kind of . . . off the job for a while."

"Off the job?"

He brushed his hair out of his eyes. "You don't work for Teeter, do you?"

"Teeter?"

"Mr. Teeter, my boss."

She shook her head. "I don't work for anyone. Well, I do. I'm a real estate broker; I'm doing this for a friend. A friend who's in trouble."

"She one of Mr. Ramirez's *assistants*?"

Nikki laughed. It wasn't probable, but it was certainly possible. "No. Not that I know of." She moved her bag to her other shoulder. "So that night. Did you . . . leave? Is that why you're not sure if Mr. Ramirez was in the building?"

"I didn't exactly leave," he said sheepishly. "See . . . my girlfriend and I got in this big fight Friday night. It was over something stupid, but she threw my crap out in the hallway of our apartment building. Then she tweeted all her friends and told them what a jerk I was.

I cut out and spent the night with a buddy. Came to work Saturday and she stopped by. Apologized. Begged me to come home." Another sheepish grin.

"Did you and your girlfriend maybe go off for a while?" she asked.

The grin grew more sheepish. "We were in the car."

"Ah." A good reason not to be peeking into parked cars, she supposed.

"But Mr. Ramirez might have been here because there was a car leaving when I got out of my girlfriend's car. And it wasn't Mr. Ramirez's."

"What kind of car?"

He thought for a minute. "A white Benz. Nice. It went tearing out of here."

"A white Benz? You're sure?" she asked, her heart skipping a beat.

"No. Wait. The car that burned rubber out of the parking lot was a BMW. The Benz was parked. Later, after I went back to work, I remember looking out the window and noticing it was gone, too."

"You saw a BMW speeding away?" Nikki asked. "What color was it?"

He thought for a moment. "Blue. Three hundred series, I think. The little one."

A blue BMW. Tiffany had a blue BMW . . .

Nikki looked up at the janitor. She was already trying to decide what her next move would be. She needed to talk to Thompson, and Rob, and maybe Edith's staff again. And the car attendant at the airport. "Thanks a lot, Teddy. You've been a big help."

She walked out of the lobby into the parking lot. But first things first. Tiffany.

* * *

Nikki was waiting for her when she walked out of Barney's Beanery at the end of her shift. When Tiffany spotted Nikki getting out of the car, Nikki thought for a minute that the girl was going to run. Instead, Tiffany walked, deflated, shoulders sagging, to Nikki's car.

"Tiffany, after you went to the party that Saturday night, did you go to Alex Ramirez's office?"

"What?" She grimaced. "No. *Wheye* would *Ah* go *tuh* his office? *Ah* don' even know where it is."

"I don't know. That's why I'm asking you. Were you having relations with Ramirez?"

The girl looked at Nikki as if she'd asked if the girl had cooties. "You mean sex? Ewww. No."

"Did you follow Rex there, then? Argue with him?"

She opened her eyes wide. "No! No, *Ah deid* not. *Ah* already tol' you exac'ly what *Ah* done."

"But you lied to me before, Tiffany," Nikki pointed out. "What if you're lying to me now?"

"*Ah'm* not. This is dif-rent." She walked to her own car.

Nikki followed her. "Tiffany, someone saw your car that Saturday night in Ramirez's parking lot. They also saw Rex's rental car there. They saw you speed away."

"They *deid* not because *Ah* wasn't there." She thrust her key into the lock of her car door. "*Ah* swear *Ah* wasn't."

"Then why would someone say you were?" Nikki put her hand on the girl's arm.

Tears ran down Tiffany's cheeks. "*Ah* wasn' there. *Ah* swear it. *Ah* left *Reyx's* house and *Ah* went straight home and *Ah hade* cup-a-noodles fur din-ner and *Ah* changed my kitty's litter box." She sniffed and turned big eyed to look at Nikki. "Ya think someone's tryin' *tuh* frame me?"

Nikki scowled. She didn't know who or what to believe anymore. "Why would they?"

Tiffany squared her shoulders. "*Ah* don't know. But

ya said yer friend didn' kill *Reyx* but he was found *deid* in *her* apartment. If someone might be tryin' *tuh* frame her, maybe he's doin' the same thin' *tuh* me."

What if Tiffany was right?

Nikki was still standing in the parking lot when Tiffany drove away in her beat-up car, smoke belching from the tailpipe. From the sound of the engine, the car was on its last legs. Could Tiffany *burn rubber* if she tried?

As Tiffany drove away in a cloud of blue smoke, it occurred to Nikki that she hadn't brought Thompson's name up to her again. In the back of her mind, she was still wondering if there was some connection between Tiffany and Thompson.

Maybe it was time to just ask him.

Chapter 24

Nikki knew that Edith knew that she'd come for more than a signature on the mold inspection report for the house. Nikki also knew that Edith knew that, for now at least, Edith's secret about knowing that Rex was alive and her argument with him was safe. It was Edith's fear that Nikki would go to the police implicating both her and Thompson as suspects that most likely motivated her to *invite* Nikki over.

Over the phone, Nikki had suggested that Thompson be available. When Nikki was escorted poolside at twelve-thirty on Wednesday, sure enough, Thompson was there. In nothing but a pair of swim shorts and surfer-boy sunglasses.

Nikki wondered if this was supposed to be some form of bribery. *I'll let you see my hunky boyfriend, nearly naked, if you won't squeal on me.* The thought amused Nikki, but she was smart enough not to bring it up. Especially since, from where she was standing, the offer might be tempting.

"Something to drink, Nikki?" Edith asked. She was

lying on a chaise lounge, in a bright blue bikini, in all her fiftysomething lumpy-bumpy glory. A big straw hat and sunglasses shaded her face.

Probably catching Nikki trying hard not to look surprised, Edith waved her over to a chair beside her. "I hope you're not offended by my state of undress. You already know all my deepest, darkest secrets. I couldn't feel any more exposed than I already do, so what would be the point of covering up?"

Nikki smiled. She had to give Edith credit; she was a tough, resilient woman. And brave. Nikki admired her. She admired her so much that she prayed the questions she had for her and Thompson wouldn't lead to a call to the police. Because if—when—Nikki found Rex's killer, she was going to call Detective Lutz and hand over all the information she'd gleaned over the last three weeks. She'd never wanted to do the police's job. She just wanted to make sure it was done right.

"I'm not offended in the least." Nikki smiled, taking a seat in the comfy chair and setting her briefcase beside her.

Thompson rolled onto his side and propped his head up with one hand. Tanned and cut, with pecs to make a girl's heart go pitter-pat, Nikki had to force herself to look out over the glistening blue water of the pool.

"I'm glad you came, Nikki," Thompson said in that sexy man-voice of his.

"You are?" She glanced back, trying to keep her gaze off his muscular chest.

He was sort of smiling, which worried her. She hadn't told anyone but Stanley and Oliver where she was going. What if Edith and Thompson *had* killed Rex? What if they intended to kill *her*? Heaven only knew whose bed *she'd* wind up in.

"Thompson," Edith said, her tone a warning.

He reached out and took her hand and brought it to his lips. It was so sweet. So sincere.

"No, Edie, you need to let me speak." He sat up, letting go of her hand. "I can't stand the idea that someone might think you could have killed a man." He looked at Nikki. "Edith never could have killed Rex; if she could have, she'd have done it years ago. But I could have."

Nikki had a million questions on the tip of her tongue, but she realized from the look on Thompson's face that she needed to keep her mouth shut and just listen.

"That day I walked into Edith's bedroom, the day of the party, when I saw Rex walking out, I swear to God I could have strangled him." He clenched his hands into fists. "I wanted to go after him, but Edie stopped me."

"I insisted I'd handle Rex myself. I didn't want Thompson involved in any way. I *had* handled it," Edith said firmly.

"But you and Thompson argued?" Nikki asked.

Edith nodded. "After Rex left, Thompson and I did have an argument. It was probably the first argument we've ever had. Certainly the worst. He wanted to go to the police. I just wanted to let Rex go and be done with him. Forever. I wanted to get on with my life. Is that so terrible?"

"Not so terrible," Nikki murmured.

"And it should have been over and done with, after that," Edith went on, bitterly. "But then Rex got himself killed. What an idiot. I don't know who did it, but I still think it was one of those hussies he was always sleeping with."

Nikki glanced at Thompson, trying to figure out the best way to question him. She didn't want to just ask

him where he went Saturday night, if it wasn't to kill
Rex. She decided to work backward. Part of the key to
the case was how Rex's body had gotten in Jessica's bed.
What if Tiffany had killed Rex and then Thompson had
cleaned the mess up for *her?*

"Okay." Nikki folded her hands on her lap. "Rex was
killed Saturday night. Where, we don't know yet, but I
have an idea. I found his rental car. Well, I didn't *find* it,
but I tracked it down. And I know where it was seen Saturday night around the time he was killed."

"You're kidding," Edith murmured.

Nikki looked past Edith, to Thompson. "You didn't
go to your casting calls that Monday. Why? I need the
truth. And I have to confess to you, I already know that
you put your condo up for sale and requested a passport."

"We've been talking for months about selling his
condo," Edith interjected. "Ever since you sold this
monstrosity." She hesitated, then looked at Thompson.
"But why didn't you make those casting calls, dear?
Where were you all day?"

Nikki kept her gaze fixed on Thompson. He looked
at Nikki, then slowly turned his attention to Edith. She
couldn't read his face. Was he afraid? Apologetic?

"I had some things to do. I didn't want to spoil the
surprise, Edith."

"The surprise?" Edith asked, obviously uncomfortable.

Nikki hoped it wasn't a dead Rex.

"I . . . put some stuff in storage, you know, to clean
up the condo. We'd been talking about me doing that,
Edie. I can account for every minute. I talked to plenty
of people that day. And I . . . I went shopping."

"Shopping?" Edith said it aloud; Nikki just mouthed it.

"The surprise isn't ready," he said, almost sounding like a kid.

"What surprise, Thompson?" Edith asked, a tremor in her voice.

He exhaled and hung his head. "I didn't want to tell you this way."

She sounded scared now. "Tell me what?"

Nikki held her breath.

He raised his head. "Tell you that I love you." The words tumbled out of his mouth. "And that I want to spend the rest of my life with you. I don't care about Rex. I don't care about my career. All that matters is you, Edie. I was so sorry about our fight. I wanted to make it up to you. I was at Cartier's that Monday."

To Nikki's shock, he pulled off his sunglasses and went down on one knee on the patio. He took Edith's hand. "So, will you marry me, Edith? Will you be my wife?"

Edith gasped.

Nikki gasped.

"M . . . marry you?" Edith asked shakily.

"I wasn't even sure, the day I bought the ring, how we could marry legally. With Rex still alive and all. Then, he really was dead." He took a deep breath. "I wasn't going to ask you until I had the ring. It's being sized. I pick it up Friday. We have reservations at Spago."

Edith took her hand from Thompson's and stroked his cheek. "You bought me an engagement ring?"

"That Monday. I felt so bad about our argument. I'd already made up my mind to ask you. I just decided that weekend that it was time." He looked down at his bare foot, and then up again, still on his knee. "So will you, Edie? Will you marry me?"

Edith threw her arms around him and Nikki turned away as they kissed. This was her cue to leave. But she couldn't. Not yet.

"I still have some questions, Thompson," she said, after giving them a moment.

He sat on the chaise next to Edith, his arm around her.

Nikki tried to mentally tick off all the unanswered questions concerning him. "The passport?"

"I wanted to take Edie on a honeymoon. To Greece. Rex never took her on a honeymoon and she's always wanted to go to Greece. But I didn't have a passport and sometimes they take forever to get these days. So I figured I better apply. I didn't know how soon she would want to get married. If she said yes."

They kissed.

"Okay, so where did you go Saturday night when you left the party?"

"He had to go back to his condo," Edith explained. "There was a kitchen fire in one of the condos on his floor. He had to check his place for smoke damage."

"There was no fire in the condo," Nikki said. She'd been in his condo. She'd spoken to his broker; he'd never said a word about a fire in the building. It wasn't something you told clients, but brokers exchanged that sort of information amongst themselves, for gossip's sake, if nothing more.

Edith looked up at Thompson.

"And then there's the problem with where you go on Thursdays," Nikki continued. She felt like a jerk for ruining Edith's special moment. But these things had to be said. Thompson had to account for his whereabouts in order to be removed from her list of suspects. If Thompson had a dark side, better for Edith to know now.

"What's she talking about? You've had voice lessons on Thursdays for as long as I've known you." Edith pressed her hand to his bare chest. "Tell her, Thompson. You have voice lessons on Tuesdays *and Thursdays*."

He hung his head. "Tuesdays, but not Thursdays."

Nikki waited.

"Thompson?"

The handsome young man's eyes teared up.

"Thompson, what's wrong?"

"I didn't want to tell you, Edie, yet. I didn't want you to . . . to think less of me."

"Think less of you? I don't understand."

He turned her hand over in his, rubbing it. "I have a daughter," he whispered.

"What?"

"It happened a long time ago. When I first came to Hollywood. She's almost ten."

"You have a *daughter?*" Edith whispered.

"It was just a . . . a one night thing. I got drunk and I had sex with this girl I met in a bar and . . . and she had a baby." He made no attempt to wipe away his tears. "She's . . . my . . . Mandy." He stopped, took a breath, and started again. "Something went wrong when she was born. Oxygen was cut off to her brain. My beautiful little girl, she's severely disabled."

Tears welled in Nikki's eyes. There was no way Thompson Christopher was this good an actor. He was telling the truth. . . . *Wow. A child. I never saw that one coming.*

"Mandy lives in a private hospital in Santa Monica," he went on. "The night of the party, the hospital called. She was very sick, Edith. They were afraid she wouldn't make it. They've said all along she won't live to adult-hood."

Edith clung to his hand. "Oh, Thompson," she breathed.

"So you were not at Ramirez's office Saturday night?" Nikki asked. "You didn't see or talk to Tiffany?"

"Tiffany?"

"Tiffany Mathews. The waitress you used to work with at Kitty's Diner."

He frowned. "Of course not. I haven't seen Tiffany in ages. What does Tiffany have to do with this?"

Nikki shook her head. "Nothing, apparently. Tell me where you go on Thursdays," she urged, already guessing the answer.

"Thursdays are my day with Mandy. We spend every Thursday together. I . . . I don't know if she can understand me, or . . . or even hear me, but I read to her. We read on Thursdays. We talk. We watch movies. She likes Disney movies."

"Why didn't you tell me?" Tears ran down Edith's plump cheeks. "Why did you not ever tell me?"

"Because I was ashamed. Not of Mandy, but of the fact that I had a child with a woman I didn't know."

"You pay for her medical care, don't you?" Nikki asked.

He nodded. "It's expensive. I couldn't make enough money on my own. That's why . . . why . . . ."

When he couldn't say it, Nikki finished for him. "Why you always date older, rich women."

"Yeah." He looked into Edith's eyes. "I was using those women because I needed their money. It's not that I didn't care for them, but . . . but I never felt anything for them like what I feel for you. I do love you, Edie, and I'll do anything for you, anything, if you'll say you forgive me. If you'll marry me." He hesitated. "But I can't give up Mandy. Or my responsibility for her care. I just can't."

"I wouldn't ask you to, darling." Edith kissed one of his cheeks and then the other and then his mouth.

This was definitely Nikki's exit cue. She rose, taking her briefcase. "I'll get your signature on this paperwork another day, Edith. Thank you. Both of you."

"But . . . but you still don't know who killed Rex, do you?" Edith asked, wiping the tears from her eyes.

"No," Nikki said, walking away from the pool. "But I know where to find out."

On the way to the office, Nikki considered calling Jessica to tell her about the turn of events at Outpost Estates, but she decided against it. Hopefully, Jessica would be at the office and she could fill her in there before she had to meet a potential client at her home in Bel Air at three.

Instead, Nikki called the car rental company and asked to speak to Ray. She was put on hold. Heading out of Outpost Estates, she marveled at the story Thompson Christopher had revealed. It was too crazy, too heartbreaking, to be made up. She'd get the details from Thompson later, but she knew they would all pan out. She knew that come Friday, Edith March was going to be flashing a big fat diamond from Cartier. She was happy for Edith. Even for Thompson. But all she could do now was eliminate them as suspects in Rex's death. She still didn't know who had done it.

While she was on hold, her phone beeped. She had another call coming in. She let it go to voicemail.

"This is Ray, how can I help you?"

Nikki identified herself as Detective Nikki Smith of the LAPD and launched into her questions concerning Rex's rental car.

"Nope. Nothing in the car, Detective. I'm looking at

the report right here in the computer. We note if something was off. Damage, or something left inside. Why're you asking?"

"I'm not at liberty to say," she explained, using a little of Victoria's *tone*. "But you definitely received the car?"

"I signed off on it, so, yeah. Definitely."

"Do you recall what the person who turned it in looked like?"

"Damn, Detective. We got a lot of cars comin' in and out of this lot in a day. That was weeks ago."

"Male? Female?" she asked. "Maybe a pretty blonde with a southern accent?" She was grasping at straws.

"I'm thinking, Detective. No, not a woman. I remember the car. Brand new Mercedes, white. Sweet ride."

"Yes, that was it."

"It wasn't a woman who dropped it off."

"A man, then? Hispanic?"

"Yeah . . ." he said slowly.

So slowly that she hoped he wasn't feeding her a line he thought she wanted to hear.

"It *was* a Hispanic guy," Ray said. "I remember now."

"Can you describe him?"

"Big guy."

"Big, like tall?" Ramirez wasn't really a tall man. He was under six feet, but tall was relative, wasn't it?

"No, big like big. You know. Three hundred. Three-fifty."

"Three hundred and fifty pounds?" Nikki said, trying not to sound disappointed.

"Yeah. Big guy with a cool tattoo," he added.

"Tattoo?" She sounded like Detective Echo, now.

"It was on his forearm. I said something to him about it. It was a hula girl."

* * *

It was a hula girl . . . Ray's last words were still bouncing around in Nikki's head as she pulled up to a red light. Traffic was moving slowly. It was going to take her forever to get to the office. She had a ton of work to do: comps, lots of phone calls to return. And tonight was Movie Night: 1965. *The Sound of Music.* Nikki hated *The Sound of Music.* But there was no way she could work late and miss Movie Night. Pretty much the only excuse that would satisfy Victoria was death. Tragic, and preferably bloody.

The light turned green. *A hula girl tattoo.* Why was that ringing a bell?

At the next intersection, she almost hit the brakes, even though she had a green.

A hula girl. A hula girl tattoo. *Mrs. McCauley.* She'd told Nikki a hula girl had tried to deliver a washing machine to her apartment the day Rex appeared in Jessica's bed.

Her heart suddenly pounding with excitement, Nikki cut into the left lane and made the next left turn, headed toward Laughlin Park.

When her phone rang, she hit the button on her steering wheel. "Hello?"

"Nikki, it's Rob. I called a few minutes ago, but I didn't want to leave a message."

She thought about telling Rob what she had found out about Rex's car and the guy with the hula girl tattoo. She wanted desperately to tell *someone.* But if she was going to tell anyone, Rob probably wasn't a good choice. It wouldn't be fair to put him in that position. After all, he wasn't on Rex's case, but he was still a cop.

"Hey, Rob," she said.

"I got your message about the autopsy report." He hesitated.

"It's okay. I understand if you can't get it for me. I

don't know what I was going to do with it anyway," she confessed.

"Yeah, I can't really give you a copy, but I did check it out for you."

"Anything stand out?"

"Not really. Standard stuff. Description of the wound, estimated time of death, which I already explained, stuff about how the ME figured out Rex's body was kept refrigerated, stomach contents, and the like."

"Stomach contents? Eww. Why would you want to know that?"

"Helps with the timeline. We once had a case where the wife claimed she came home from church to find her husband dead. Thing was, he still had the steak dinner from the night before in his stomach."

"Oh my gosh! So he died the night before?"

"Yup. The missus had to have stepped over the body to get dressed to go to church the next morning."

"Crazy," Nikki said, hanging a right. "Okay, so what was in Rex's stomach?" She was curious now.

"Um. Looks like he'd just eaten." He sounded as if he was reading the report. "ME says a burger, fries, a strawberry milkshake, and . . . a salad with Thousand Island dressing. Interesting. From what Marshall said, he didn't seem like a salad kind of guy."

It all sounded like fast food. Maybe Rex was eating on his way to Ramirez's office? But the salad didn't make sense. How did he drive and eat a salad? "Interesting," she repeated. She was almost at Jessica's apartment complex. "Well, thanks for the info."

"You bet. Marshall says he wants to have you over for dinner. Maybe next week?"

"Sounds good." She pulled into the parking garage.

Five minutes later, Nikki was standing in front of Mrs. McCauley's door.

Chapter 25

"Mrs. McCauley, good afternoon."

Mrs. McCauley was missing her dentures today. When she spoke, her mouth was pink and gummy. "I wondered when you'd be back."

"Pardon?"

The old lady winked. "The dog circus intrigued you, didn't it? Would you like to come in? I usually don't have cocktails until five, but exceptions can be made."

Nikki tried not to stare at her. She was wearing an orange tutu over a pink-and-blue flowered bathing suit, topped with a cute black cardigan that even Victoria would have approved of. The knee-high fringe moccasins, showing off bony knees, were what really made the ensemble.

"I'm sorry. I don't have time for a drink right now." Nikki tried to look disappointed. "Maybe another day?"

"And if I don't live to see another cocktail hour?" Mrs. McCauley leaned on her walker. Today she had a black garland around it with little bats swinging from the corners. "You'll wish you'd taken me up on the opportunity, won't you?" she said with her slight Eastern Bloc accent. "I make an excellent dry martini."

"I bet you do," Nikki said.

"So why are you here? I don't have tickets, you know."

Nikki waited.

"For the dog circus."

Nikki wondered why she had thought for a second that Mrs. McCauley might be of any help. She sighed. Smiled. "I don't need tickets. But thanks. I wanted to ask you about the hula dancer that tried to deliver a dishwasher to you a couple of weeks ago. Do you remember, he or she had the wrong apartment?"

"It was a refrigerator."

"You said it was a dishwasher."

"You think I don't know the difference between a dishwasher and a refrigerator?"

Nikki regrouped. "Mrs. McCauley, the person who tried to deliver the appliance to you, to the wrong apartment, was it a man or a woman?"

"Not many female delivery *men*, sweetie." Mrs. McCauley spoke slowly, as if to a none-too-bright child. "A refrigerator comes in a big box. It's heavy, even on a handcart."

"So it was a man." Nikki hesitated. "You said it was a hula dancer who tried to make the delivery."

Mrs. McCauley got a funny look on her face. "I said that?"

Nikki nodded. "Yes, ma'am."

"Well, that's crazy. Hula dancers are women. Women don't deliver refrigerators. Why didn't you tell me that was craziness when I said it?"

Nikki wondered if she should mention the absurdity of the dog circus. No need. "I guess it didn't seem that important at the time, but it is now. Can you describe for me the man who tried to deliver the refrigerator?"

The old lady leaned on her walker again, obviously deep in thought. "My memory's not what it once was, but you already knew that." She pressed her lips together over her gums. "It was a big man, not a hula dancer. He was too fat for one of those grass skirts."

"Did he happen to have a tattoo?" Nikki dared.

"Darn if he didn't!" she exclaimed, slapping her hand on the walker. The bats swung. "You know him?"

"I . . . might know *of* him. Was the tattoo, by chance, of a hula dancer? On his forearm." Nikki demonstrated with her own.

Mrs. McCauley looked up at Nikki with great surprise on her wrinkled face. "I believe it was. That makes a lot more sense than having a hula dancer delivering refrigerators, doesn't it?"

Nikki grinned. "Thank you, thank you." She reached out and squeezed her arm. "One more question. Then I promise I won't bother you again today. When you told the man with the tattoo that he had the wrong apartment, do you know where he went next?"

Again Mrs. McCauley had to think. "I was closing the door," she said. "But I believe he stopped at Jessica's apartment. Did she get a new refrigerator?"

"I don't know, Mrs. McCauley," she said. "But I'm sure going to find out."

Nikki's appointment in Bel Air went on for what seemed like an eternity. The entire time she was touring the house and chatting up the potential client, she was thinking about the case.

The guy who returned Rex's rental on Sunday had to

be the guy Mrs. McCauley had seen Monday. A refrigerator box was definitely big enough to hold a body . . . even Rex's. Which meant she had to find the guy with the hula tattoo.

Her mind kept going back to what Tiffany had said about suspecting Alex Ramirez. Ramirez was definitely a part of this mess; she just didn't know what part. And she still had no explanation for the blue BMW the janitor had seen taking off from the parking lot, if it hadn't been Tiffany's. Could someone have borrowed her car? Or was it just a coincidence that Tiffany had a blue BMW and a blue BMW was seen speeding away from the office? It was certainly possible; there were plenty of them in L.A.

It was after six when Nikki left the 9,000 square foot Mediterranean-style home, headed for Ramirez's office. She was going to have to hurry if she was going to make it home to change before she went to Mother's for Movie Night. *The Sound of Music* . . . it was almost more than she could bear to think about.

By the time Nikki arrived on Sunset Plaza Drive, Ramirez's parking lot was empty. Teddy met her in the lobby. "I figured you'd be back."

"Did you?" she asked. "What made you think that?"

He was wearing the same uniform as the day before. Today he was carrying a broom. "I don't know. You didn't seem like someone who would give up easy." He took a step closer to her and leaned on the broom. "So what's up with you and Mr. Ramirez?"

"N . . . nothing."

"Because I got to thinking. I know you're not his wife because I've seen her here before. She's in a wheelchair. But all those questions you were asking about what Mr. Ramirez was doing that night, I wondered if maybe you were his girlfriend or something."

"No." She cringed. "Of course not. I told you. I'm helping out a friend."

"*She* his girlfriend?"

"She is not." She slung her Prada over her shoulder. "Listen, Teddy, I need you to show me where the white Mercedes was parked that night."

He exhaled and picked up his broom. "Guess it can't hurt." He leaned the broom near the door as they went outside. It was already dark out, but the parking lot was well lit.

"Over there." Teddy pointed.

Nikki looked in that direction. "Could you show me exactly where?"

He shrugged and walked across the lot. She followed.

She stood in the parking place he led her to and studied the pavement. There was nothing there. Nothing that looked like blood. Nothing that indicated it was any different than any of the other parking spaces. She groaned. "Can you tell me where you saw the BMW?"

"It was here." He pointed to the next space. "And then it took off that way, down Sunset Plaza Drive. Going that way." He pointed north.

Nikki stood in the parking place and turned slowly in a circle, not sure what she was looking for, but hoping she'd know it if she saw it. "Could you see the person driving the BMW?" she asked.

"I was just getting out of my girl's car, and like I said, it was going fast."

"How long between the time you saw the BMW leave and when you looked out the window and noticed that the Mercedes was gone?"

"I don't know." He ran his fingers through his hair. "A long time. Couple of hours. It was probably after midnight. I had to wax floors."

"But you don't know if Mr. Ramirez was in the building?"

"Nope. I was buffing the halls. Didn't go anywhere there was carpeting."

Having spun in a complete circle, she studied the two-story building. "Are those his office windows?" She pointed.

He looked. "Um . . . yeah."

She stared at the windows, then turned suddenly to him. "Is Mr. Ramirez here now? I can see there's no car here, but is this one of those evenings when his car is parked down the street?"

"Nope. I saw him leave earlier. He was on his cell. He was saying something about going to his son's soccer game."

She studied the bank of windows. "Do you have a key to Mr. Ramirez's office?"

Teddy took a step back. "Man . . . I can't do that. You're nice and all, but I could lose my job."

Nikki kept staring at the windows. She needed to get up there and poke around his office. Maybe he would have a date book with details of his meeting with Rex. Maybe a bloody ice pick lying around?

She turned to Teddy. "I really need to get in there, Teddy. My friend has been accused of murdering someone and Ramirez has something to do with it; I just don't know what yet."

Teddy hooked his thumbs in the waistband of his pants. "I don't know . . . this is a good job. Best I've ever had. Pay's good and I don't have to do that much work."

He looked as if he was considering it. She wondered if it would be worthwhile begging. If only she hadn't given the guy at Barney's the gym membership gift card . . . But Teddy didn't look like a gym rat.

She wondered what she had in her handbag . . . He probably wouldn't be willing to break the law for a bag of peanuts.

She looked up suddenly.

Jeremy would kill her. If Victoria didn't get to her first.

"You a Lakers fan, Teddy?" She sashayed up to him.

He looked at her quizzically. "How'd you know that?"

Because every twentysomething guy in L.A. is. She smiled. "Ever seen the Lakers play? I don't mean on TV. I mean at Staples Center. Live. *Courtside,*" she said, dangling the carrot closer.

Teddy's eyes got big. "You saying what I think you're saying?"

She dug into her bag and came up with the envelope with the tickets on the first try. Was it Providence? "Two tickets. Courtside, Saturday night, against the Kings."

He swore under his breath, staring at the tickets she held out in front of him. He was practically panting. "And you'd give me those tickets?" he said. "Just for letting you in Ramirez's office?"

"Give me five minutes. Ten, tops." She waggled the tickets.

Teddy had a look on his face like Stanley and Oliver did when she was opening a bag of dog treats. "Do I have to go in with you?"

"Nope. It would be better if you didn't."

"And you're not, like, gonna steal anything?"

"I just want to have a look around."

He glanced at her quickly, then back at the tickets. "Cops ask, I'll say you broke in."

That made no sense since there would be no forced entry, but she wasn't going to tell him that. "Fine. They are for Saturday night, though. You work."

"Screw work. Me and Buffy are gonna see Jack, Kobe, and the Lakers!"

Five minutes later, Nikki was alone in Ramirez's personal office. She already knew her way around since she'd been there the week before with her mother. She sat in his chair behind his desk and looked over it. No appointment book. No bloody ice picks. Just the picture of him and his family and a pile of folders with nothing of interest inside.

Cursing was strictly forbidden by Victoria. Nice ladies didn't resort to such base behavior, but Nikki was sorely tempted. She felt as if she were so close to a revelation, and yet . . . she still had nothing substantial.

With a sigh, she got out of his chair and walked along a row of cherry bookcases. She found nothing but books on various dull subjects such as tax law and entertainment law. She poked her head in an open doorway and spotted a large conference table. There was a door that apparently led to the hall. She was reaching for a light switch when she heard a male voice in the hall.

She almost called out to Teddy, then realized it wasn't Teddy. But she knew the voice.

Holy hell! It was Ramirez!

Nikki did what any self-respecting amateur P.I. would do; she dropped to all fours.

The office door swung open, a woman giggled, and Ramirez walked in. Entangled in his arms was a woman Nikki had never seen before. Nikki crawled backwards into the dark conference room, praying they were too busy in their lip-lock to notice her.

As she crawled into the dark room, her bag fell off her shoulder and hit the floor. She froze, cringing.

Apparently, they were too busy for Ramirez to notice that the lights were on, even though he'd left them off, or that he had an audience.

Ramirez closed the door and pushed the young brunette up against it. She squealed, but it wasn't from pain.

Another lip-lock. With tongue.

Nikki blushed and scooted back. It was definitely time to hit the road. She just prayed that the door she'd seen in the conference room led out into the hall.

Nikki saw the woman's blouse flutter to the floor. There was another peal of giggles. The brunette appeared to be barely out of high school.

The Sound of Music was beginning to sound better with every passing moment.

Nikki propelled herself further backward as Ramirez wrapped the woman in his arms and waltzed her to the leather couch. High heels went flying as he pushed her onto the leather cushions.

And Nikki had sat on that very couch . . .

She heard what had to be Ramirez's pants drop.

Just as she backed out of view of the show that she feared would quickly drop from PG to X, she heard the door open again.

"Get out! Get out, you little bitch!" a woman shouted from the direction of the doorway.

Nikki froze. The giggler screamed.

"Get out," the female intruder ordered. "Get out before I shoot one of those implants off!"

Nikki crawled forward again, dragging her Prada behind her like an old feedbag. She couldn't help herself; she had to see who it was.

"Constance." Ramirez was wide-eyed.

Nikki hovered on all fours in the dark conference room doorway.

The giggler was scrambling for her blouse and shoes. Ramirez was sitting up on the couch, straightening his tie, his pants around his ankles. In the doorway, Mrs. Ramirez sat in her wheelchair holding a handgun.

"Get out!" Mrs. Ramirez shouted, pointing the gun in the general direction of the bimbo.

The woman hopped on one foot and then the other to put on her shoes. Then, pressing her back to the wall, her blouse somewhat covering her lacy pink bra, she slipped behind Mrs. Ramirez and disappeared into the dark outer office.

"Constance, put that down. You're being ridiculous."

"*I'm* being ridiculous? You're having sex with a sixteen-year-old on the couch I bought you for your birthday and *I'm* the one being ridiculous?"

"Give me the gun before you hurt yourself and we'll talk."

"I'm not the one who's going to get hurt." She rolled closer to him with a simple tap of the controller under her left hand. In her right hand, she still held the gun on him. "Every Wednesday night."

"Every Wednesday night, what?" Ramirez sounded cool and controlled, but he looked scared.

"Women. You have a woman here every Wednesday night when you're supposedly at your Rotary Club meeting. That's what she told me."

"That's what *who* told you?"

"I don't know who she was. She didn't give me her name when she called me. Does it matter? She was right. She said you were a cheat."

"Constance—"

She thrust the gun toward him, tears welling in her eyes. "She was right about the cheating. That means she was right about the rest, doesn't it?"

"What rest?"

"A thief and a murderer," she choked.

Nikki trembled. She needed to get out of here. She needed to call the police.

"Constance, I don't know what—"

"Shut up!" Mrs. Ramirez shouted. "Shut up. For once I'm going to speak and you're going to shut up. It wasn't enough for you to help Rex March stage that plane crash. Make people think he died. What he was paying you wasn't enough. You had to steal from him, didn't you?"

"Constance, no. Please—"

"I told you to shut up!" She rolled closer. She was a pretty woman, with dark hair and gorgeous dark eyes. "Shut up this second or I'll shoot you, Alex, I swear I will. You stole from Rex and when he came back from wherever the hell he'd been and demanded his money, you killed him."

"You don't know what you're saying." Ramirez rose from the couch and the next thing Nikki knew, the gun went off. It was so loud that time stood still for a second. Then the reality of the situation bombarded her.

She heard Alex scream and fall to his knees, grasping his leg. The room smelled of gunpowder.

"Get up again and I'll shoot the other leg," Mrs. Ramirez threatened.

Now Nikki was scared. Where was Teddy? She scooted back and fumbled in her bag for her phone. She had to call the police!

But what if they heard her on the phone? Would Mrs. Ramirez shoot her, too?

Nikki was breathing hard, so scared she couldn't think. But she had to think.

What would Victoria do in this situation?

She'd get help. It wasn't safe to speak aloud, but
what if she could get to a landline? If she dialed 911,
they'd trace the call.

Her heart pounding, her gaze fixed on the
Ramirezes in the other room, she got up into a crouch-
ing position and began to run her hands along the conference table. Surely there was a phone somewhere.

"I didn't do it," Ramirez groaned. "I did help him
stage the plane crash. I did take more than my share
from his bank account, but I swear on my son's life, I
didn't kill Rex."

"You swear on your son's life, but not your daughter's!"

"Constance. You're not making any sense. Listen—"

"You expect me to believe you didn't kill him? When
you lied about everything else? About our whole life together?"

Nikki's foot hit some sort of console behind her and
she spun around, feeling her way over its top. A phone!
Her hands shook as she sat down, her back to the console, and fumbled with the phone, trying to be as quiet
as possible.

"I didn't kill him. I swear I didn't." Ramirez was
breaking now. He was crying.

Nikki lifted the receiver, dialed 911 and cringed as
the phone beeped. She watched the doorway, but the
Ramirezes hadn't heard it. She put the phone on the
floor, her heart pounding so hard that she could barely
catch her breath.

"I swear. I swear I didn't kill him. He . . . he was already dead, Constance."

"What do you mean, he was already dead?"

Nikki crawled back toward the doorway.

"In the parking lot," Ramirez moaned. "She killed

him in my parking lot. All I did was get rid of the body. I swear. I called Loco."

"You called my cousin and got him involved in a murder?" she screamed.

"Not a murder. No, no. I just needed to get the body out of my parking lot. I called Loco and he took care of it. He borrowed a buddy's refrigerator truck. He left Rex's body in Jessica Martin's apartment."

Nikki couldn't believe what she was hearing. She had so badly wanted to believe Tiffany was innocent. But Ramirez's story made sense.

"Why?" Mrs. Ramirez begged. "Why, if you were innocent, didn't you just call the police?"

"I did it for us, baby. For you and our son and our daughter. If the police had found him dead in my parking lot, they'd have investigated me. They might have found out I was in on Rex's staged death. They would have found out I was embezzling money from him. I could have gone to jail, baby."

Nikki felt like she was sitting in the dark watching a movie. But the pain she heard in Mrs. Ramirez's voice was too real to be fiction.

"Why that woman's apartment, Alex? Why would you put Rex's body in that innocent girl's apartment? Why would you try to frame her?"

"I wasn't framing her," he scoffed, his voice turning bitter, despite the obvious agony he was in. "I was just removing the trash she left in my parking lot."

Nikki held her breath, her ears ringing as she realized what Ramirez was about to say. No . . .

"What are you talking about?" the woman in the wheelchair demanded.

"It was Jessica Martin who killed Rex in my parking lot, Constance. I saw her drive away in her green BMW."

Chapter 26

Tears filled Nikki's eyes. It wasn't true. It couldn't be. Jessica hadn't killed Rex. Ramirez was a liar and a cheat. Why would she believe *anything* he said?

"The woman accused?" Mrs. Ramirez was saying. "She actually did it?"

"She did it, I swear." Ramirez crumpled over, gripping his leg. His leg was covered with blood. It was seeping into the carpet in front of him.

Mrs. Ramirez raised the gun again.

"Connie, please. I'm telling the truth." Tears ran down Ramirez's cheeks. "Don't shoot me. I swear to God I'm telling the truth. You can talk to Loco. He'll confirm my story. I didn't kill Rex March."

Mrs. Ramirez rolled her wheelchair closer to her husband. "You stupid bastard! I don't care about Rex March," she shouted at him. "I'm not going to kill you over him." She rubbed her teary face on her shoulder while keeping the pistol steady. "I'm going to kill you because I warned you that if you cheated on me again, I would."

He tried to back away from her, slide left or right, but there was nowhere to go. She had him pinned against the couch.

"You can't kill me," he blubbered. "You'll never get away with it. You'll stand trial and go to jail and our children will be without a mother *or* a father."

It was when Mrs. Ramirez laughed that Nikki realized she was *really* going to do it. Until that moment, Nikki had assumed she was just an angry wife. Not a vengeful one.

"I'll never do a day of jail time. No jury will convict me, Alex. Not for killing the cheating, lying, thieving husband who put me in this wheelchair."

The look on Mrs. Ramirez's face made Nikki scramble to her feet. She knew she should stay out of sight until the police arrived, but she couldn't let the woman kill her husband. No matter how much he deserved it.

"Mrs. Ramirez, no!" Nikki stepped into the room.

Startled, Mrs. Ramirez swung the gun around and pointed it at Nikki.

Nikki raised her shaky hands. Her heart was pounding so hard in her ears that she could barely speak. "Put the gun down," she managed. "Let him go to jail for what he's done; let him suffer. He's not worth killing."

Slowly, Mrs. Ramirez lowered the gun, and for an instant Nikki thought she had given in. Ramirez had got up on the couch and was sliding down to the far end. Then, without warning, his wife swung the pistol around and pulled the trigger.

The gun fired and Alex Ramirez's body fell back against the couch under the impact of the bullet. From the size of the hole in his head, Nikki knew he was dead before he slumped over.

Nikki heard the gun hit the floor and she slowly turned to look at the woman in the wheelchair. Her eyes were dry, now. She sat there staring at her dead husband, his brains splattered on the leather couch.

Sirens screamed in the distance.

The office door flew open and Teddy rushed in. "What the hell is going on here? I just went down the street for a pack of—" Ramirez's dead body caught his attention.

Teddy gagged and looked away.

Nikki moved toward the door, as dazed by Ramirez's accusation as by his death. Could Jessica *really* have killed Rex?

"Teddy," she said, feeling as though she were moving and speaking in slow motion. She gripped his shoulder. "I need you to hold yourself together. Are you going to be sick?"

He shook his head.

"Good, because I need you to wait here with Mrs. Ramirez for the police." She paused. The sirens were getting louder. "Tell me something." She slowly lifted her gaze to meet his. The bag on her shoulder felt as if it weighed a thousand pounds. "The car you saw speed away that night. The BMW. Could it have been green?"

"I . . . I thought it was blue," he said, his voice gravelly. "But it was dark and I just saw it for a second."

"Was it an old, beat-up blue BMW or a new green one?"

He thought for a second. "It was new," he said softly. "Definitely a new one. It had one of those little fin antennas."

Nikki's brain was suddenly bombarded with a million thoughts. A green BMW. Jessica's secret affair with Rex. After Edith's party, Jessica said she went home. She said Pete could vouch for her. But she hadn't gone straight home. . . . Nikki recalled the conversation she and Jessica had had just before Jessica left. Jessica was hungry;

she was going for a burger where she always went. In & Out.

The autopsy report . . . Rob said Rex had fast food in his stomach. A burger and fries and a salad. It wasn't a salad. It was the lettuce, tomatoes, and onions on his burger. Topped with In & Out's "special sauce": Thousand Island dressing.

"Oh, my God," Nikki muttered. Jessica had run into Rex at the burger joint.

"Mrs. Ramirez," Nikki said, barely recognizing her own voice. "Does your cousin Loco have a tattoo of a hula dancer?"

The woman looked up, dazed. "Here," she answered, touching her forearm.

Nikki's heart tumbled. "Teddy," she said. "You stay right here. You understand me? You don't move until the police arrive."

"Shouldn't we . . . shouldn't we be doing CPR or something?" He looked petrified.

"No," she said, sparing him the gory details of the fatal wound. "He's dead. Just wait here. Give the police my name and tell them I'll be right back."

"Where are you going?" he called after her as she went out the door.

"To see a friend."

Nikki rang Jessica's doorbell three times. There was no answer. Where the hell was Jessica? She felt like she needed to get inside. Maybe to have a look around? Maybe just to wait for her. She wasn't thinking all that clearly. Or maybe too clearly. Surely Ramirez was wrong . . .

Nikki rang Mrs. McCauley's doorbell and waited as

the old woman rolled her way to the door on her walker and went through the same ritual she did every time. Nikki knew the drill by heart.

"I thought you weren't going to bother me again today," Mrs. McCauley said as she opened the door.

"Do you have a key to Jessica's apartment?" Nikki exhaled. "I know you have a key. I need to borrow it."

"You all right?"

Nikki took a deep breath, closing her eyes for a second. "Mrs. McCauley, please. The key."

The old woman stared at her for a moment, then rolled away. She came back two minutes later, holding up a key on a Windsor Real Estate key chain. "You have to bring it right back. It's a big responsibility, having a neighbor's key. I need it back."

"I'll bring it right back," Nikki said.

She was at Jessica's door, letting herself in, before she realized she hadn't even thanked Mrs. McCauley.

In the pristine white living room, nothing seemed out of place. But Nikki didn't know what she was looking for. The police had combed the apartment for clues. Surely nothing was here to prove or disprove what Ramirez had said. She wandered down the hallway to Jessica's bedroom. The closet doors were open.

Nikki stared numbly at the clear plastic coffins holding the shoes and handbags. She studied a code on a box containing a pair of snakeskin Gucci heels. The other boxes had three letters, but this box had three letters and a number. J-M-L-4.

J-M-L . . . J-M-L . . .

Jessica's last boyfriend had been James Mitchell Landon, the fourth. A land mogul. James had given Jessica the snakeskin shoes. Nikki remembered the first night she had flaunted them at an office cocktail party.

J-M-L-4.

It hit her so hard that she found the epiphany almost physically painful.

The code didn't match shoes with handbags. They were the initials of the men who gave them to her. The expensive shoes and bags weren't gifts, in Jessica's eyes. They were trophies.

Nikki looked at the other boxes. She spotted the red Jimmy Choo heels Jessica had worn the night of the party. She grabbed the box off the shelf and opened it, letting the lid fall to the carpet. She picked up a shoe. Something looked different from the night Jessica had worn them.

The box had the code A-R-M printed on it.

Still holding the shoe, Nikki dialed a number on her BlackBerry. "Edith, this is Nikki. Tell me something," she said into the phone. "Rex's first name. It wasn't Rex, was it?"

"Nikki, are you all right? You don't sound—"

"I may have figured out who killed Rex," she said numbly. "His first name, Edith?"

"He never wanted anyone to know, but it was Artemis."

"Artemis," Nikki repeated, holding up one shoe with a deadly looking spike heel. *Deadly.* "I'll call you back," she said as she heard the apartment door open.

"In here," Nikki heard herself call to Jessica.

"Nikki?" Jessica came rushing into the bedroom. She took one look at the shoe and set her handbag on the chair near the door. Her tone was distant. Aloof. She knew Nikki knew. "You need to put those back."

"Tell me the truth." Nikki wanted to cry, but she was too angry for tears. "The heels have been replaced, haven't they? They were red leather that night. Now they're red silk. We took them to the repair shop."

Jessica walked slowly toward Nikki. "I didn't know he

was alive. I swear I didn't. It wasn't premeditated. I saw him at In & Out that night, after the party. I couldn't believe it was him. It was him, all right." She gave a little laugh. "I followed him."

Nikki held Jessica's gaze. "To Ramirez's office."

"To Ramirez's office." Jessica walked around her, going to her closet. "We argued. I was so hurt. So angry with him." She pulled one of the boxes from the closet; it had the initials L-K-G. Inside was a velvet bag. "He told me he loved me."

"Apparently, he told a lot of women that," Nikki said gently.

Jessica didn't seem to hear her. "We were supposed to go to Tahiti *together*. We'd been making plans. Then his plane went down." Tears filled her eyes as she took the bag from the box. There was something heavy inside. "I couldn't understand how he could have left me like that. How he could have let me think he was dead. He was full of platitudes, but he had no intention of taking me with him, not ever. He never loved me. I was so angry, I took my shoes off. Shoes he gave me when he told me he loved me. I was going to throw them at him."

Nikki stared at the shoe in her hand.

"I hit him with one," Jessica said. "The heel went right through his eye. Who would ever think something like that could happen? He fell over dead." She slid her hand into the velvet bag. "I didn't mean to kill him, but I wasn't sorry he was dead." There wasn't a hint of emotion in her voice.

"But . . . but Pete vouched for what time you arrived home that night. He talked to the police for you. "

"People lie to the police, Nikki. For all sorts of reasons." Jessica smiled. "Pete lied for me. I offered to sleep with him if he would vouch for me. He did."

"And you did," Nikki said, thinking back to Sunday,

when she had run into Pete on the stairs. He'd looked
like he'd already been to the gym. Jessica hadn't answered the door right away because she'd been in the
shower. They'd just had sex.

Nikki was so busy staring at the shoe, then Jessica,
then the shoe again, that she didn't see the pistol. At
first. When she saw it in Jessica's hand, she wasn't even
all that shocked. Nothing would shock her tonight.
"Where did you get that?" she blurted. Stupid question,
considering the circumstances.

"Lawrence Karl Gelpin. L-K-G," she read off the box,
seeming pleased with herself. "I like to keep all my belongings in order."

"You're going to shoot me, are you?" Nikki considered the red Jimmy Choo still in her hand as a weapon.
What were the chances it would work twice in the same
month?

"Afraid I have to," Jessica said, almost apologetically.

"But . . . but we're friends. I . . . I was trying to protect you."

Jessica sighed. "If you'd given me another hour, I'd
have been in the clear. This wouldn't have had to happen. You should have gone to Movie Night. I was going
to take care of Ramirez. Or have Mrs. Ramirez take care
of him for me. And that would have been that. It would
have been easy to pin it all on him, once he was dead."

Nikki held on to the shoe for dear life. "You called
Mrs. Ramirez."

"Yup."

"And now he's dead. She killed him."

"As I expected she would." Another smile . . . "But
then you made a mess of things." She leveled the gun.

Nikki raised the red high heel. She was going to miss
The Sound of Music . . . and maybe every Movie Night
thereafter.

A sound in the living room startled them both.

"Hello!" a distinctly accented voice called.

Nikki heard a rolling squeak. "Back here, Mrs. McCauley!" she shouted. "In the bedroom."

"I told you to bring me back that key. I suspected you were up to no good. Then I saw the giraffes going in after you and I knew it for sure." She rolled into the bedroom with her walker, followed by the building's superintendent. "Mr. Jordon let me in." Spotting Jessica with the gun still held on Nikki, the old woman made a sound in her throat. "Good thing I did."

Nikki lowered the shoe to her side. "You can't kill us all, Jess," she said. "You're done. Mr. Jordon, could you call the police?"

Jessica flipped the safety on the gun, leaned down, and picked up the velvet bag it had come from. She carefully returned it to the bag, then the plastic box, and walked to the closet to place it on the correct shelf.

Nikki wanted to throw the shoe at Jessica, at the wall. At something, someone. But, of course, the police would need it for evidence. She tossed it on the bed and reached into her handbag to call her mother.

Jessica calmly tidied her closet while Mrs. McCauley watched, maybe keeping an eye out for the giraffes.

Nikki got Amondo. "I know Mother's in the theater with her guests, but I need to speak with her," she said, her voice cracking with emotion.

It took a couple of minutes, but finally Victoria came on the line. "Nicolette, where are you? What's wrong? I'll come at once."

"I . . . I wanted to tell you I'd be late, is all," Nikki said, fighting tears. She couldn't believe she had so misjudged Jessica's character, but she was glad she'd live to attend another Movie Night.

And then ...

It was Victoria who met Nikki at the door on Roxbury the next evening. Stanley and Oliver flew past her, through the foyer, headed straight for the kitchen and the heavenly smells coming from there.

"You're late, Nicolette." She was wearing a vintage white floor-length Chanel gown. Her hair was done up, her makeup perfect, down to her rose-colored lips. She looked as if she were on her way to the Oscars.

"I'm sorry. I had to go back to the police station. Detective Lutz had some more questions for me." She stared at her mother, feeling completely underdressed in a gray flannel skirt, black sweater, and boots. "Are we going somewhere?"

"Certainly not. I'm dressed for dinner. I thought we'd eat on the terrace. It's a beautiful evening." Closing the door, she linked her arm through Nikki's. "And I have a surprise for you for after dinner."

"I hope it's a bottle of wine. One for each of us." Nikki sighed and rested her head on her mother's shoulder. Nikki was so much taller than Victoria that she had to stoop, but she smelled heavenly.

For a couple of moments, there in Jessica's apartment the previous night, she had thought her life was over. She didn't know how she could have misjudged Jessica so completely, but she was thankful her mistake hadn't been fatal. Live and learn.

"So you didn't get arrested?" Victoria said.

Nikki raised her head. "No. Why would I be arrested? I didn't do anything wrong."

Arm in arm, they walked through the black-and-white tiled foyer. "Aiding and abetting a criminal? Interfering in a police investigation? Breaking and—well, not breaking, but certainly entering. And heaven knows what else you did, Nicolette!"

Nikki laughed. She could hear the dogs barking in the kitchen and Ina soothing them, with treats, no doubt.

"I'm serious," Victoria insisted. "I hope you've learned your lesson. Criminal investigations should be left to the professionals."

"Mother! You were in on it, too. You're lucky Detective Lutz didn't call *you* down to the police station today."

Victoria lifted a brow as they walked through the living room to the French doors that opened onto the terrace. "If he had, I'd have been well dressed, wouldn't I?"

Nikki stopped where she was, looking out over the stone terrace. "Wow, you did this all for dinner for just the two of us?"

A small round table had been elegantly set with her mother's favorite Waterford crystal and china. Around the table, a hundred candles sparkled in the darkness. More floated in the pool.

"It's beautiful," Nikki murmured, truly touched.

"Well, it's not every day that my daughter comes close to death and lives to see the killer thrown in the pokey."

Nikki turned to her mother, laughing. "The pokey? No one has called it 'the pokey' in forty years."

"Sit down, Nicolette, before the lobster bisque gets cold." Victoria glided to one of the chairs at the table and Nikki took the other. "There's the bisque, then a buttercrisp salad, then a filet mignon with roasted carrots, and bananas Foster for dessert. You always did like the flaming desserts."

Nikki picked up a linen napkin and laid it in her lap. "And there *is* wine," she said as Amondo approached the table, dressed in a black dinner jacket, carrying a bottle of wine. "So, what's the surprise?"

"Well, I know how upset you were about missing Movie Night last night, so . . ." Victoria sat back in her chair, obviously pleased with herself. "Amondo has agreed to run the movie again tonight. A private showing just for the two of us!"

"Let me guess." Nikki held her glass up to Amondo, not knowing if she wanted to laugh or cry. "*The Sound of Music?*"

Cheryl Crane, daughter of movie icon Lana Turner, brings her Hollywood insider expertise to the second book in a star-studded mystery series featuring celebrity realtor-turned-sleuth Nikki Harper and her screen goddess mother, Victoria Bordeaux . . .

Nikki Harper is a superstar among Hollywood realtors. Among private investigators however, she's strictly amateur, and her first case was a *Waterworld*-sized disaster. But when a body turns up in a Dumpster behind Victoria Bordeaux's mansion, Nikki feels duty bound to get involved.

Before his demise, Eddie Bernard was the uber-privileged son of one of the biggest TV producers of all time, and a spoiled, violent, party-boy loser. The list of people glad to see him gone could stretch from one end of Bel Air to the other. In fact, about the only person Nikki's sure is innocent is the prime suspect: Jorge Delgado, her childhood friend and the son of Victoria's housekeeper. With the D.A. and the media throwing the words "death penalty" around, Nikki has to help.

Victoria, of course, can't wait to delve into another Tinseltown scandal, and soon Nikki is submerged in a secret world of celebrity drug dealing, dangerous cults, conniving stars, illegal aliens and, of all things, the Food Network. With the aid of a voyeuristic neighbor and some good old-fashioned bribery, Nikki starts to close in on the truth. But can she keep Jorge from facing the final curtain . . . while keeping herself out of a killer's spotlight?

Please turn the page for an exciting sneak peek of the next Nikki Harper mystery

IMITATION OF DEATH

coming next month from Kensington Publishing!

Chapter 1

Nikki walked into her mother's kitchen, flip-flops slapping on the Italian tile floor, and opened the huge commercial stainless steel refrigerator.

"If the bomb detonates, we don't have a chance," came a deep, sexy male voice from the terrace.

The sun was just beginning to set over the stone and wrought-iron privacy fence that framed the property and the sweet smell of bougainvillea drifted into the kitchen through the French doors. Her Cavalier King Charles Spaniels spotted the open doors and shot through them, out into the backyard.

Nikki frowned, glancing in the direction of the escapees, then peered into the fridge: foie gras, hummus, star fruit, duck eggs. No plain old peanut butter and jelly here. She sighed. She wasn't really hungry, just bored. Friday night, all dressed up in sweatpants and a ratty tee, and nowhere to go.

"A hundred thousand American lives?" cried the voice of Victoria Bordeaux, silver screen goddess of the fifties and sixties.

"Gone." There was a snap of a thumb and an index finger. "In a fiery explosion that'll be felt for a thousand miles in every direction."

"Please tell me you're not getting on that train, Dirk. You'll die!"

Cocking her head to hear better, Nikki let the refrigerator door close. *I should write a book,* she thought. *Because no one could make this crap up.*

"Probably, but I have to try. Otherwise, I couldn't live with myself," came the dramatic male voice.

"Let me go, too!" cried Victoria. "Maybe I could disarm the bomb myself!"

"And risk our unborn child's life? Out of the question."

Nikki stepped out onto the stone terrace and heard the sound of Lynyrd Skynyrd wafting in the air . . . which made for an interesting musical score for the scene unfolding in her mother's Beverly Hills backyard. "Marshall?"

"Shht!" Victoria warned, bringing a manicured finger to her pale peach lips. She was dressed in a white Michael Kors jogging suit, her platinum hair tied up in a cute silk scarf, and her trademark pearls on her slender throat. This was *her* Friday night staying-in attire, versus Nikki's. Victoria Bordeaux was one classy lady.

Victoria sat on a chaise lounge, her legs stretched out, with pink foam spacers between her bare toes. She held a script in her hand, reading glasses perched on her nose. "A kiss! One more kiss before you go. Oh, Dirk, I can't believe you're going to get on that train."

"What the heck are you two *doing*?" Nikki asked, glancing at Marshall, her dearest, nearest friend.

Marshall Thunder, recently voted Sexiest Man Alive by *People* magazine, and box office boy wonder, drew a brush over Victoria's delicate toenail. The nail polish was pink. "Just one kiss." He pursed his lips. At six-foot-two, the forty-two-year-old Native American had one of those hard bodies that could have launched a thousand ships. A thousand ships of screaming, fainting female fans. And his face . . . a chiseled masterpiece with dark eyes and high cheekbones.

Victoria, probably thirty years Marshall's senior—Nikki didn't know exactly how old her mother was, and Victoria wasn't telling; her birth records were *allegedly* lost in a hospital fire in Idaho—pursed her lips and kissed the air.

"Tell our son I loved him." Marshall spoke the words poignantly as he grabbed an orange stick from the basket at his feet and touched up the polish on one of Victoria's toenails. "Good-bye, my love."

Victoria drew her hand over her forehead, fluttered her eyelids, and lay back in the chair in what would have been a swoon in her early days in cinema. "No, noooo."

"Mother! Marshall!" Nikki looked at one and then the other. "What are you *doing*?" She glanced around as the seventies southern rock song got louder. "And where is that music coming from?"

Victoria opened her eyes and sat up, pulling off her reading glasses. "What does it look like we're doing, Nicolette? My pedicurist cancelled my appointment and one can't very well go the entire weekend with chipped polish. Marshall kindly offered to do my pedicure and manicure for me." She smiled her perfect smile, flashing the Bordeaux blue eyes she was still famous for, even after years in retirement. Then she scowled. "The music is coming from next door. The Bernards'. Where else?"

"She's going over my script with me," Marshall explained. He glanced at Nikki's bare toes in her worn flip-flops. "I could do yours, too, sweetie." He lifted a dark eyebrow. "Your feet look awful. When was the last time you had a pedicure?"

Nikki dropped into one of the chairs and tried to nonchalantly hide the foot from which she'd scraped the polish off her toenail with a fingernail while on the phone. "I've been busy."

Her mother lifted her eyebrows.

Victoria was never seen in public without her hair done and makeup on her face. She didn't own a single ratty t-shirt or, God forbid, a pair of baggy sweatpants. It just wasn't in her genetic composition.

"Don't tell me you're doing this movie, Marshall." Nikki motioned to the script, trying to shift their attention to anything or anyone but her toes. She loved her mother, sometimes even adored her, but Nikki didn't find it easy to be Victoria Bordeaux's daughter. While gracious to her fans, Victoria could be critical of those closest to her, particularly Nikki. And Nikki, admittedly, could get defensive. The friction between them seemed worse since she'd been forced to move back in with her mother after a major water main break in her own home, followed by a painting disaster. Marshall had come for the evening, at Nikki's request, to serve as a buffer. He and Victoria *always* got along; he never took offense at anything she said. "That script's awful," Nikki observed.

"It's not so bad. I'm going to do it if Zoe what's-her-name does. It's going to be the hit of next summer, with or without me." Marshall screwed the cap back on the pink nail polish. "Let's let that dry a few minutes, and then we'll add a clear coat." He sat back and relaxed, returning his attention to Nikki. He was wearing a pair of corduroy shorts, a tight surfer tee, and Gucci sunglasses, making him look even hunkier than usual. (Of course, it was sunset. Only stars wore sunglasses in the dark.) "It might as well be me."

"I thought you were going to take a break." She found herself mouthing the words to "Freebird" as the song continued to blast from next door. "You said you and Rob talked it over and agreed you were working too hard. That when you finished the film you're shooting, you were taking a year off."

"Year off, shmear off." He waved his hand dismissively. "But don't tell Rob I said that," he warned, pointing his finger at her. "It's a delicate subject. I feel like I need to work while I can. You know how fickle fans can be. A year from now the only offers I might be getting could be made-for-TV movies and OxiClean commercials."

"I'll drink to that." Victoria raised a margarita glass and sipped from it.

Victoria liked her evening cocktails and Marshall like making them for her. They were best buddies, these two. An interesting combination: the retired screen goddess and the still-in-the-closet blockbuster action star.

"What's going on next door?" Nikki asked, glancing around to see what mischief her *boys* were getting into. Stanley, a black, white, and tan tri, was on the trail of some bug or rodent, his nose to the ground. Oliver, a Blenheim, had parked himself under a hydrangea bush and was busying himself grooming his tail. "Has it been going on for long? I didn't hear the music from inside."

"We already worked our way through the *Nuthin' Fancy* album. We've moved on to their (Pronounced 'Leh-'nérd 'Skin-'nérd) album. It was their first."

Nikki looked to Marshall, duly impressed. "Hey, you know your Skynyrd."

He grinned. "Rob has all their albums, on vinyl."

Victoria cocked her ear in the direction of the Bernard mansion next door, then shook her head in irritation. "I told Abe that he'd better get control of his worthless son. I warned him, next time Eddie threw one of his parties and disturbed my peace and quiet, I was calling the cops. It's only a matter of time before his guests start climbing over the wall and crushing my begonias."

Their neighbor, Abe Bernard, was probably the best television writer and producer in Hollywood, certainly the most successful. His company, Bernard Television, reported higher earnings the previous year than the late Aaron Spelling's company. His current law drama had hit number one in the Nielsen ratings, two years running. While Abe was one of the most respected, most revered names in Hollywood, his thirty-five-year-old son was a loser. Eddie Bernard had tried his hand at being a model, an actor, and a businessman, all unsuccessfully. Eddie drank too much, had a drug problem, and was constantly in trouble with the law: drunk driving, possession of illegal substances, assault. So far, his father's money had been able to keep him out of a lengthy jail sentence, but the guy was bad news. He had none of the integrity or work ethic of his father.

"You're not going to call the cops, Mother," Nikki said dryly. "You always threaten, but you'd never do it."

"True. I don't have much use for the police." She waved a delicate hand. "No offense meant toward Rob," she told Marshall.

"No offense taken." He smiled sweetly.

Nikki noticed her mother was wearing the Howard Hughes sapphire ring: platinum, 3 carats, art deco, studded with very high-clarity diamonds. Hughes had given her several nice pieces of jewelry back in the day when he'd been trying to woo her to RKO Studios.

Nikki had the feeling there had been more than business wooing going on there, but for decades, Victoria had remained calmly but firmly silent on the matter.

"I've never forgiven them," Victoria continued, "for the way you were treated that time you were picked up for—"

"Mother," Nikki interrupted. "Could we not talk about that?"

Victoria crossed her legs at the ankles and took another drink of her margarita. "You're certainly touchy this evening. Where's Jeremy? You should be out dining and dancing with your beau, not sitting around the pool with an old lady and her favorite bear."

Nikki and Marshall made eye contact. Nikki lifted an eyebrow.

"Oh, for heaven's sake," Victoria said, which was as close to swearing as she ever came. "I know what a *bear* is: a big, burly, man." She waved in Marshall's direction, frowning. "Although, I suppose they're supposed to be hairy, too."

"Weren't Eddie and Lindsay Lohan in rehab together?" Marshall artfully started a new topic of conversation and ran with it. "I thought I read that somewhere."

"In one of your tabloids?" Nikki asked. "You, of all people, know you can't believe a word they print."

"I read regular newspapers, too," he defended. "Just not about this," he added in a very small voice. "But this was his third or fourth stint in rehab in the last five years."

"Conniving, worthless little punk," Victoria muttered. "He's like the nephew in *Fifteen Green Street*. Remember that film I did with Willi Wyler?"

"The one set in New Orleans?" Marshall clutched his hands over his heart. "I adored you in that film. You were *so* beautiful. So strong-willed, right to the end. Do you remember that green gown you wore in the dinner scene, you know, when you discovered that your nephew had had your sister committed so he could take over the family business?"

Victoria smiled at the memory. "It was Persian silk. And that emerald necklace I wore—"

"Exquisite," Marshall finished for her, both of them lost in the moment.

"Were you nominated for an Oscar that year, Mother?"

Victoria's smile tightened. "No. And Julie Andrews ended up winning for *Mary Poppins*, of all things. But Audrey Hepburn wasn't nominated for *My Fair Lady*, either. I don't know what the Academy was thinking."

Nikki smiled. "You always said—"

The sound of an explosion next door cut Nikki off. She shot out of her chair, looking at Marshall. "Was that—"

"A gunshot!"